Yummy Cowboy

Snowberry Springs Ranch, Book 1

Ophelia Sexton

Philtata Press, LLC

For Liv Brywood, with many grateful thanks for her hospitality in her beautiful Montana home, and for helping me brainstorm this series.

Chapter One – Summer

Snowberry Springs Ranch, Montana
Saturday, June 11

"Summer, I'm so happy that you agreed to stay for a while," said Grandma Abigail as she entered the ranch house's old-fashioned kitchen.

As usual, her frosted blonde hair was flawless and her makeup was impeccable above a severely cut blazer and pleated skirt of unrelieved black. But even skillfully-applied foundation and concealer couldn't entirely erase the marks of sleeplessness and grief from her fine-boned face.

"Anything to help. I owe you so much," Summer replied.

Her phone, tucked into the back pocket of her checkered chef's pants, suddenly squawked like a chicken while simultaneously vibrating.

She'd found the ringtone hilarious when she first installed it, but now it sounded jarringly out of place.

She pulled out her phone and glanced at the number. Then she stabbed her finger at the screen, forcefully rejecting the call.

"Sweetie, are you *sure* you can stay until Labor Day weekend?" Grandma sounded uncharacteristically hesitant. "You really aren't needed at your restaurant?"

Summer shook her head. She'd hoped to put off this conversation for a while longer. "It's closed right now," she said, sticking to the official story. "We're making some major changes. Planning to reopen in the fall with a whole new look."

Then the oven timer went off. *Saved by the bell*, she thought with relief.

Knowing that her mother's vintage avocado-green wall oven ran hot, Summer hastily opened the oven door and pulled out a pan of mushroom caps stuffed with a mixture of breadcrumbs, Parmesan cheese, fresh herbs from the garden, garlic, and the ranch's own Italian-style pork sausage.

She was relieved to see that the appetizers were perfectly browned on top. As the professional chef in the family, it had fallen to her to cater Grandpa Frank's Celebration of Life here in her childhood home. And she had been happy to do it.

She loved feeding people. Especially people she cared about. And being able to cook like this felt like a tribute to the man who had paid to send her to the Culinary Institute of America in Napa, California.

As she set the baking tray down on a metal trivet to protect the old but well-kept desert gold Formica counter, she listened to the sounds of conversation drifting in from the living room and through the open windows.

Outside, on the ranch house's wraparound porch, some of Grandpa's longtime friends were drinking beer and sharing memories.

It was a beautiful June day in Montana. *Much too nice for a funeral*, thought Summer.

She overheard a few snatches of speculation about what would become of the Snowberry Springs Ranch now that Mom and Dad had inherited the place.

Truth was, Dad and Summer's older brother Spring had been doing most of the day-to-day work of managing the property for a few years now, ever since Grandpa Frank's first stroke.

"I mean, I do feel bad about keeping you away from San Francisco," Grandma Abigail continued, "but I really need your help right now, Summer."

Bullet dodged, Summer smiled at her grandmother. "And I'll be happy to do whatever you need," she said in her most reassuring tone.

Then she picked up a spatula and began transferring the mushroom caps and their savory golden-brown toppings to a serving dish.

"But your restaurant?" Apparently, her grandmother wasn't ready to let go of the subject.

"It's fine. Really," Summer said, glad that she had her back turned. Grandma had always been sharply observant, and Summer didn't want her expression to betray her. She added, "In fact, I can stay as long as you need."

"Are you *sure* about that?" Grandma's tone was politely disbelieving. "We all know how hard you've been working, sweetie. Why, you couldn't even make it home for the holidays last year!"

"Thanksgiving, Christmas, and New Year were our busiest time," Summer explained. She couldn't suppress a pang when she thought of the restaurant that so proudly bore her name. "But things are going just fine without me right now. I can handle anything that comes up by phone or email."

She ruthlessly suppressed the stab of guilt at the half-truth. *It wouldn't be fair to burden Grandma with a full explanation*, she told herself. *Not on the day of Grandpa Frank's funeral.*

On cue, her phone squawked again. She silenced it with an apologetic glance at her grandmother. "And *nothing* is more important right now than being here, for you," she added, and returned to arranging the appetizers on the serving dish.

"I don't know if I ever told you how proud Frank and I were of you when we read about all those reviews you've received. I've saved copies of all those newspapers," Grandma said.

Summer's gut twisted in pain at the reminder.

Just a few months ago, those reviews had been the brightest light in her world. They'd been proof that she'd succeeded in her long struggle to make it in the male-dominated world of high-end restaurant kitchens.

Then a fresh worry intruded. *If Grandma is following my career so closely, did she hear the news?*

Crap. Summer swallowed hard.

She tried to reassure herself that Grandma wouldn't be acting so worried about Summer's availability to stay if she knew the truth.

"Frank and I always knew you had a special gift, and I'm so glad the rest of the world is seeing that, too," continued Grandma. "I'm so grateful that you could come home to help me out." She sighed. "You see, we finally convinced the Livingston Vintage Rail company to run trains down to the North Gate of Yellowstone, with a stop here in town, just before Frank... left us. Left *me*."

At the desolate note in Grandma Abigail's voice, Summer put down her spatula, turned, and folded her grandmother into a hug.

She'd always known Grandma Abigail as a force of nature —dynamic, stubborn, and hard-working. She felt strangely shrunken now, as light and fragile as a bird in Summer's embrace.

"I still can't believe Frank is really gone. Every time the phone rings, I can't help thinking that it's him, phoning from the hospital yet again to make sure that your father and your brother are handling everything just the right way here at the ranch." She gave a sad little huff of not-quite-laughter, followed by a heavy sigh. "It's not *fair*. We both worked so hard to close that deal with the LVR. It's going to be a whole new start for our town, and Frank won't be around to see it!" Her arms came around Summer's waist. "Thank God you're here, Summer!"

Summer held her grandmother tightly as grief and guilt surged through her.

Truth was, her life in San Francisco been in full meltdown when she got word that her beloved Grandpa Frank was in the hospital. In bitter retrospect, she should have dropped everything right then and rushed home. But she'd still been nursing a tiny spark of hope that maybe she could salvage the disaster.

"I'm so sorry I wasn't there to say goodbye to Grandpa—" she began, feeling a renewed surge of guilt.

Then her phone squawked again. Grandma quickly ended the hug and stepped back.

Summer decided that chicken ringtone needed to go. Now.

She'd barely finished rejecting the call when her text notifications began chiming and scrolling down her screen at an alarming rate. *Bok-bok-bok.*

Oh, shit. She absolutely could not deal with any of this right now. Not with her grandmother standing right next to her. *And it's not like I can do anything about the situation at the moment.*

"Sweetie, do you need to answer any of those calls? You've been getting an awful lot of them," observed Grandma Abigail.

Summer grimaced. "I must've gotten on some spammer's list," she lied.

Then, quickly swiping, she put her phone into Do Not Disturb mode. She'd deal with the inevitable voicemail and text messages later. *After* all the guests had departed, and once she'd cleaned the kitchen from top to bottom and put away all of the pots and pans she'd used to cater the funeral repast.

And changed that damned ringtone for something less obnoxious.

Right now, though, according to the schedule she'd fastened to the refrigerator door with a magnet, Summer needed to prep a tray of canapés.

For the base, she sliced a crusty, fresh-baked baguette from Jenna's Java & Bakery in town. Next, she would top them with swirled rosettes of herbed cream cheese and thinly sliced applewood-smoked trout from fish that her brother had caught and smoked himself.

As she filled a pastry bag with the cream cheese mixture, she asked, "What kind of special project did you need help with?"

"It's The Yummy Cowboy Diner," replied Grandma Abigail.

"Are you kidding me?" Summer asked in shock. She had begun to pipe cream cheese rosettes onto the bread, but stopped. "That place is still in business?"

For most of Summer's life, The Yummy Cowboy Diner had been the town's only restaurant. If you could even *call* it a restaurant. It had always appeared to be hanging on to life by its fingernails.

She remembered it as a no-frills breakfast and lunch place with dingy decor stuck somewhere in the middle of the last century. Her grandparents owned the building, just like they owned most of the commercial buildings in town, and were silent partners in the business. For as long as Summer could remember, Mrs. Michaels had run the diner's day-to-day operations.

Summer had heard from her mom when Mrs. Michaels passed away last year. At that time, she had assumed that the place would go out of business.

"It is," Grandma confirmed. "The young man who took over running the diner is a very hard worker and an excellent cook. But he's self-taught, and I believe that's the reason The Yummy Cowboy Diner is still struggling. Just before Frank passed—" She paused for a moment to collect herself, then continued. "He and I discussed reworking the place into something a little more... upscale."

Summer pursed her lips, swiftly piping rosettes of herbed cream cheese onto the baguette slices. "No offense, but do you really think a town this size can support an upscale restaurant?"

Grandma nodded. "Frank and I believe that we could make this place a tourist mecca like West Yellowstone once the LVR begins running trains here next year. We want Snowberry Springs to be ready when people do start coming... and hopefully staying here, too."

"Next year? When?" asked Summer.

"Joshua—he's the LVR's director—promised that service will start next May or June. Just in time for tourist season," Grandma replied. "Though it might be a little later. Since it's been such a long time since there were trains running down this way, there's a fair amount of restoration work needed on the old tracks, you see."

"That makes sense." Summer put aside the nearly-empty piping bag and opened the refrigerator. As she pulled out the tray of sliced, smoked fish she'd prepped earlier, she added, "I always wondered why more people didn't stay here. I mean, Snowberry Springs is less than an hour's drive to the North Gate."

"Exactly!" Grandma Abigail nodded. "And that's where you come in, sweetie. Frank and I felt that the first step was to make The Yummy Cowboy Diner more attractive to tourists. Once I find someone to renovate the old Snowberry Springs Inn, it'll be easier to convince people to stay here. In the meantime, why not snag hungry park visitors on their way back to Bozeman after a day in the park? If we had a good restaurant, we could spread the word to the bus tour companies and have them stop here for dinner."

"That does sound like a good idea," Summer agreed as she began draping translucent, paper-thin slices of smoked trout over the cream cheese rosettes, topping them with delicate fronds of fresh dill harvested from the ranch's kitchen garden. "There aren't a lot of restaurants along this stretch of the highway, and most of them are either hamburger joints or barbecue and beer."

Her mind automatically began going through possibilities for revamping the old diner. New American cuisine was probably the best bet for something upscale but familiar to both tourists and a hometown client base.

"Wonderful! I'm so glad you agree." Grandma smiled. "Why don't we go there for lunch tomorrow? I want you to see what's become of the place since you left. You could give me your thoughts regarding a makeover for it."

Fresh guilt surged through Summer. *Would Grandma Abigail even want my help if she knew the truth?*

She hadn't told anyone about what had happened. Not even Winnie, who might the only person who could truly understand the situation.

"I'd be happy to do that," she said, ruthlessly suppressing her feelings. "I mean, I would never have been able to attend the CIA if it wasn't for you and Grandpa paying my way. This is the least I can do to pay you back."

"'Pay us back'? That's nonsense, sweetie," her grandmother scoffed. "You don't owe us anything. Frank and I both agreed that it would be a sin not to nurture our grandchildren's gifts." She paused. "Would one o'clock be all right?"

"That would be great." Summer finished arranging the fish, then washed her hands.

She shoved a tray of mini-quiches she'd prepared earlier into the oven and set the timer. Then she picked up the platters of stuffed mushrooms and canapés, and followed her grandmother out of the kitchen.

As Grandma Abigail rejoined Mom, Dad, and the other family members in the wood-paneled living room, Summer circulated among the funeral guests with her appetizers. While she did so, she found herself thinking about what kind of changes she might suggest for the diner that didn't involve demolishing the place and building a whole new restaurant.

Maybe I can suggest that the business move into one of the nice brick buildings on the other side of the town square.

This morning, while shopping for ingredients, she'd noticed a large storefront for rent next to Jenna's Java & Bakery. Of course, moving The Yummy Cowboy Diner from its present location would also mean having to build an entire new commercial kitchen from scratch.

She sighed. It was impossible to make any real plans without knowing Grandma's budget, but it was fun to fantasize about designing a new restaurant from the ground up that would take advantage of the town's vintage brick buildings.

Tomorrow should be interesting, she thought as she ventured out onto the porch to offer the appetizers to Grandpa's friends. *At least it will keep my mind off what happening back in San Francisco.*

Chapter Two – Summer

S nowberry Springs Town Square
  The next day

"Don't worry," Grandma Abigail assured Summer forty-five minutes after they were seated in one of The Yummy Cowboy Diner's peeling burgundy vinyl booths. "The food here is worth the wait."

"I sure hope so," Summer said. "I'm *starving*."

This morning, after reading the long string of increasingly nasty texts and emails that had arrived during Grandpa Frank's funeral and Celebration of Life yesterday, and listening to five annoyed-to-angry voicemail messages, her stomach had been churning so badly that she hadn't been able to manage more than a slice of dry toast and some very milky coffee for breakfast.

She was in more trouble than she'd ever been in her life. And she had no idea how to fix the situation. Coming back to Montana felt like running away. But she desperately needed some breathing room. Some time to *think* and figure out her next move when she returned to San Francisco.

Hanging out with her grandmother, her parents, and her three siblings this morning had been good. After breakfast, she and Mom had spent some time weeding and tending to the ranch's large vegetable-and-herb garden. The calm, repetitive rhythm of the work, combined with the fresh air and the birdsong, had helped calm her shattered nerves.

By the time her lunch date with Grandma Abigail rolled around, Summer's stomach had settled.

Now, she added, "And I'm super-interested to see if a basic dish like meatloaf can *ever* be worth this kind of wait."

"Good food takes time." Grandma sounded like she was repeating something she'd heard.

"For fine dining, maybe. But even then, you prep dinner service so that you don't keep the customers waiting *this* long. The timing on the courses is supposed to be 'leisurely,' not 'slow.' Besides, this isn't a fine dining restaurant… it's a *diner*." Summer pointed out.

Grandma Abigail sighed. "You're right, of course. And I really wish they hadn't run out of the fish and chips."

"Or the lamb chops?" That had been the first item that Summer had tried to order off the crowded menu, since it had jumped out at her from the list of usual burgers, soups, and salads on the menu. "Or the elk chili?"

After their third attempt to order something off the menu, Terri, their high school-aged server, had finally suggested either the breakfast or lunch specials.

Grandma Abigail had brightened at learning that the breakfast special was a waffle topped with house-made huckleberry compote and whipped cream from the Stevenson Dairy, just down the road.

After hearing that the bison in the meatloaf lunch special originated at the Snowberry Springs Ranch, Summer had ordered it. The price of the dish seemed absurdly low, considering the cost of the ingredients.

True to the small-town spirit of Snowberry Springs, all the diner's patrons had greeted them when Grandma and Summer entered the place.

Summer had forgotten how nice it was to be back in a place where everyone knew you.

While she and her grandmother waited... and waited... and waited for their lunches to arrive, Summer used the time to study the front-of-house operations.

At least the place was crowded with locals. That hinted that the diner's problems might be fixable. A business that couldn't attract loyal patrons wouldn't survive the slower winter months, when the flood of tourists died down to a trickle.

"Is the diner normally this busy?" she asked, looking around.

Her Diet Coke was down to a quarter-inch at the bottom of a tall plastic cup filled with crushed ice, and Grandma's coffee cup had run dry a while ago.

Behind the long Formica-and-chrome counter, Terri had her back resolutely turned to the diner's patrons. Her phone was stuck to her ear, and even above the hubbub of conversation, Summer could hear that the girl was having a loud argument with someone named Ashley regarding Noah (or possibly Noel).

Grandma Abigail nodded. "Oh, yes. It's even busier at breakfast. Everyone loves the waffles and pancakes here. There's a line going down the sidewalk most mornings." She paused. "That's a good sign, right?"

She had given Summer the rundown on The Yummy Cowboy Diner's bleak financial situation on the drive into town.

"Sure," Summer agreed, but couldn't help asking, "but are you sure the line isn't just because the kitchen is so slow?"

"Trust me, it's worth the wait. I've never had waffles like the ones they serve here," Grandma repeated. "But you see why I need your help."

She hadn't said much about the diner's new owner, other than that he'd been the head cook and still worked in the kitchen.

"The front-of-house operations are a hot mess," Summer reported. "And if you want to turn this into an upscale dining establishment, the first thing this place needs is a major facelift."

She swept her hand around the diner's interior, taking in the dingy brown wood paneling cluttered with old license plates, metal signs, vintage photos, tacky cowboy memorabilia, and a very dusty taxidermied bison head mounted above the door leading to the bathrooms and kitchen.

"The booths, tables and chairs are all in rough shape," she continued. "The decor in this place hasn't changed since I was in high school. Heck, Grandma, maybe not since *you* were in high school!"

Grandma Abigail laughed, but Summer wasn't exaggerating.

Wherever she looked, she saw seat cushions either peeling or torn and patched with silver duct tape. A row of ugly, fake-wood Formica-topped tables marched down the center of the dining room, with even uglier metal chairs that looked like they'd been purchased at a flea market somewhere.

A long counter with beaten-up turquoise vinyl barstools ran along one wall of the diner. Behind it was a backbar crowded with big industrial coffeemakers, a wide conveyor belt toaster, a soda fountain, and a vintage chrome and sea-foam green enamel milkshake machine straight out of the fifties. Hideous yellow and brown linoleum tiles covered the floor.

"I don't think you can salvage much here. Just hire a dumpster —or a fleet of dumpsters." Summer could already envision the changes that her grandmother should make here. "Take this dining room down to the bare walls and—"

"Abigail dear," interrupted a woman's voice. "I'm so sorry for your loss."

Jolted out of the mental list she was furiously compiling, Summer looked up to see Mrs. Jeffries standing next to their booth. The gray-haired lady with the stylish black-framed glasses had been Summer's sixth-grade teacher, though she was probably long retired by now.

"Thank you, Susan," Grandma said as Mrs. Jeffries bent to hug her. "I'm sorry we didn't have a chance to speak at the funeral. You remember my granddaughter, Summer?"

"Of course!" Mrs. Jeffries straightened up and smiled. "Abigail's kept us informed of your success. I'm waiting for the day when you get a TV show just like your sister!"

Summer grinned at her. "I'm camera-shy. I prefer to work my magic behind the scenes."

"Well, it's always nice when my students grow up and become successful adults," Mrs. Jeffries told her warmly. "Abigail, I was so sorry to miss Frank's funeral yesterday. My first great-granddaughter had her christening over in Three Forks, and I couldn't bear to disappoint my grandson and his wife."

Grandma reached up to pat Mrs. Jeffries' arm reassuringly. "I understand. And I think you made the right choice. You'll text me some photos? I can't believe that Chris is all grown up with a daughter of his own!"

"Of course, I'll send you some photos," Mrs. Jeffries promised. "I was just on my way out, but I couldn't leave without offering my condolences in person."

"It's very kind of you," Grandma responded. "I don't know what I'd do without everyone here supporting me."

Mrs. Jeffries bent to give Grandma another hug, then beamed at Summer. "Are you thinking of moving back home?"

Summer shook her head. "No, I'm just here for a few weeks."

"Oh, that's too bad," Mrs. Jeffries told her. "It seems like all of our young people are leaving the town. I guess the big cities are more exciting. Well, it was lovely to see you again, dear."

The diner's smudged glass door had barely closed behind Mrs. Jeffries when lunch finally arrived.

Or at least Summer's food arrived. Grandma Abigail's waffle with a side of scrambled eggs and fried ham was still MIA.

"Oh, I think he's making it now," the waitress said with a shrug when Summer asked about it. "I'll bring it out when it's ready." She cast an eye over the table with its empty coffee cup and soft drink glass. "You guys need a refill on anything?"

Summer bit back a snarky rejoinder. Instead, she nodded. "Yes, please."

And silently added another couple of items to her "Must Fix" list for The Yummy Cowboy Diner.

"Please go ahead and start without me," urged Grandma Abigail. "I don't want your food getting cold."

"If it isn't cold already," muttered Summer.

The large beige plate with the dark brown rim was sloppy and the presentation terrible, even for a diner.

Her heart sank as she noted the drips on the table where the gravy overflowed a mountain of mashed potatoes that had been plopped on the side of the plate.

This is going to be terrible. Summer braced herself as she reluctantly scooped up a forkful from the thick slice of meatloaf and lifted it to her lips.

To her astonishment, the meatloaf was moist and flavorful, and above all, well-seasoned. The sloppy pool of thick brown liquid turned out to be a caramelized onion gravy, clearly scratch-made rather than from a packaged mix. It was so good that she wanted to lick every last drop from the plate.

Most surprising of all, the mashed potatoes had clearly been made from fresh Yukon Gold potatoes laced with butter, milk, garlic, and salt.

Clearly, the cooks in this kitchen didn't believe in using either instant gravy or instant mashed potatoes. *Good.*

"Well?" Grandma Abigail asked, smiling. "What do you think?"

She'd been observing Summer's changing expression as she took her first few bites.

"It's good," Summer admitted. "I mean, *really* good. I can see why you think this place is worth saving. When you and your co-owner redo the menu, I think this meatloaf needs to stay."

Grandma Abigail nodded. "And the waffles are the best I've ever had. They should stay, too."

Her gaze drifted over Summer's shoulder. The crow's feet radiating from the corners of her bright blue eyes deepened as her smile turned into a mischievous grin. "Ah, and speaking of which, here comes my special."

"Mrs. S!" a male voice called, the deep tones cutting effortlessly through the buzz of talk in the dining room. "Terri told me you were here! So, I thought I'd serve you myself... and tell you how sorry I was to hear about Mr. S's death."

Summer twisted around and peered at the man approaching from the kitchen. He balanced a pair of the ugly beige-and-brown plates in his hands, one mounded with whipped cream and laced with purple huckleberry sauce, and the other holding scrambled eggs and a slab of fried ham.

Her first impression of Grandma's business partner was of intense dark brown eyes fringed by sinfully long lashes. He had short, dark hair, and sexy scruff highlighting a firm jaw. He was tall, with long, jeans-clad legs and broad shoulders stretching the fabric of a red The Yummy Cowboy Diner t-shirt that looked like it had been spray-painted on him.

Summer's mouth went dry. All of her hormones revved into overdrive.

Holy moly, I'll have what Grandma's having!

Then came the gut-punch of recognition. *Brock.*

Brock Michaels, the late Mrs. Michael's son.

The boy who had cruelly rejected her when she finally worked up the courage to ask him to Senior Prom after months of nursing a hopeless crush on him. Back then, he'd exuded an unshakable confidence.

He still did... along with a hefty wallop of sheer animal magnetism.

Oh, crap.

Chapter Three - Brock

Summer Snowberry was back in town.

Even worse, she was *here*. In his diner.
The star of Brock Michael's high school wet dreams was currently sitting across the table from sweet old Mrs. Snowberry, his chief investor and business partner.

If the blonde teenaged girl had been a diamond in the rough, the woman looking him over right now was a polished gem, her gaze as hard and cool as sapphires set in platinum.

The weight of her gaze pressed on his chest like a boulder, squeezing the breath from him.

Shit.

Brock had spent all four years of high school trying to push down his feelings for her.

Even as a dumb-ass kid, he'd known he had nothing to offer the smart, pretty girl from the richest family in town. That knowledge hadn't stopped his brain from featuring her in a nightly parade of X-rated fantasies, though.

She'd left town right after high school graduation to attend some fancy-pants culinary academy in California. In the years since then, Brock had done his best to forget her.

Impossible to do when her grandparents were the richest people in Paradise Valley, and both Summer and her younger sister Winter were celebrities these days.

Everyone in town eagerly followed them on social media and in the news. He couldn't escape hearing all the breathless gossip about Summer's award-winning restaurant for rich people in San Francisco, and Winter's popular HomeRenoTV show about restoring old houses in Seattle.

Right now, though, he was relieved to note that despite the one-two punch to his gut, his legs were still moving smoothly and he hadn't dropped the plates he carried. Because ruining Mrs. S's brunch would just be the cherry on top of today's dirt sundae.

"Brock!" Mrs. S's bright blue eyes, the same shade as Summer's, lit up as he approached the booth. A delighted smile stretched her lips, and warmth radiated from her, as if seeing Brock had made her day. She was like that with everyone, but that didn't make it feel less real. She made him feel like he *mattered*. "How are things going, dear?"

"Doin' okay, Mrs. S," he lied. Despite her repeated urging, he just couldn't bring himself to call her "Abigail." It felt disrespectful. "Been a busy day so far," he added, placing her waffle and sides in front of her.

"Busy" was a total understatement.

His day had been complete shit so far, starting with the realization that Kenny, the diner's longtime manager, had forgotten to phone in the week's orders to the restaurant supply place in Bozeman. *Again.*

Since this was Kenny's second fuck-up in a month, Brock hadn't tried to restrain his temper. He'd yelled that maybe, *just* maybe, Kenny should stop fucking relying on his memory and actually *write out* a fucking To Do list.

In response, Kenny had quit on the spot. The old guy had stormed out of the kitchen right before the morning rush started.

Brock wasn't sure whether to be relieved or panicked at Kenny's departure.

Sure, he'd had been Mama's right-hand man, helping her keep the place afloat after Dad left. Back when Brock was still washing dishes before and after school and on weekends, Kenny had taught him how the restaurant business worked.

But Kenny hadn't adjusted well to Brock becoming his boss after Mama's death last year. And Brock was never sure if Kenny's screw-ups were deliberate sabotage or just a sign that it was finally time for him to retire.

In any case, Mrs. S didn't need to know about any of that. Especially not with Ms. Fancy Pants Executive Chef right there.

"Brock, you remember my granddaughter, Summer?" Mrs. S asked, right on cue. "She came back home for Frank's funeral. I thought I'd bring her by and show what you've done with the diner."

Summer's smile looked forced. She said nothing, but the way she avoided his gaze told Brock she probably thought his place fell short.

A spurt of resentment etched through his gut like acid. *He* hadn't been lucky enough to have rich grandparents willing to pay for culinary school!

"I *think* I remember her, Mrs. Snowberry." He forced his best easy-charm grin, the one that had always worked Saturday night wonders at the Elk's Head Tavern, back when he still had time to date.

And he'd be double-damned if he let Summer know how strongly her presence still affected him.

"Didn't we go to high school together?" he asked Summer, trying to keep his tone casual.

Her eyes widened in surprise. For an instant he thought he saw hurt flash across her expression.

Her tone cool, she replied, "Uh, maybe? What year were you?"

Fuck. That stung, but good. Was she *really* trying to pretend that she didn't remember him? Or maybe she really didn't.

He wasn't sure which was worse.

Brock's temper flared. "Aren't you the one on TV? Pink tool belt?" He did his best to fake ignorance. "Restores old houses in Seattle, or something like that?"

He cursed himself as soon as the words slipped out. *Now she knows I'm just yanking her chain!*

"No, that's my sister Winnie." If Summer's tone had been cold before, it positively dripped icicles now.

"Summer's an executive chef and owns her own restaurant in San Francisco these days," Mrs. S interjected proudly.

As if everyone in town doesn't already know that! Brock thought.

Scowling, he crossed his arms.

He saw Summer's gaze dart to his biceps, and fought the urge to smirk at her. *Guess she likes what she sees.* It made him feel fractionally better.

"Last year, she made *Golden State Foodie Magazine's* list of California's ten best chefs under thirty," Mrs. S continued.

"Oh, right, you're the famous chef, huh?" Some stupid impulse made him add, "Isn't my meatloaf is the best you've ever had? I sourced the bison from your family's ranch and ground the meat myself."

To his surprise and pleasure, she nodded. "It's excellent." Then she spoiled everything by adding, "Too bad about everything else."

What the hell? He scowled down at her. "Oh, yeah? You think you could do better?"

Her golden brows shot up, and her bright blue eyes met his

squarely for the first time. A hot jolt of desire raced through him, seasoned with irritation and dislike.

He didn't want to want her, not when she was sitting there, all smug and superior in *his* restaurant, criticizing *his* food.

"As a matter of fact, yes," she said calmly. "For one thing, I'd ensure that all of a table's orders came out at the same time. And I wouldn't make my customers wait for nearly an hour for their food."

He hated she was right. "Well, I pride myself in cooking each dish to perfection before I serve it," he shot back. "Quality's worth waiting for."

"Mm-hmm," she said, looking unimpressed with his bullshit. "Look. Your food *is* good. But I came in wanting to try your lamb chops. You were out. Same story for the elk chili, *and* the fish and chips." She actually rolled her eyes. "The meatloaf was my surrender in the face of overwhelming outages."

Brock blew out a frustrated breath. *Why the hell did she and Mrs. S have to come in today, of all days?*

"Any other criticisms, Ms. Executive Chef?" He didn't try to keep the growl out of his tone.

"Plenty of them," she shot back. "Starting with the observation that nothing about this place does your food credit. This plate was such a sloppy mess when it came out that I was bracing myself for a terrible meal."

Yeah, well, from what he'd heard, the places she worked specialized in serving fancy shit, like a plate holding a single roasted carrot surrounded by a few dots of sauce. That kind of pretentious crap would never go over in a place like Snowberry Springs. People in these parts expected a meal that filled them up and stuck to their ribs.

He smirked down at her. "Well, you know what they say—don't judge a book by its cover."

Summer raised her brows at him and reached for one of the menus. She lifted it by her fingertips, as if it were contaminated with something nasty. "Or a restaurant by its tacky, *sticky*, laminated menus?"

He opened his mouth, but nothing came out. Which made him even madder than he already was.

"I read through it while I was waiting." Her lip curled as she hefted the comb-bound tome. "You have way too many items and some truly terrible food photos in here. How the heck are you making any money? These prices can't possibly cover your costs for ingredients plus overhead."

Brock's scowl returned. He knew she was right. But that didn't mean he liked her pointing it out in her snotty voice.

He'd been meaning to update the menus and review the pricing. But with eleventy-million other things clamoring for his attention, he hadn't gotten around to it yet.

Not to mention, Kenny had repeatedly warned him that he'd upset his loyal customers if he raised his prices.

"And while I'm on the subject of your menu—" she continued.

He groaned. *Why? Why is she still talking?*

The very last thing he wanted or needed this morning was this lecture from a stuck-up big-city chef.

Not to mention, every minute he spent out here meant tickets piling up back in the kitchen. At this rate, he'd still be cooking orders at closing time.

He opened his mouth to tell her off, but a glance at Mrs. S showed her hanging on Summer's every word. *Fuck me.*

"—your wait staff should be more familiar with your specials," Summer was saying. "Terri was very friendly, but she couldn't tell us whether my grandmother's order came with country fried potatoes or toast or both. And she had no idea what sides came with the meat loaf."

Brock crossed his arms. He tried—and failed—to keep the frustration out of his voice. "Look, Summer, I get it. I do. But I'm really short-staffed at the moment, and I'm not inclined to be picky with the waitresses who actually bother to show up for their shifts."

That was a real sore spot with him. Sure, this might just be a summer job for Terri and the others, but he'd been raised to believe that you always did your best by showing up and working hard.

"Hm," Summer said again, and he gritted his teeth at her tone.

While they'd been sparring, Mrs. S had begun demolishing her huckleberry waffle with every sign of enjoyment. Now, she wiped her lips delicately on the paper napkin. "Summer, dear, are you telling me that you could help transform this diner into the kind of place that could handle a crowd of Yellowstone tourists?"

"Of course," Summer said without hesitating. Her challenging blue gaze never left Brock. "These are exactly the kinds of problems I was trained to solve. In fact, while I was waiting during the hour or so it took for my lunch to arrive, I started making a list. I've already noticed fifteen major problems that need fixing."

A list? She had the nerve to come into my *place and make a fucking* list? *Who the hell does she think she is?*

She smiled up at him, clearly inviting him to ask about her fucking list.

He glared down at her, refusing to take the bait.

His jaw began to ache from clenching his jaw muscles so hard. His dentist was going to have a conniption from all the teeth-grinding he was doing right now.

Silence stretched between them. Then, still looking coolly

superior and more beautiful than anyone so annoying had a right to be, Summer gave a tiny shrug and turned back to her lunch.

Mrs. S stepped in to fill the conversational gap. "What did you have in mind, dear?" she asked Summer.

"Well, the very first thing would be to give this dining room a refresh to make it more modern and inviting."

Brock couldn't suppress the low growl rumbling through his chest. His diner was *plenty* inviting. Hell, he had a full house most days, and people waiting outside for a table.

"The food is great," Summer continued. But before Brock could bask in the compliment, she went on, "So it would make sense to add a dinner service, since that's always the primary moneymaker for a restaurant. You did mention that this diner was currently struggling to maintain a positive balance sheet—"

A combination of burning humiliation and smoldering anger heated Brock's face. Mrs. S had shared the diner's financial information with her snotty granddaughter? *Why the hell did she do that?*

As if his day wasn't already scraping the bottom of the shit barrel!

"—so, I'd also recommend that Brock here spend some time costing out his most popular menu items and adjusting the prices." Summer turned back to Brock. "Analyze your receipts. Keep only those dishes that your customers are actually ordering, and cut the rest of them. Then you won't need a, um, *binder* for a menu." Her cute nose wrinkled. "And for God's sake, no photos. Get someone to design a cute logo for you, and keep the menu to one or two pages, tops."

"Costing out?" Brock hated having to ask, thereby handing her a win. But neither Kenny or Mama had ever mentioned doing anything like that.

Summer's brows rose in surprise, as if she couldn't believe he didn't know what that meant. "Food costs for a *profitable* breakfast and lunch place normally run about eighteen to twenty percent of the menu price. I know what my dad and brother charge for the ranch's wholesale bison, so I'm guessing that you're actually losing money on this meatloaf special once you calculate in your food costs plus overhead, like labor and utilities."

Mrs. S nodded agreement.

The heat scorching Brock's face now flooded through his entire body. But he couldn't argue that he'd fucked up pricing the daily special. He'd never heard of the magic percentages she was quoting, but they made instant sense to him.

How did I not figure that out for myself? And why the hell did I listen to Kenny when he told me what my customers would be willing to pay?

Neither the late Mr. S nor Mrs. S had said much to him after they reviewed the diner's accounts last month, but Brock had seen the concerned glances they traded.

But he wasn't sure how he could work any harder. He was already pouring his entire fucking life into this place, and it was still bleeding red.

He wondered why Mrs. S was humiliating him like this in front of her granddaughter. Was she trying to pressure him into selling the place and buying her out? Was she regretting her investment in Brock's dream?

Mrs. S didn't seem like the sadistic type. But what other explanation was there for this public takedown of the diner he'd dedicated the past year of his life to?

"Next, I'd recommend setting up an integrated point-of-sale system to help with this place's inventory management problems," Summer said, ticking off points on her fingers. Like it or not, he was going to hear the entire list. *Great.* "If you did that, I can guarantee that The Yummy Cowboy Diner would never be embarrassed by running out of staple menu items again."

He concentrated on breathing, pushing down his anger—and his urge to defend himself—with a supreme force of will.

She continued, "Plus, a good POS would streamline operations. For one thing, all orders entered into the system automatically print out as tickets for the kitchen. Terri and the other servers wouldn't have to keep running between the front and back of the house. Plus, the POS we use at SummerTime in S.F. also ties into our food inventory management by automatically placing orders with our restaurant's suppliers as soon as stock begins to run low on anything."

We? he wondered. *Who the hell is "we"? I thought Summer owned her restaurant.*

"—not to mention handling reservations, card transactions, and tying into our electronic bookkeeping sys—"

"That all sounds great for a big-city restaurant," Brock interrupted her. The ache in his jaw was beginning to spread through his neck, and the effort of choking back his temper was giving him a pounding headache worthy of a killer hangover. "But that kind of fancy system sounds like way more than I need." *Or can afford,* he added with silent bitterness. Unlike *some* people, he wasn't made of money. "Besides, this diner has always used a paper ticket system, and that's worked just fine for the past fifty years."

Summer sighed loudly and made a point of looking around the crowded dining room. "Things are *not* working 'just fine' when your customers are waiting this long for their food during lunch rush, *and* you don't actually have enough inventory to cook the items on your menu. And I haven't even set foot in your kitchen to inspect it. Who knows what issues I might uncover there?" Her pink lips curved in a saccharine smile.

"Inspect? *My* kitchen?" he snarled. "Over my dead body, Summer."

"Why? What are you trying to hide?" she shot back. "Are we talking mice? Roaches? Hood vents clogged with grease? Believe me, I've seen it all."

"Why, *you*—" he began.

How dare she! He cleaned his damned kitchen from top to bottom after closing every day.

Then Mrs. S raised her hand and the not-so-sweet old lady dropped the bombshell she'd no doubt been planning since she got a look at his diner's books.

"Then it's settled. Summer and Brock, you're going to work together to turn this place around before the LVR begins operations here next May. I want The Yummy Cowboy Diner to become the best restaurant in the area, better even than any of the places in Ennis or Livingston."

"What?" The word tore loose simultaneously from Brock and Summer's throats.

A sudden silence descended over the dining room. Everyone was staring at them—Terri, the regulars seated at the counter, all of the locals at the tables and in the booths.

"No way," Summer protested. "Is this some kind of joke?"

Brock fervently hoped so.

Chapter Four – Brock

Brock couldn't believe what he'd just heard.

He'd grown up in this diner, spending every day after school and on weekends helping in the kitchen while his mama ran the front of the house, trying to make ends meet after his jerk of a dad walked out and never paid a cent of child support.

Brock had sworn that if he ever had a family of his own, he'd make damned sure to provide for them in the way his dad never provided for him and Mama.

"No way," he told Mrs. S. Keeping his tone polite took every ounce of will he possessed.

Summer crossed her arms and scowled. She wasn't any happier about her grandmother's plan than he was.

Brock continued, "This is *my* diner, and with all due respect, ma'am, I've been doing a good job so far. I don't need someone else coming in here and trying to turn The Yummy Cowboy Diner into some fancy hipster joint with twenty-dollar burgers."

Mrs. S's lips thinned as her blue eyes turned sharp and stared right into his soul.

Brock met her gaze, his own eyes narrowing.

He'd been putting in twelve-hour days, seven days a week, ever since Mama went into hospice, and the diner was *still* bleeding money. But maybe if he just worked a little harder, he could make this place work without Ms. Fancy Pants Chef telling him what to do.

Because this was *his* place.

More importantly, it had been his mama's place. And his second home, growing up. No way in hell was Brock going to disrespect her memory by saying or even thinking that Mama had done a bad job with this diner. Even if it was a little worn around the edges, it was comfortable. It was part of the town's history... and his.

Business partner or not, if Mrs. S thought that he was going to throw away the fruits of Mama's blood, sweat, and tears, she had another thing coming.

It was bad enough that Kenny had quit. The old guy had been Mama's right hand for years, and Brock could only imagine what she was thinking right now, looking down on him from heaven.

Mrs. S's expression abruptly softened. She sighed. "Yes, of course I respect your decision to keep the diner open after Pamela passed away. I agree with Summer that your food is outstanding, and Frank always thought so, too."

Brock relaxed fractionally. *Okay, maybe she's on my side, after all.*

But she wasn't done talking yet. "You're a very hard-working young man, Brock, and I have faith that you *can* make this diner a success. But, based on the financials that Frank and I reviewed just before he passed, you really do need some help on the business side of things. Especially if you're going to expand operations as we discussed when we... *I*... invested in this diner."

Brock saw the shadow of grief cross her expression before she lifted her chin resolutely and continued. "My granddaughter is a professional chef from one of the best culinary institutes in the country, and she has experience running a world-class restaurant in San Francisco. She could help you figure out a way to make necessary changes while still keeping the spirit of your mother's diner."

"No. No way." He shot his best death-glare at Summer, the one that lit a fire under his kitchen staff's asses when they were slacking off.

She returned the gaze, her cornflower eyes wide and innocent, and shook her head minutely. As if she hadn't been in on her grandmother's plan.

Hah, serves her right! he thought darkly. *Looks like that damned list of hers has come back to bite her in the ass.*

That rankled. Especially since he was well aware of The Yummy Cowboy Diner's shortcomings.

But, dammit, I'm already working all day and night! What else can I do? Aloud, he said, "And even if I wanted to do some kind of fancy dining room renovation, I can't afford to close the diner for weeks or even months of construction."

"It wouldn't have to be a *complete* tear-down," Summer said. "Just a refresh of things like the booth upholstery, maybe some new tables and chairs, a fresh coat of paint, and... decluttering." She turned to Mrs. S. "Grandma, I know I promised to help you, but even if Brock wanted my help—which he doesn't—this is a *much* bigger project than I feel comfortable tackling while I'm in town."

"Yeah, that's right," Brock agreed eagerly. With an effort, he added, "I know you mean well, Mrs. S, but I can handle this. I've got some plans in the works." That part was a half-truth, but he didn't want to encourage Mrs. S to offer any more "help."

Summer caught her lower lip between her teeth as she stared down at her half-finished plate of meatloaf. Her brow creased, as if she was thinking of more ways to criticize his food and his diner.

Liquid fire pooled in Brock's groin as he imagined what it would be like to kiss those sweet, plump lips.

Maybe he could just fuck that expression of superiority right off her face. He hadn't gotten laid in... *Holy hell, has it really been that long?*

Trying to keep this diner afloat had consumed pretty much his entire life over the past year. He'd walked into the kitchen the day after Mama's funeral and submerged himself in work to keep his grief at bay.

"Promise me you'll at least sleep on it before making your final decision." Mrs. S's voice derailed Brock's lust-filled train of thought.

His face heated, and he hoped to God that his expression—and, more importantly, the front of his jeans—hadn't betrayed his dirty fantasies about her granddaughter.

"Fine," he said grudgingly. "I'll think about it."

"Good." Mrs. S smiled sweetly at him, her blue eyes the same cornflower shade as Summer's. "We'll be back for lunch tomorrow. We'll talk then."

"Great," he said, unable to fake any enthusiasm. "Enjoy your food, ladies."

He spun on his heels and marched back to the kitchen.

The sight that greeted him as he strode through the swinging door was the opposite of what he wanted. Instead of frantic activity, everything seemed to have ground to a halt while he was away.

Marlene Wittenmeyer, his line cook, had her back turned to the big flattop where a row of burger patties sizzled away. She shook her spatula at her teenaged son Austin, who worked as Brock's dishwasher.

"—and then I told her, 'Katie, you shouldn't settle for someone who doesn't put you first.'" Marlene sounded indignant.

She was a short, stout woman somewhere in her fifties, with

wisps of bleached blonde hair escaping from her black cap. She was reliable and hard-working, but she also liked to talk. And when she talked, she got distracted from whatever else she was supposed to be doing. Like cooking.

Austin huffed and rolled his eyes. "Jeez, Ma, I know we both think Chris is a loser, but you *know* how Katie gets when someone tries to tell her to—"

"You two, get the fuck back to work!" Brock roared, finally free to unleash his anger at Ms. Fancy Pants Chef coming into *his* diner, and criticizing *his* food and *his* place with her big-city snobbery.

Startled, Marlene spun around to face Brock. Her mouth, outlined in bright red lipstick, opened into an indignant O. "*What* did you just say to me, young man?"

He glanced pointedly at the big stainless steel ticket wheel, still filled with outstanding orders. "We're running an hour behind."

Marlene planted her hands on her generous, apron-clad hips. "Don't you *dare* talk to me like that! I don't care how upset you are, but you keep a civil tongue in your head. Or I'll be following Kenny out that door." She pointed down the short hallway that led to the walk-in cooler, tiny office, and the diner's back door.

Brock groaned. Like Kenny, she'd starting working at the diner when Brock's mother was still running things. Unlike Kenny, Marlene did her job well and competently… if she wasn't distracted.

In fact, she and Mama had been friends for years, which hadn't made it easy to suddenly become Marlene's boss. Especially when she insisted on calling him "young man" every time he did something she didn't like.

But he had to admit that she was right. It wasn't fair for him to take out his frustration on the people who worked for him, and especially not someone like Marlene.

"You're right, and I'm sorry, Marlene," he said. "I shouldn't have yelled at you. But I just got an earful out there about how long people are waiting for their lunches."

She nodded, mollified. "These burgers'll be done in just a minute," she promised, reaching for the bag of buns. "And that'll close out six of those tickets."

He looked at the tickets and began working on the next non-burger order.

∞ ∞ ∞

After the lunch service finally ended and the diner closed for the day, Brock, Marlene, and Austin cleaned the kitchen. Then Marlene and Austin clocked out and left, while Brock stayed to take inventory of his walk-in cooler and his shelves.

As he'd feared, Kenny had made a mess of things. And Brock knew he shared the blame for not being on the ball and just trusting in the old guy to handle things.

Thanks to the long June days in Montana, the sun was still high when Brock finally arrived home.

He lived in a small two-bedroom cottage that he'd inherited from Mama, set on a couple of acres just outside town, across the disused railroad tracks and down the road a ways.

Brock fetched a can of Coke from his fridge and drank half of it down in one thirsty gulp. Then he went out into his vegetable garden to do some thinking while he pulled weeds and harvested the first of the green beans and strawberries.

He needed to come up with a plan to keep Mrs. S off his back. Instead, as he worked, he found himself worrying that he was on the verge of losing everything he'd worked so hard for.

After Mama died, Brock had met with Mr. and Mrs. S on the day after the funeral. They'd promised him they'd let him take over

Mama's half of The Yummy Cowboy Diner, if he proved he could run the place.

What if Mrs. S fires me and replaces me with Ms. Fancy Pants Chef? Or someone like her, who went to culinary school and everything?

Nausea rolled through his gut at the thought.

He couldn't let that happen. Not after everything he'd done and sacrificed for his place. He hadn't even had a day off—or a date— in the past year. All he did right now was work at the diner, do his chores at home, and go to sleep.

It's not fucking fair if I lose everything now! He ripped out a bunch of houndstongue and flung it onto his compost heap, then vengefully attacked the long tendrils of bindweed sneaking up his beanpoles.

The clock was ticking. Between now and lunchtime tomorrow, he had to come up with some kind of plan to satisfy Mrs. S's concerns... and keep Summer Snowberry the hell out of his business.

Chapter Five – Summer

Sunday, June 12

Winnie: Hey sis, you still awake?

Summer: Yeah. What's up?

Winnie: ::angry face emoji:: I need to vent about something. But first, how long are you staying at the ranch?

Summer: I promised GA I'll stay until Labor Day Weekend.

Winnie: Seriously? Must be nice to get some time off. I'm sorry I had to rush back to Seattle this morning.

Summer: You missed out on Dad's BBQ brisket. But everyone understands that you're in the middle of filming the next season of Restoring Seattle.

Winnie: My producer is really riding my butt about this stupid Dream House project. As if they need me there. Geoff and Mel have everything under control. And it's not like I get any input into the design.

Summer: Wait, what? The show isn't letting you pick your own stuff for your dream house? I mean, I know that you're Construction Girl and Geoff and Melanie are the design team on the show, but this is going to be your HOME. Can't you talk to Karla or something? I mean, as the producer, she can override their decisions, right?

Winnie: Sigh. I wish. Actually, I wish that Geoff and I had just eloped or something. Turning our engagement and this stupid

Tudor Revival project into a TV circus is exhausting. It's making me hate the house and everything to do with weddings.

Summer: I'm sorry. For what it's worth, it's a gorgeous house. I love that medieval half-timbered look.

Winnie: I actually had my heart set on a gorgeous Jud Yoho Craftsman in Ravenna. ::crying emoji:: Got overruled on that one, too.

Summer: Oh no! Why?

Winnie: Geoff, Melanie, and Karla decided the Tudor Revival house in First Hill looked more photogenic and more "fairy tale." Whatever the hell that means.

Winnie: Not gonna lie. "Restoring Seattle: Geoff and Winnie's Dream House" is turning into a nightmare.

Winnie: Vegas and an Elvis wedding chapel are sounding better and better.

Summer: I'm so sorry. Your Dream House season sounded like such a sweet idea.

Winnie: Oh, and did I mention my producer just vetoed my wedding gown?

Summer: No! WTF? I loved the dress you picked!

Winnie: That's why I wanted to vent tonight. Karla just told me that the show is getting a free wedding dress from some up-and-coming designer, so I'm going to have to wear that one instead. I'm supposed to be happy because it's way more expensive than the one I picked, but honestly, I think it's butt-ugly. It's all lacy and floofy and shit. Not my style at all. I'm going to hate my wedding photos.

Summer: I am SO sorry. I hope the network is paying you a crapload of money for going through all this.

Winnie: I feel like I sold my soul to HomeRenoTV. Anyhow, enough about me. Tell me about your vacation plans.

Summer: Not really a vacation. GA is putting me to work while SummerTime is closed for renovations. She wants me to upgrade The Yummy Cowboy Diner and turn it into something a little more upscale.

Summer: Which could be fun, except guess who's running the place these days?

Winnie: Mrs. Michaels… wait, no, she passed away last year. I heard it was cancer. Who?

Summer: Brock.

Winnie: No way! ::shocked emoji::

Summer: Yeah, GA really put me on the spot today. Did not appreciate that. Plus, he was *such* an asshole when we offered to help him.

Winnie: OMG. Is he still hot?

Summer: Maybe. Yes. And you didn't hear it from me, but he's actually a great cook. But his attitude is ::poop emoji:: NOT a sexy look, no matter if he IS "the yummy cowboy." Gah. I hope I can talk GA out of her plan for the place. Maybe we can just dynamite it and start over with a new owner.

Winnie: Yeah, good luck with that. You know how GA gets when she has a Plan for World Domination.

Winnie: Crap, Karla's calling. Probably some fresh disaster for the show. TTYL

∞ ∞ ∞

The Yummy Cowboy Diner
Monday, June 13

"But Brock made it perfectly clear yesterday that he doesn't want my help." Summer tried her best to sound reasonable. "Wouldn't it make more sense to upgrade a business that actually *wants* to be upgraded? I noticed that there's a new café-bakery place on the other side of the square. Maybe *they'd* be interested in expanding into the building next door. It's been vacant for years, ever since Phillips & Son went out of business."

Grandma Abigail stretched her neck, then rubbed it as if it ached.

"Are you all right, Grandma?" Summer asked.

"I'm fine. I think it may be time to replace my pillow." Grandma folded her neatly manicured hands, with their flawless pale-rose polish, on the scratched fake-wood Formica tabletop. Her blue gaze met Summer's. "And Jenna's Java doesn't need my help," she said firmly. "But this place does."

Trapped, Summer looked around the crowded diner. "Okay, but if that's the case, Grandma, then where is Brock? Wasn't he supposed to meet with us?"

And if he bailed on them, then too bad, so sad. It wasn't like he was open to advice, anyway.

"I'm sure he's very busy right now," Grandma replied, "but I expect he'll join us when our food is ready."

"Awesome. So, that'll be in an hour?" Summer couldn't keep the snarkiness out of her tone. She smiled tightly at her grandmother. "Don't worry, I ate a substantial breakfast."

Grandma Abigail sighed. "I know he didn't impress you yesterday, but sweetheart, I really need your expertise to save this diner. It's been part of this town for fifty years, and it would be a shame if it went out of business when the food has improved so dramatically over the past year."

"But I'd only be able to offer a Band-Aid fix," Summer countered. "I mean, how much can I *really* do when I'm only here for a few weeks? Plus, it's pretty clear that Brock Michaels still hates my guts." She grimaced. "You saw the death glares he was shooting my direction yesterday, right? What makes you think he's going to listen to anything I say?"

Unexpectedly, Grandma Abigail grinned at her. "Well, for one thing, those awful laminated menus are gone now."

"What—? Oh." Summer spotted a white sheet of paper propped behind the salt and pepper shakers.

She reached for the new menu. It looked like it had been created using one of those free templates from the Internet, then printed on an ink jet printer. And it was still a hundred times better than the laminated phone book from yesterday.

The revised menu listed a short set of breakfast options, with pancakes and waffles getting top billing, and omelets and breakfast burritos beneath. She turned the menu over and found lunch entrees plus various milkshake combinations on the other side.

Gone were the old menu's massive selection of fourteen different kinds of hot and cold sandwiches, twelve omelets, ten pasta dishes, seven salads, six burgers, five different kinds of steak, and four different soups.

The new lunch menu listed a single Soup of the Day (ask your server), hamburgers with a choice of toppings, a Sandwich of the Day (Monday was classic grilled cheese sandwich served with house-made tomato soup), plus a rotating list of daily specials.

Today's special was chicken pot pie with a side salad, with a note that each pie was baked to order and would take about twenty minutes.

The prices were all higher, too.

She was grudgingly impressed. Despite his defensiveness yesterday, Brock had apparently listened to at least *some* of her recommendations, and acted on them overnight.

Maybe he's not a complete idiot.

But he was still an ass, and she'd rather help her brother shovel manure than work with Brock.

She opened her mouth to tell Grandma Abigail just that, when Terri came by to deliver their sodas and take their lunch orders for the chicken pot pie.

When the young server left their table, Grandma Abigail leaned forward. "Before he passed, your grandfather and I did a lot of thinking about what needs to be done to attract tourists traveling between the Bozeman Airport and the North Gate of Yellowstone. We both agreed that the two most important things were to have a real restaurant and a hotel in operation before the LVR begins service next summer. And of those two things, only the restaurant is actually doable between now and then." She frowned and rubbed her upper left arm, as if it ached, too.

Summer nodded. The old Snowberry Springs Inn, which had occupied a Gold Rush-era mansion on the outskirts of town, had closed twenty years ago, after the death of its longtime owner. The grand old house, like so many other historic buildings in town, had been left vacant since then. Even the presence of a turn-of-the-century spa building around the private hot spring on the property hadn't been enough to entice someone to buy the place and fix it up.

"None of our plans to save this town will succeed unless The Yummy Cowboy Diner becomes profitable," Grandma continued. "Sweetheart, Frank and I believed in your dream enough to help you start your new life in San Francisco. Now, I need you to believe in *my* dream. And with Frank gone, I can't do this alone."

Summer noticed that her grandma looked pale and drawn under her tastefully applied makeup. "Are you feeling all right?"

Grandma Abigail waved off her concern. "I'm just tired, and very worried about the future. I need you, Summer. I need your help to save this diner."

Summer shuddered. "I'd rather give up my culinary career than have to deal with Brock Michaels on a daily basis," she said flatly. "And in case you didn't notice yesterday, it's clear he feels the same way about me. The two of us working together would be an absolute disaster."

Grandma Abigail frowned. The overhead fluorescent light glittered on the fine beads of perspiration that suddenly appeared on her face.

Summer's gut clenched in warning. *Something's wrong.*

"Sweetheart, I'm *begging* you—" Grandma Abigail's breath rasped in her throat as she took a shuddering gasp of air. An instant later, her eyes rolled back. She slumped backwards against the booth's burgundy vinyl seat, her mouth half-open.

"Oh shit!" Summer gasped. *This can't be happening—not so soon after Grandpa Frank!*

She lifted her head and looked around frantically. No one in the diner had noticed anything wrong yet. She caught the server's eye—at least the girl wasn't busy with her phone today.

"Terri!" she shouted. "Call 911! Now!"

Chapter Six – Brock

"Young man, are you hung over?" Marlene demanded as she lowered a basket of French fries into the deep fryer.

"No. Why?" Brock looked up from his skillet, where he was sautéing a mixture of mushrooms, onions, and garlic for a burger topping.

"Because you look like you've been rode hard and put away wet, and you're grumpy as hell," she shot back.

"I'm just tired," he admitted. "Didn't get a whole lot of sleep last night. And before you ask—" he raised his hand to forestall her next question, "—not because I was out having a good time. I was trying to sort out the mess that Kenny left."

Her red-painted mouth turned down unhappily. "Kenny was a good guy," she countered, her tone defensive. "He was just doing his best, you know."

With an effort, Brock bit back his vitriolic assessment of Kenny's "best" and just shook his head. He didn't want to discuss the sorry state of the diner's finances with her, not when he knew she'd tell the whole town about it by tomorrow.

"How's that burger coming along?" he asked instead, turning his attention back to the skillet. He'd cooked the excess moisture from the mushrooms, and the onions were browning up nicely.

"It's coming," Marlene snapped. "Just another thirty seconds."

Brock's head ached and his eyes felt gritty, as if he'd been out in a dust storm.

He had worked late into the night reviewing the past month's worth of receipts to see which menu items were the most popular, and then costing them out, as Ms. Fancy Pants Chef had suggested.

To his horror, he discovered that most of the dishes he was serving cost at least half of what he was selling them for.

When he added in his monthly overhead—wages, insurance, utilities, etc.—the resulting numbers forced him to confront reality.

Summer had been one hundred percent right about the reason that The Yummy Cowboy Diner was still running in the red despite a crowded dining room every breakfast and lunch service. *Dammit.*

Right now, no matter how hard he worked, he was losing money on each dish he cooked.

Worst of all, it was his own damned fault for listening to Kenny's bad advice instead of sitting down and doing the math himself.

After his mother's death, it had been easier for Brock to retreat to the kitchen and use the hard work of cooking to hold the raw pain of loss at bay. Kenny had kept the diner's books and done the payroll for as long as Brock could remember.

At the time, there hadn't been a compelling reason to change a system that seemed to be working. The pricing might have worked for Kenny, and the restaurant, back in the day, but with rising prices due to inflation, it was well past time to make some adjustments if Brock wanted to make ends meet.

After he went to bed last night, his seething anger at himself for letting things get this bad kept him awake for a long time.

When he finally fell asleep, he dreamed he was frantically hunting for a missing ingredient in his walk-in cooler while a blizzard of tickets swirled through the kitchen and Marlene shouted that she was quitting.

Then Summer appeared, wearing a white chef's coat, her arms crossed and her sweet mouth curled in scorn.

"You messed up bad, Brock. Everyone knows you're a loser," she purred. "So, why don't you let me take over the diner?"

Then, she pressed her soft curves against him and wound her long, sun-kissed golden legs around his hips. Her nails stabbed him in the back, sinking deep into his flesh like knives.

The pulsing shriek of his alarm clock shattered the dream into fragments of disturbing images.

Brock lay in the pre-dawn darkness, his heart pounding. His cock aching with morning wood and the phantom sensation of having his skin clawed to ribbons clung to him.

The sense of wrongness had persisted as he dragged himself through his morning routine, then headed for the diner.

Now, Terri popped into the kitchen. "Mrs. S and Summer just showed up," she reported. "They want to talk to you... oh, and they both ordered the chicken pot pie."

She stuck the ticket on the round, stainless steel ticket holder, grabbed the plate with the finished burger and fries, and disappeared back into the dining room.

Brock groaned and headed for the cooler, where the rounds of buttery puff pastry dough he'd prepped this morning were stored.

"Bad news, boss?" Marlene asked when Brock returned.

"Nope," he said, with more confidence than he felt as he began ladling the rich chicken and vegetable chowder from a stockpot simmering on the stove. He filled a pair of ramekins and topped each of them with a round of chilled dough, pressing firmly to seal the edges.

He shoved the ramekins into the oven to bake for twenty minutes, and started assembling the side salads for the specials. While he worked, he rehearsed what he was going to say to Mrs. S when he brought out her meal.

To start with, he was going to point out all the changes he'd already made overnight.

He imagined the look of triumph on Summer Snowberry's face when she noticed that he'd taken some of her advice. It made his stomach churn.

But just because she'd given him some valuable tips didn't mean that he wanted Ms. Fancy Pants Chef breathing down his neck. He had to convince Mrs. S that he'd be okay without her granddaughter's "help."

Hell, Marlene would probably quit on the spot if Summer tried bossing his assistant cook around.

"Boss!" Terri burst into the kitchen. "You gotta come quick! Mrs. Snowberry is having a heart attack or stroke or something!"

Brock's stomach dropped. He stopped slicing tomatoes. "Did you call 911?"

Wide-eyed, Terri nodded. "But you're with the fire department, right?"

"Not anymore." Regret lanced through him as he grabbed the kitchen's first aid kit from the wall and sprinted for the dining room.

Before Mama died, Brock had been one of the town's volunteer firefighters. He'd been forced to resign his position once he started running The Yummy Cowboy Diner. But he still missed the work—and the respect he'd finally earned after years of being known as Mrs. Michael's wild kid.

The first thing he saw upon entering the dining room was a group of curious diners gathered around one of the booths. A babble of suggestions and instructions rose from the onlookers, most of them dead wrong.

"Back to your seats, everyone," he shouted, pushing his way ruthlessly through the onlookers. "Give us some room."

The crowd melted away, though not without lingering, avidly-fascinated glances at the tableau.

Mrs. S's eyes were closed and her carefully made-up face shone with sweat as she slumped, apparently unconscious, against the back of the same booth she'd occupied yesterday.

Summer had pulled the table out of the booth. As Brock approached, she was bent over her grandmother, taking her pulse.

"Is she breathing?" he demanded.

Summer nodded. "Her pulse is weak but not dropping noticeably," she reported, cluing Brock in that she'd had some kind of first aid training.

Oh thank God! thought Brock.

Despite his current opposition to her plan, he liked Mrs. S a lot.

"I think she's having a heart attack," Summer said. "Just before she passed out, it looked like her neck and left arm were bothering her. I should've *known* something was wrong!"

Brock nodded. Those were classic heart attack symptoms.

He reacted to the distress in Summer's voice by automatically placing a comforting hand on her shoulder. The warmth of her smooth skin startled him.

That was when he noticed that she was wearing a pretty sundress in bold floral print today, with a high round neck that left her shoulders bare.

He snatched his hand away as if the contact burned him, but the sensation of silky heat lingered against his palm, inviting him to stroke and caress.

Oh, hell no.

He forced himself to focus on the crisis.

"Let's get her shifted around." He dropped the first aid kit on the bench behind him, and bent to lift Mrs. S's legs.

With Summer's help, he repositioned the old lady so that she sat with her back to the wall, and her legs on the bench. He raised her knees, angling her legs in a bent position to encourage blood flow to her heart.

"Do you know whether she's taking any medications for heart problems?" he asked.

Summer shook her head. "Not that I know of... though she isn't the type to admit any weakness."

Brock huffed out a humorless laugh. "Yeah, I noticed."

Mrs. S groaned and stirred weakly.

"Help's on the way, Mrs. S," Brock told her. "While we're waiting, I want you to chew and swallow an aspirin. Do you think you can do that?"

Her lids fluttered open. "I really wish you would call me Abigail," she whispered.

Relief spread warmth through Brock's chest. "Tell you what... if you hang on, and get better, I promise I'll try to remember to call you by your first name." He grinned down at her. "Though my mama's ghost might show up and smack me upside the head for sassing my elders."

Summer chuckled. His enmity momentarily forgotten, Brock turned his head and shared a smile with her before opening the metal first aid kit case and digging out a packet of aspirin.

"I'll give it to her, if you hand me one of those glasses of water," she said, indicating the table with her chin.

He straightened up and handed Summer the aspirin and water,

then surveyed his watching customers. "Anyone got a coat they can lend Mrs. S until the EMTs arrive?"

His first aid training had emphasized keeping a heart attack victim warm and comfortable until an ambulance arrived.

He and Summer did what they could for Mrs. S. It felt like an eternity before the Snowberry Springs Fire Department arrived, but in reality, it was less than ten minutes.

Brock knew both of the firefighters entering the diner. One of them was his childhood neighbor Evie, who now ran E.V. Carter Automotive, and the other was his high school buddy Jason Lund, who owned his own cabinetry business here in town.

"Brock, dude, do I need to post a warning about your Daily Specials?" Jason joked as he pushed a gurney through the door that Evie held open for him.

"Not funny, Jayce," she snapped as she followed him in, lugging a huge blue soft-sided first aid case.

Her concerned gaze met Brock's. "What happened, Brock? Terri said it was a possible heart attack or stroke?"

He briefly described the situation. Summer chimed in with her grandmother's vitals. Before he'd emerged from the kitchen, she'd apparently been timing Mrs. S's breaths and pulse using her vintage wristwatch.

"Good job, guys," Jason said as he pushed the table further out of the way and squeezed into the booth. "We'll take it from here."

The town's lone ambulance came and went, rushing Mrs. S off to the nearest hospital, located forty-five minutes away in Livingston.

Crisis over, Brock said goodbye to Jason and Evie, then turned to head back to the kitchen.

That was when he noticed Summer just standing next to the vacated booth. She looked pale and shaken. And surprisingly uncertain.

"Hey, aren't you going to the hospital?" he asked.

"When my folks get here," she replied curtly. At his expression, she added, "Grandma was the one who drove us into town. I didn't think about grabbing her car keys from her purse before the ambulance left."

"I'll drive you," he said, before he had time to think about it.

Her eyes widened in shock. "Uh, no, that's okay," she protested. "I can wait until Mom gets back to me and gives me a lift."

But he saw the way that her gaze darted to the diner's front door, as if straining for a glimpse of the departed ambulance. "It's the middle of lunch rush and you're really busy," she added.

That settled it.

"Well, I'm going to the hospital, with or without you," he growled. "So, stop arguing and ride with me, Summer. I'm parked out back."

"Thanks," she muttered without meeting his eyes. Her cheeks flushed under her golden tan.

Stiff-backed, she marched through the diner, heading for his kitchen without a backwards glance.

It was probably killing her to accept a favor from him. Despite his worry for Mrs. S, he couldn't help smirking as he followed her.

"Young man, how's Abigail doing?" Marlene demanded as soon as he entered the kitchen.

"Not good," he said without slowing down. "She's been rushed to Livingston Memorial."

"Oh no!" Marlene dropped her spatula onto the flattop with a clatter. "Is she going to be okay?"

"Don't know," Brock said, heading for the short hallway that led to the back door. "I'll know more when I give Summer a lift to the hospital. You think you can handle the rest of lunch service on your own?"

"I'll manage," Marlene said firmly. "Please let me know the moment you get any news about Abigail's condition."

"Will do," Brock promised.

Ahead of him, Summer pushed open the diner's back door and marched through, her back straight and her golden hair neatly braided in a long plait that hung between her shoulders.

Brock followed her out into the small parking lot. "It's the black pickup over there," he said, indicating his Tacoma and wishing it wasn't so dusty and spattered with dead bugs.

He figured that nothing he owned would meet her high falutin' standards, but he hated handing her ammunition.

"Thanks. I—I really appreciate this," she said, stopping next to his truck.

He could tell how much it cost her to acknowledge the favor.

The next forty-five minutes were going to be fun. Just him and Ms. Fancy Pants Chef in his truck.

Wonder what we're gonna talk about? Senior prom? Or how she's gonna spiff up my diner?

Chapter Seven – Brock

He and Summer didn't talk much during that long drive to the hospital.

Summer spent most of the time frowning down at her phone, furiously texting her family.

Brock couldn't help noticing that her nails were short and neatly trimmed, free of polish. A couple of half-healed burns showed vividly pink against her tan, and there were pale scars from older injuries marring her fingers and backs of her hands.

His hands bore a similar collection of injuries, old and new. It was the inevitable consequence of working with sharp knives and hot metal surfaces all day.

Her thick braid, the color of sun-ripened hay, hung over one bare shoulder, and rested on the tantalizing curve of her breast.

Brock's mouth went dry as he imagined cupping its soft weight in his hand.

His cock stirred, and he forced his eyes back to the road. Thanks to the North Gate of Yellowstone, located a half-hour drive south of Snowberry Springs, the highway through Paradise Valley was straight and well-paved.

On the downside, having such a good road also meant having to pass plenty of big, lumbering tour buses that were driving at exactly the speed limit.

As he drove, he couldn't help thinking about Mrs. S's outrageous proposal, and what it might mean for him if the worst came to pass. He hated himself for wondering about what would happen to his diner, but she held the mortgage on the building, not to mention the business loans she'd made over the years to Mama, and later, to him.

If Mrs. S dies, is Summer gonna inherit her grandma's half of the diner?

Brock shuddered. He didn't want to think about how quickly he could lose all of his hard work and family history.

When they arrived at the hospital, Brock dropped Summer off at the entrance to the large, single-story building and went in search of a parking space.

He considered waiting out here in the parking lot instead of going in. He fucking hated hospitals. Once he stepped foot through those doors, he knew that the smells and the sounds would flood him with memories of his mother's surgeries, and her monthly visits here for chemo treatments.

Don't be such a fucking weenie, he told himself. *After everything the Snowberrys did for Mama, this is the least I can do for Mrs. S and her family.*

He parked on the street, then began walking across the hospital's front lawn towards the low, tan brick building. Then he saw a familiar white extended-cab Ford pickup approaching, and spotted Bob and Priscilla Snowberry, Summer's parents, sitting in the truck's cab, with Spring sitting behind them.

He stopped and waited for them to park.

"Brock! How is Abigail doing?" Priscilla Snowberry demanded as she emerged from the truck and hurried over to him. She wore somewhat raggedy jeans shorts and a tank top. With her blonde hair pulled back in a loose ponytail, she looked like an older version of Summer.

"I don't know. Summer and I just got here a couple of minutes ago," Brock replied.

"And thank you so much for driving her!" Priscilla enveloped Brock in an unexpected hug. "I was out in the stables and didn't check my phone for a while."

"It's no problem," he assured her, surrounded by the comforting smell of sweet hay and horses. "I'm worried about Mrs. S, too. I hope she's gonna be okay."

Priscilla nodded. "Bob's taking it pretty hard," she confessed, her gaze moving to the two men approaching them.

She reached out and took her husband's hand. Bob Snowberry was a big man, with graying hair and the deeply tanned, weathered complexion of someone who spent his days outdoors in all kinds of weather.

Summer's brother Spring—his real name was Zachary, but no one ever called him that—nodded in Brock's direction. "Hey, Brock."

He was a tall, serious-looking guy, a few years older than Brock. The news had apparently pulled him away from haying—green bits of alfalfa and golden wisps of timothy grass were stuck to his t-shirt and cowboy hat.

Brock nodded back. "Hey, Spring."

Priscilla's phone chimed. She glanced down. "Autumn says she's on her way. She'll be here in a half-hour."

Autumn was Summer's younger sister. She'd married an older man shortly after graduating from high school and moved to Bozeman.

"Let's go inside and hear what the doc has to say about how my mom's doing," Bob suggested in his soft voice.

Feeling like a fifth wheel, Brock tailed them into the hospital.

They found Summer sitting in the ER waiting room. She sprang up as soon as her parents and brother walked in, and everyone exchanged hugs.

Now that everyone's here, I should probably get back to the diner, Brock thought, trying to push down a sudden stab of envy at this display of family closeness.

With Mama gone, he didn't have any close kin in the area. His grandparents had passed a few years ago. He was an only child, and his father had walked out when Brock was in the fourth grade.

The year after high school graduation, Brock's old man had gone off the highway somewhere in Idaho and wrapped his car around a tree. The medical examiner had found his blood alcohol level was twice the legal limit.

Brock's only reaction had been relief that his father hadn't hurt or killed anyone else in the accident.

Lunch rush would be over by the time Brock returned to Snowberry Springs, but it wouldn't be fair to leave the cleanup to Marlene and the rest of his staff.

Besides, he was eager to review the day's receipts and see if the changes he'd made had paid off.

But first, he had to know whether Mrs. S was going to pull through.

"What happened to Abigail?" Priscilla asked Summer. "Your texts were a little confusing."

"We were having lunch at the diner," Summer began. "Grandma was pretty stressed out about the whole situation with Brock—"

"Hey, wait just a minute," he interrupted, his temper flaring. "If she was stressed out, it was because of all that stuff *you* said yesterday about fixing up my place!"

Summer glared at him before turning back to her parents.

Spring leaned against one of the waiting room's walls, silent as usual, his expression watchful.

"Anyway, as I was saying, Grandma Abigail was really worried about the diner," Summer continued. "She wanted me to fix the problems there before I go back to San Francisco, and I told her it was a bigger job than I felt comfortable—"

"—not to mention I don't need you breathing down my neck, telling me how to run my business—" Brock interrupted again.

Summer tried to ignore him. "—anyway, I told her I didn't think it was a good idea—"

"Got that right," Brock muttered. That earned him a faint smile from Spring.

"—and that's when she started looking really ill and fainted," Summer finished.

"And you're blaming me for that?" Brock demanded. "I wasn't even there!"

Despite his denial, he felt a twinge of guilt. *Had* he contributed to Mrs. S's heart attack?

"Well, you're the reason she was so worked up in the first place!" Summer shot back. "Mom, you would not believe how badly—"

"Now wait just a God-da—" Brock remembered that Bob and Priscilla were faithful churchgoers, and hastily edited himself. "I mean, gosh darn minute! If anyone was stressing out Mrs. S, it was *you* and all of your fu—uh, *stupid* ideas for fancying up *my* place!" He glared at her. "Everything was just fine until *you* showed up!"

Summer produced an unladylike snort. "You're delusional. You can't even—"

"Stop it!" Priscilla ordered. Summer drew breath to protest, and her mother added in a quelling tone, *"Both* of you. You're behaving like children."

"Sorry, ma'am," Brock muttered.

His face heated with embarrassment. She was right. This wasn't the time or place for Summer and him to argue.

"Sorry, Mom," Summer said, a moment later.

"My mother's been having heart issues for a while now. She didn't want anyone to know," Bob said softly. "Summer, that's why your grandma was so happy to hear that you were staying at the ranch for a while. Now that my dad's gone, she can't really manage all the family's businesses by herself. I'd appreciate it if you put some thought into how you can help her."

Summer turned red. Her shoulders slumped and her gaze dropped to her strappy sandals. "Sure," she muttered.

Brock felt his own face heat. Maybe he wasn't one hundred percent at fault here, but he couldn't deny that he'd contributed to the situation.

"Priscilla and Robert Snowberry?" someone asked from the waiting room doorway. Brock saw a young Indian woman in a white coat standing there. "Hi, I'm Dr. Gupta, Mrs. Abigail Snowberry's attending physician."

"Yes, we're the Snowberry family," Bob said, with a gesture that included everyone in the waiting room, including Brock. "How's my mother doing?"

"I'm thrilled to report that her condition is now stable," Dr. Gupta replied, smiling. "We are preparing her for a percutaneous transluminal coronary angioplasty, commonly referred to as cardiac catheterization procedure to place a heart stent."

She continued with a brief explanation of the procedure, which she described as much less invasive as bypass surgery, and with a much faster recovery time.

When she had finished updating everyone on Mrs. S's condition and prospects for a full recovery, Brock felt the crushing burden of dread lift from his shoulders.

Mrs. S is gonna be okay, thank God!

"I should get going," he said after Dr. Gupta left the waiting room. "Please let me know how Mrs. S is doing."

To his surprise and pleasure, Priscilla came over and gave him another hug. "Thank you so much for bringing Summer. Give me your number and I'll text you as soon as Abigail is out of surgery."

$$\infty\infty\infty$$

"Hi, Mrs. S," Brock said from the doorway of the hospital room the next afternoon. "I came by to see how you were feeling after your surgery."

He'd driven up from Snowberry Springs after the diner closed for the day. As promised, Priscilla had texted him last night to report that Abigail's surgery had gone smoothly, and that she was hoping to come home in the next day or so.

To add to the good news, when Brock reviewed his receipts last night, he realized that the changes he'd made to the diner's menu and pricing were working. Yesterday was the first day in a long time that he hadn't lost money.

"I'm bored. Daytime television is terrible, and I'm overjoyed to see you, dear." Mrs. S was sitting up in bed, and looking a lot better than the last time he'd seen her, unconscious at his diner.

She added, "And I thought you'd agreed to call me Abigail if I pulled through?"

"I did, but it's gonna take some getting used to," Brock admitted. "Uh, *Abigail*."

It felt wrong, and it went against everything his mama had taught him about being polite… but he'd *promised*.

Mrs. S—*no, Abigail*, he reminded himself—looked pleased. "That's much better, dear. Well, come on in. Don't be a stranger."

He approached the bed and remembered something. "Here, I brought these for you. They're from my garden."

He offered her a large glass pickle jar holding the bouquet he'd hastily cut when he dashed home to change into clean clothes before driving up to Livingston.

Abigail's face lit up as she took the flowers from him. "Oh, they're beautiful! Pamela always grew the most beautiful heirloom roses. I'm so glad they're thriving in your care." She buried her nose in the mass of white, yellow, and pink blossoms, and inhaled deeply.

Brock's throat tightened. Growing up, there had never been much money, but there had always been fresh flowers perfuming the house from the first daffodils in April to the last zinnias and chrysanthemums in October. After Mama passed, keeping her beloved garden going felt like the best way to honor her memory.

He placed the bouquet in its humble vase on a side table, then pulled up one of the plastic visitor's chairs. "So, how are you feeling... Abigail?"

If he said her name often enough, maybe it would stop sounding so *wrong*.

She grimaced. "Well, my leg is really sore where they inserted the stent through my femoral artery. Would you believe that the nurses already have me up and walking?" She shook her head. "At least I'll be able to go home tomorrow."

"Oh, that's great news." Brock felt some of the tension ease from his shoulders.

He owed her a great deal for all of her support over the years. And he liked her, despite her bossy ways. Or maybe because of them. She made him feel like he *mattered* to her. Like she cared whether he succeeded or failed, and not just because of the money he owed her.

"I'm so glad you drove all this way to visit me," Abigail said. "I wanted to have a private chat with you before Bob and Priscilla show up."

Uh-oh, he thought. *And I walked right into this trap with an armful of roses.*

"About?" he asked, as if he didn't already know.

Abigail threw him a look. He wasn't fooling her. "Believe me, dear," she began, "I know and appreciate how hard you've worked so far to improve things at the diner. Your food is outstanding, and I'm not the only one who thinks so. Everyone in town loves eating there."

Oh yeah, she's buttering me up, all right.

"But...?" Brock asked. "I know there's a 'but' buried in all of your sweet-talkin', Mrs., I mean, Abigail."

"Touché." She grinned at him. "*But*, from here on out, Brock, it's going to be about working smarter, not harder. You can't do everything yourself, and you'll kill yourself trying." Her smile turned wry. She patted her chest. "It's a lesson I forgot to apply to myself."

He nodded warily.

"All this to say, I believe in you, Brock, and I want you to succeed."

Here it comes, he thought. "I'm already making changes—" he began.

"I saw. And I admire you for not letting your pride get in the way of taking good advice," Abigail said, her expression serious now. "Which is why I have a proposal for you."

"What kind of proposal?" Whatever it was, he was sure he wouldn't like it.

Chapter Eight – Brock

L ivingston Memorial Hospital
Tuesday, June 14

"If you're willing to reconsider your opposition to having Summer help you make the diner profitable," Abigail said, "and if some additional conditions are met, then I'll forgive the mortgage and all of the diner's outstanding business loans."

Brock's breath caught. He'd inherited all of Mama's debts along with the business, and they'd only grown over the past year as he struggled to run the place. "What conditions?"

"Here's what I'm thinking," Abigail replied. "I'm willing to give you and Summer each a fifty percent stake in the diner, debt-free, if you agree to the following conditions: first, the two of you have to work together while Summer is in town, and you split the profits evenly. Second, the diner must be operating with a minimum five percent profit margin by September fifteenth. Third, if either of you ever quit this project, you must sell your stake to the other partner. You can't bring in any outsiders."

She smiled benevolently at him and folded her hands on the thin hospital blanket. She waited for him to catch his breath, then said, "Now, how does that sound? Can you bring yourself to work with my granddaughter for ninety days?"

Brock swallowed hard. *Debt free!* he thought, dizzy at the prospect. On the surface, this was an unbelievable stroke of good luck.

But of course, amazing offers always came with a catch. This one was no different.

"That's a really generous offer," he said cautiously.

"But?" Her smile vanished.

He decided on brutal honesty. "But it'll be a nightmare if I'm answerable to a business partner who swoops in to criticize what I'm doing at The Yummy Cowboy Diner before swanning off to her fancy, big-city restaurant again."

And that was the best-case scenario.

Worst case, he'd be stuck with Summer breathing down his neck for the next three months.

Should I risk it? Can I put up with Ms. Fancy Pants Chef trying to run things in return for the next step up in my dream?

Because if he could make the diner profitable, he'd finally have the financial stability he needed to pursue his *other* dream.

He wanted a wife and a family of his own. And that was impossible if he couldn't pay his bills.

Not to mention that he didn't actually have time for dating right now.

"Summer has promised me that she'll stay in Montana until September. If your partnership doesn't work out, you could offer to buy her out anytime after the ninety-day period ends," Abigail pointed out. "If I know her, she's champing at the bit to return to San Francisco. I'm sure she'd be more than happy to sell you her share of The Yummy Cowboy Diner once the two of you have made the place profitable."

Brock thought about it. Summer Snowberry was bossy, annoying as fuck... and disturbingly attractive. And whatever happened, he'd probably be stuck with her until he could afford to buy her out... which wouldn't be for a while, not at five percent profit.

But he could put up with her for three months, if it meant owning his diner free and clear. Right?

Right. He made his decision. *I can put up with* anything *for ninety days. Even Ms. Fancy Pants Chef.*

He stood and offered Abigail his hand. "Okay. I'll work with Summer for the next three months and make the diner profitable, and in return, you'll cancel out the diner's mortgage and all of the outstanding loan balances."

She beamed up at him, and closed her cool, dry fingers around his. "Brock Michaels, you have yourself a deal. I'll talk to Summer as soon as possible, then have my lawyer draw up the necessary paperwork." She released his hand and settled back against the pillow. "Now, dear, tell me about the changes you've already made..."

When Brock left Abigail's room a half-hour later, he couldn't help wondering whether he'd just scored a win or made the biggest mistake of his life.

Then he spotted Summer heading straight towards him. She wore a pair of stylish khaki shorts and a pink crop-top that left her midriff bare. Her head was bowed and she was apparently so deep in thought that she wasn't aware of his presence.

He halted and waited for the inevitable fireworks.

And damned if he wasn't looking forward—just a little—to seeing her expression when she realized she wasn't going to have the last word in changing *his* diner.

Summer

Summer sighed as she walked down the hospital corridor, heading for her grandmother's room. Yesterday, she'd been determined to stand her ground in the face of Grandma Abigail's outrageous request.

Then everything had changed in an instant.

She had done a lot of thinking last night, after they all returned from the hospital.

Dad never asked for much. So, it was a big deal that he'd requested she help Grandma Abigail.

And then there was the fact that she owed her grandmother a debt she could never fully repay. Without Grandma Abigail's generosity, Summer could have never set out on the road that had led to her very own restaurant, SummerTime.

It had been a dream come true... until last month.

That was when her business partner Gregory Brandywine had emptied the restaurant's bank account and vanished. His theft had forced Summer to cover the week's payroll from her personal funds.

She'd filed a complaint with the police, of course, but not much had happened since then. And she didn't have the funds to hire a private detective, not with all of her other debts right now.

At least the local news hadn't picked up the story, thank God.

But Summer wasn't willing to admit defeat, not yet. She'd worked too long and too hard to just walk away from SummerTime. She *knew* her restaurant could turn a profit. All she needed was enough money to pay her staff and suppliers to re-launch it.

So, she'd decided to keep paying the rent, but closed the restaurant while she tried to find a way to finance its reopening. The official story was SummerTime was undergoing a major renovation. Of course, everyone in San Francisco's restaurant community knew real story.

Most of her fellow chefs expressed support and sympathy, but they all considered her place DOA. Even her general manager and friend, Maggie Tang, thought Summer was crazy for continuing to pay the rent on her closed restaurant and not calling it quits.

Summer was determined to prove them wrong. But there had to be a better way than working with Brock! She was going to talk to Grandma Abigail and see if—

A flash of red fabric warned her an instant before she walked right into Brock's hard chest.

Startled out of her deep immersion in her thoughts, Summer squeaked and stumbled back. A pair of large, sinewy hands gripped her upper arms and steadied her.

"W-what are you doing here?" she demanded, her heart pounding.

"Havin' a talk with your grandma." He gave her a crooked grin, his brown eyes warm and appreciative as they met hers.

Her heart began pounding crazily. She suddenly felt like she was back in high school, when every casual encounter with him sent her into transports of dizzy joy.

"Oh. It's, um, really nice of you to visit her." Summer stepped back, trying to wrestle her hormones under control. She eyed him suspiciously. *Talking about what, exactly? My perfectly reasonable suggestions for improving the diner?*

She couldn't help noticing that Brock's worn jeans molded perfectly to his long, muscular legs, and that he wore another one of those sinfully tight t-shirts with "The Yummy Cowboy Diner" printed across his broad pectorals.

He was definitely hotter than he'd been in high school. *And he was so nice to me and to Grandma Abigail yesterday, too.*

She didn't want to like him, not after the way he'd stomped on her teenage heart.

Maybe he's changed.

She sure had. Restaurant kitchens were brutal. You had to be strong to survive and thrive there, especially if you were female. Her first year of working had been hell. She'd toughened up in a hurry.

These days, she kicked ass when she had to, and she sure as heck didn't take crap from anyone.

"We had a lot to talk about. Looks like we're gonna be partners... at least for the next three months."

"What?" Summer felt shock run through her body like a splash of ice water. "You mean you're actually going to let me help you give the diner a makeover? Why? You hated all my suggestions!"

"Let's just say that Abigail just made me an offer I couldn't refuse." His grin deepened and became devilish. "I'll see you tomorrow, *partner.*"

His repeated use of the term pinged in her head.

"Wait, what do you mean by 'partner'?" Now she was confused... and a little worried. *What the heck did Grandma Abigail tell him?*

"You'll see," he shot back. "Your grandma has an interesting proposition for you."

Oh, no, she thought. Impending doom gathered over her head like a dark purple thunderhead.

Still grinning, Brock strode away, leaving her to shake her head before she tapped on the door to her grandmother's room.

"Sweetheart! You're just the person I wanted to see!" Grandma Abigail said brightly when Summer poked her head in. "Did you see Brock just now?"

"I did," Summer replied. She entered the room and bent to kiss Grandma's cheek. "You're looking a lot better than yesterday."

Grandma Abigail chuckled. "Well, I feel like a mule kicked me in the leg, and I'm still a bit shaky, but I've already walked up and down the corridor twice today. Please, sit." She indicated the plastic chair at her bedside.

"Those are beautiful roses," Summer said as she took a seat.

Grandma Abigail grinned at her. "They're from Brock's garden."

Summer suppressed a groan. *Why is he being so darned sweet? What does he want?*

Then Grandma Abigail's grin vanished, replaced by a serious expression. "He really is very thoughtful, sweetheart. And a hard worker, too. I really wish you'd reconsider working with him to fix up the diner."

Summer drew a deep breath. "About that—" she began.

"So, I'm going to make you the same offer I made Brock just now," Grandma Abigail interrupted.

I knew it! I knew there had to be some reason he was acting so smug!

Summer listened without comment as her grandmother outlined the conditions for the proposed partnership. But her heart began beating fast at the extremely generous terms.

She didn't want another business partner. Not after the way Greg had betrayed her trust. And she sure as heck didn't want to partner with *Brock*, of all people.

But he was right. This was an offer she couldn't refuse. Not with SummerTime's fate in the balance. She was certain she could make the diner even more profitable than Grandma's stipulation.

If I can make The Yummy Cowboy Diner a success, I'll get Brock or Grandma Abigail to buy me out in September. Then I'll go back to the city and reopen SummerTime.

Grandma didn't know it, but she had just thrown Summer a lifeline. Her offer couldn't have come at a better time. Even if it meant swallowing her pride and working with Brock for three months.

All Summer had to do was keep the wolves at bay until she could cash out her half of the diner.

"All right," she said when Grandma had finished speaking. "I'll do it. I'll turn The Yummy Cowboy Diner into a cash cow for all of us. And I think I know how."

Grandma Abigail reached out and clasped Summer's hand. "Oh, sweetheart, you've made me so happy. You know how much the diner means to this town... and how much it meant to your grandfather."

"I won't let you down," Summer promised.

Silently, she added, *And I'm going to show Brock the difference between a cook and a real chef.*

Chapter Nine – Summer

The Yummy Cowboy Diner
Wednesday, June 15

"No way," Brock said firmly.

The only light in the diner's tiny parking lot came from an old barn lamp mounted over the diner's back door. But it was enough to illuminate the muscle twitching in his jaw as he glared down at her. "The last thing I need during breakfast rush is *you* breathing down my neck, Ms. Fancy Pants Chef."

Dawn was a promise of bright pink over the mountains to the east, but it was still dark in town. Summer fought back a yawn as a cool breeze swept out of the darkness. She hadn't gotten up this early in a long time, but she was determined to show Brock that she was serious about her half of their new partnership.

Upon her return from the hospital yesterday, she'd spent the rest of the afternoon and evening contacting various friends and acquaintances to spread the word that she wanted to sublet her apartment and parking space for three months.

No sense in paying all that money if she wasn't going to be there, and both housing and parking were always in demand. She'd driven the sixteen hours to Snowberry Springs rather than flown, so that she could bring her knives, pans, and other equipment to cater Grandpa Frank's Celebration of Life.

Now, Brock crossed his arms and leaned against the back door, clearly intent on blocking her.

Summer tried to ignore his bulging biceps and muscled forearms with their dusting of dark, wiry hair, and glared right back up at him. She'd faced down a lot worse in her years of working at the busiest restaurants in San Francisco.

"You don't get to tell me 'No,'" she pointed out in her most reasonable tone. "I'm your partner now, remember?" She couldn't resist the temptation to meet his angry, dark eyes with a smirk. "Fifty-fifty partnership until the middle of September. And if I'm 'Ms. Fancy Pants,' do I get to call you 'Mr. Grumpy Pants'?"

In response, he actually *growled* at her. "Fuck you."

"Only if you're real nice to me... and buy me dinner first," she shot back.

And instantly regretted it when she saw his jaw drop.

Where did THAT come from? she asked herself in shock. *I sure as heck don't want to give him the wrong idea.*

She had a brief, vivid fantasy of him backing her against the door and kissing the hell out of her with the same aggression that had marked most of their exchanges so far. Her throat went dry, and an unexpected pulse of desire, hot and aching, kindled between her legs.

Crap. No. That would be such a bad idea.

It was his fault for being so sexy when he was angry. Or maybe she had a thing for big, angry men with big muscles and tight butts.

Brock wore his working clothes—a trucker's cap, brim turned backwards; another one of those sinfully tight t-shirts; jeans; and comfortable sneakers.

Summer couldn't be sure if the lamplight was playing tricks on her, but was he actually *blushing*?

She wore her loose, comfortable black-and-white checkered

chef's pants, with her white chef's coat buttoned over it. The breast pocket of her coat had her name embroidered on it, along with the spray of delicate pink-and-white snowberry blossoms that formed her restaurant's logo. The same snowberry design decorated the brim of the flat black skullcap jammed over her tightly braided hair.

"Brock, like it or not," she said in her firmest tone, "I'm going to observe your breakfast service so that I can make more recommendations."

"Oh, great. And then let me guess: you'll have another fucking list for me?"

She grinned cheerily at him. "Yup. Guaranteed. But it's all for a good cause. You want this place to turn a profit? I can help you do that... but only if you play nice."

He glared at her for a moment longer, then straightened up.

"Fine," he gritted, and turned to unlock the door.

To her surprise, he held it open for her. She stepped into the dark hallway and felt the heat radiating off his body as he entered behind her.

An instant later, the lights snapped on. He brushed past her and marched towards the kitchen.

"While you're prepping for breakfast, I'm going to inspect your storeroom and your kitchen," she called after him.

His back stiffened, but he kept walking. "Whatever. Just don't move or reorganize anything without asking first."

She bit back her first response and forced herself to say, "Okay."

Despite his tone, it wasn't an unreasonable request. Each chef had their preferred way of arranging equipment and inventory.

As Brock began working in the kitchen, Summer looked at the two doors on either side of the hall. One bore a plastic wood-grain sign with the word "Office."

She opened the door and found a windowless room that resembled a walk-in closet.

A metal desk stood on one side of the room, the workspace crowded with a monitor, keyboard, laptop docking station, and an all-in-one copier/scanner/printer. A large, dented filing cabinet and bookshelves crammed with binders and hard-copy accounting ledgers took up the remaining wall space.

She shut the door, reminding herself to sit down with Brock after the diner closed today, and go over the week's bills and receipts.

Based on his reaction to her request to observe breakfast service today, he'd probably blow his stack when she asked to see his income and expenditure.

Too bad. Grandma Abigail trusted her to come up with a plan to turn this place around. And to do that, Summer needed hard data.

The other door led to a storage room twice the width of the office, crowded with tall metal racks that held a variety of spice containers, cans, bulk staples like flour and sugar, plastic bags of hamburger buns, and sacks of potatoes and onions.

A smaller rack, separate from the food items, held cleaning supplies.

The linoleum floor looked worn and stained, but clean, even under the shelving.

The back of the room was a featureless wall of stainless steel, with a latched metal door of a relatively modern walk-in cooler.

Summer stepped inside. A chilly blast of air greeted her. She checked the thermometer settings and found everything in order. Then she inspected the contents of the cooler.

Like the dry storage area, the diner's walk-in cooler was clean and neatly organized, which was a relief, with all the perishables stored according to food safety principles.

The only things missing were date/content labels on the storage containers. She'd have to remedy that… "first in, first out" was the iron-clad rule of good food storage management. With the way the diner had been running out of ingredients, she didn't think anything in here was past its expiration date, but even with that, better to be safe than sorry.

Impressed with the food storage areas' overall neatness and cleanliness, Summer jotted down a few notes for improvements, then checked her watch.

It was almost time for the diner to open, so she headed for the kitchen.

"Hi, Summer!" said an older woman who was busily cracking eggs into a large stainless-steel bowl. She wore a long white apron, a colorful scarf folded over her hair, and bright red lipstick. "Don't you look all grown up in your chef outfit!"

Outfit? Does she think I'm playing dress-up? Summer blinked, then recognized Marlene Wittenmeyer, who'd been working at the diner ever since Summer could remember. Her annoyance vanished immediately. "Oh, hi, Mrs. Wittenmeyer! It *has* been a while. How are you?"

"Oh, I can't complain," Marlene said, smiling as she began rapidly dicing onions. "Is it true that you're gonna be working with us now?"

"Yes, I'll be here until September." Summer could feel the heat from Mr. Grumpy Pants' angry eyes drilling into her back like laser beams. She ignored him.

"How's Abigail doing?" Marlene demanded.

"Much better. She's supposed to be coming home from the hospital this afternoon," Summer reported.

She began her inspection. The floor, countertops, and appliance surfaces all looked clean. Likewise, the walls, with their vintage subway tile. So far, so good. She bent to peer under the stove and asked, "How are Katie and Austin doing?"

"I'm doing just fine," said the tall, brown-haired teenage boy who sat on a stool in one corner of the kitchen, peeling potatoes. "I graduated a couple of weeks ago. I'm heading to Gallatin College in the fall. Got accepted into the Culinary Arts program."

"Congratulations," Summer told him. "I know that's a hard program to get into."

He grunted, then asked, "Is it true that you own your own restaurant in San Francisco?"

Before she could answer, Brock snapped, "Less talking, more peeling, Austin. Or we're gonna come up short again today."

He stood in front of a tall, heavy-duty Hobart mixer, mixing up a batch of pancake batter from scratch.

Again? Summer made a note to follow up with him. Exactly how often was the diner running out of basic items?

But she was pleased to see that Brock wasn't using frozen fries and hash browns. Not only did fresh potatoes taste better, they were much cheaper.

Summer completed her inspection, aware of three pairs of eyes intently tracking her around the kitchen. "Everything looks great, guys," she announced. "This is one of the cleanest commercial kitchens I've ever seen."

Brock snorted, but didn't stop scooping flour into the Hobart's giant mixing bowl.

Terri entered the kitchen from the dining room, and began clipping the first orders to the ticket wheel, calling out the items as she did so.

Summer sighed. She really needed to talk to Brock again about purchasing an integrated POS system that would print order tickets directly to the kitchen.

Now that the diner was open for business, it was time to order some waffles and coffee, and observe how the front of the house handled breakfast service.

With only a few customers, things started off smoothly, even if both of the young servers on duty paused frequently to look at their phones.

Grandma Abigail mentioned that the diner's manager had quit a few days ago. So, it didn't surprise Summer when things descended into chaos a half hour later.

The diner was at full capacity, with more customers lined up outside. Summer observed as Austin's older sister Katie and her fellow server Terri panicked at the flood of orders.

As Summer watched, customers began complaining that they'd been served the wrong orders. Some tables never received their food, while other tables had one person still waiting for their order while their companions were nearly finished eating.

Finally, Summer couldn't take it any longer. She'd seen enough, and the customers needed help. She set her coffee cup down with a thump and marched to the back of the diner.

"Everyone stop what you're doing!" she shouted in her most authoritative tone. "Now!"

Everyone in the kitchen froze. Even Brock.

Summer turned to the servers. "Terri, Katie, what the heck are you doing? You're just randomly grabbing plates as they come up, without looking at the tickets! That stops right now."

Both servers looked at each other in dismay.

"She's right," Marlene said. "You girls are making more work for us. As if we weren't already busy enough!"

"All right, this is how things are going to work from now on," Summer began.

She explained the system in a few terse sentences, ignoring their cowed looks. This was Restaurant Operations 101, something

Katie and Terri should already be familiar with.

It had been a few years since she'd worked as an expediter, but Summer still knew how to manage tickets and the flow of dishes out of the kitchen. She set to work unsnarling the mess that Terri and Katie had made, and got everything running smoothly within fifteen minutes.

The hours flew by, with no real break between breakfast and lunch, but Brock and his staff had prepped sufficient quantities of everything, so nothing ran out.

After the lunch rush ended and the last customers departed, Summer gathered everyone together in the front of the house for a meeting.

She began by critiquing Terri and Katie for ignoring the ticket system and making the already-swamped kitchen re-do orders. Marlene and Brock both nodded in agreement at this.

Terri began sniffling halfway through, but Summer ignored her. She ended with "…and if I catch either of you using your phones while you're supposed to be working, you're gone."

"But you can't do that!" Katie shot a wide-eyed look of appeal at her mother, then Brock.

Summer braced herself for opposition. But Marlene nodded in agreement.

"Yeah, she can," Brock growled at the two young women, catching Summer by surprise. "I catch either of you girl slacking off where customers can see you, I'll fire your asses."

Terri's sniffles turned to tears and outright sobs. Katie sat there stone-faced, pale with shock.

"Go," Brock ordered them. "You guys are done for the day."

They practically ran for the back of the diner to clock out.

Warmed by the unexpected support, Summer continued. Next, she presented her ideas for reorganizing the locations of the kitchen's appliances and prep stations to reduce the amount of unnecessary running between the stove, grill, and fridge.

She expected Brock to argue with her suggestions, Instead, he sat, listening intently. From Grandma Abigail, she knew he'd learned on the job, rather than through any formal training. At least he seemed open to some basic improvements.

Then, she sat at the diner's computer and reviewed the past month of income and expenses while Brock and his staff cleaned the kitchen.

Once everyone else had clocked out, Summer emerged from the office to collar Brock. "Hey, do you mind staying a few more minutes? We need to talk."

He threw her a wary look. "About what? You got another list for me?"

Apparently, his show of cooperation earlier had been just that —a show for the staff. "I wanted to run some ideas by you for making the diner profitable by Grandma Abigail's deadline."

He sighed loudly. "Fine. There some huckleberry pie left, and I'm starving."

She followed him out to the dining room and filled a pair of mugs with the last of the coffee while he served up two large wedges of fragrant purple pie.

Summer waited until they were both seated, then said, "You made a great start with your menu overhaul, but you need to reduce your portion sizes to keep ingredient costs under control. Bigger is *not* better."

"I've been told otherwise," he said, absolutely deadpan.

To her horror, giggles rose in her throat and spilled out of her mouth as her brain came to a complete halt. It didn't help that heat rose from the neckline of her chef's coat to her cheeks, and she knew she'd turned bright red.

Brock sat back and grinned at her. "What else?" His tone was mild, but there was a wicked glint in his brown eyes.

"We need to add a dinner service."

His grin vanished. His dark brows knitted together in a frown. "I can't afford to hire extra people right now. Hell, I'm not even sure I can afford to replace Kenny."

"Wait. Hear me out," she blurted. "The profit margins on dinners are higher because people order things like appetizers, desserts, and drinks. Plus, we can charge more for dinner entrées. And it would make staying in town more attractive to tourists once the LVR begins service next year." He was still frowning, so she added, "It looks like Fridays are your slowest days for breakfast. We could start by shifting the diner's Friday hours to lunch and dinner service, no breakfast. Then expand to other days if the experiment works out."

He blew out a breath. "I'll think about it." His tone was grudging. "What else?"

"I noticed you don't have an Alcoholic Beverage License."

His frown deepened. "That's right," he said flatly.

Now what's his problem? She fought down her annoyance. If he insisted on being stubborn, she had to be the reasonable one.

"I mean, that's normal for a breakfast/lunch only place," she continued, "but you're losing out on major potential lunch and dinner revenue without an ABL. If we put beer and wine on the menu, the checks would increase, and with a nice profit margin, too."

"No," he said in the same flat tone. He set his fork down and put both palms flat on the tabletop. "My dad was an alcoholic. Drank himself to death. No booze in my diner. And that's final."

Summer recognized what that confession must have cost him. "Okay. No ABL. The next best option to increase a diner's check is to offer a gourmet dessert menu with dinner. Let's look into getting an espresso maker, too."

She saw the mutinous expression on his face and groaned silently. *Stubborn idiot! Is he really going to shoot down every single idea just to score points against me?*

But she wasn't ready to give up on this item, not when she'd just conceded on the liquor license. "Look, I know commercial espresso machines run in the thousands of dollars. But the coffee distributor for SummerTime will lease us those machines cheaply, and burr grinders, too, if we sign a contract with them for coffee bean deliveries. It wouldn't hurt to offer fancy espresso drinks for breakfast and dessert, right? Especially once the tourists come."

She saw Brock pause to think about it. Sensing victory, she added, "There's an excellent profit margin on coffee drinks. At my restaurant, our average cost to produce an after-dinner cappuccino was about ninety cents. We listed them on our dessert menu for $3.95."

His eyes widened as that sank in.

Then he growled, "Fine. If you can get us a good deal on an espresso maker, go for it. But if you want fancy desserts, you're gonna be the one baking them, because I don't bother with that kind of fiddly shit."

She folded her arms and gave him her sharpest look, the one that made line cooks and dishwashers cry.

He stared back at her for a long moment, then admitted, "I know how to make a mean berry shortcake using my gran's recipe, but that's it."

Summer nodded. "Shortcake is a great seasonal item, especially if we can get fresh berries from a local farm. For the rest, let's outsource dessert since we'll both have our hands full with everything else."

"*Outsource?*" Brock asked with a sneer. "You think those fancy bakeries in Bozeman are gonna deliver all the way out here?" He shook his head. "This isn't San Francisco. You can't just order delivery from any old place."

With an effort, she ignored his attitude. "What about the new bakery right here on the square?"

"Jenna's Java? That's mostly Danishes and cookies and stuff." Brock waved his hand dismissively.

Summer shrugged. "I'm willing to give it a shot. If I like what I see and taste, I'll commission a set of custom, seasonal desserts to offer with our weekend dinner service. It won't be the same old huckleberry pie you can find at every diner in Montana."

"Nothing wrong with this huckleberry pie, Ms. Fancy Pants." As if to prove his point, he shoved a large forkful into his mouth.

"And there's nothing wrong with being open to change, Mr. Grumpy Pants," she retorted, rolling her eyes.

If he didn't have an attitude adjustment soon, it was going to be a *long* three months until she could take her money and head back to San Francisco.

Someone rapped on the diner's front door, making the old-fashioned shopkeeper's bell quiver and chime. Brock looked past her. "It's Kenny. What the hell does he want?"

Chapter Ten – Brock

Espresso maker. Dinner service. A fucking gourmet dessert menu, for crying out loud!

Listening to Summer's ideas, it sure sounded like she didn't merely aim to make this place profitable. She wanted to turn Brock's homestyle diner into some kind of fancy big city restaurant.

While he couldn't argue that a lot of her business suggestions made sense, he didn't like where her proposed changes were leading.

The Yummy Cowboy Diner had *never* been an espresso and gourmet desserts kind of place.

He might not know the finer details about running a restaurant like Ms. Fancy Pants Chef did, but Brock knew his customers.

And despite the enthusiasm that made Summer's beautiful features glow, he had the feeling that it wasn't just her pushing for these changes. Before Frank Snowberry passed away, he had told Brock that Snowberry Springs needed to offer the kinds of things that would make tourists want to pull off the highway and stay in town.

I knew Mrs. S's offer was too good to be true! Brock thought. But he'd thought that working with Summer would be his biggest challenge, not fighting for the heart and soul of his diner.

He couldn't deny that The Yummy Cowboy Diner was in deep trouble. Or that Summer knew what she was doing.

But there had to be a better way to save this place than change it past recognition and destroy a lifetime of Brock's memories. He'd grown up here, spending afternoons doing his homework at the counter, helping as soon as he was big enough to hold a broom or carry plates. He'd worked every job in this diner, from busing tables and washing dishes to cooking.

Every corner of this building held precious memories of his mama smiling and laughing with her customers, joking around with Marlene and Kenny, and making Brock her special mugs of hot chocolate sprinkled with cinnamon on snowy days.

Nope, he didn't intend to roll over and let Summer and Abigail destroy the things that made the diner special to him and the town.

"Well?" she asked. "What do you think?"

He chewed and swallowed the last bite of his pie, and prepared to lay down the law to his new partner.

Okay, if he was honest with himself, what he *really* wanted to do right now was get up, walk around the table, and kiss Summer until she forgot about cappuccinos and seasonal berry shortcake. She had no right to look that sexy in a coat that covered her from neck to wrists. He itched to loosen her tight braid and run his hands through her golden hair. It would feel so soft, sliding through his fingers.

And it would look mighty fine spread out over his pillows. Even better if her lips were parted and moaning in pleasure.

Then someone knocked on the diner's front door and derailed his X-rated train of thought.

Brock glared at the intruder.

Just because he and Summer were sitting in the dining room didn't mean that the diner was still open to the public. Besides, everyone in town knew his place closed at three p.m.

Then he recognized the thin, slightly stooped figure peering through the large glass panel set in the door.

Summer, seated with her back to the door, gave him an inquiring look.

"It's Kenny. What the hell does he want?" Brock asked.

He shoved his chair back and rose to his feet. Four quick strides brought him to the door.

"Hey, kid, can I talk to you for a minute?" the diner's former manager asked with a sheepish expression.

Brock peered at him, trying to guess what he wanted.

The old guy looked freshly-shaved, and his thinning hair was combed neatly. He wore an actual buttoned shirt, stain-free. His pants looked a size too big, and a well-worn leather belt cinched them tight around his skinny hips.

Brock unlocked the door. The shopkeeper's bell chimed, a sweet, cheerful sound as he pulled it open. "Hi there, Kenny. What brings you here?"

"Well, uh, you see," Kenny began, looked acutely uncomfortable.

Brock's spidey sense began tingling. Whatever Kenny wanted, he knew he wouldn't like it.

Then Kenny's gaze moved to somewhere behind Brock. "Hey, is that Summer Snowberry? I heard she came back for Frank's funeral."

"Hi, Mr. Stinson," she called. "Long time no see." To Brock's relief, she stayed put at the table.

"How's Abigail doin'?" Kenny asked, craning his neck to look around Brock, who stood in the diner's doorway.

"Much better. She's supposed to come home from the hospital today," Summer replied.

"What can I do for you, Kenny?" Brock asked, deliberately interrupting what threatened to turn into a long conversation.

"Well, now," Kenny cleared his throat, discomfort reappearing in his face. He shuffled his feet. "I've been doing a lot of thinking these past few days. I may've been a bit, uh, *hasty*, in quitting."

"You sure did walk out at a bad time," Brock agreed. His gut tightened. He knew where this conversation was headed.

"Yeah, about that..." Kenny looked up and finally met Brock's eyes. "I came to tell you I've changed my mind. I'll be here first thing tomorrow morning."

Dammit. Brock hesitated, torn between loyalty to the old man and his simmering anger at the huge mess that the diner's general manager had left behind.

Could Kenny still handle the job? Or would Brock be inviting a fresh round of mistakes and important tasks forgotten or neglected?

And then there was the matter that Kenny hadn't actually asked Brock for his job back. He'd *told* him he was coming back. As if it was a done deal.

"No, I don't think that's a good idea," Brock said, and braced himself.

Kenny's eyes widened. "What?" he demanded, sounding incredulous. "You *need* me, kid. I kept this place running for forty years! I taught you everything you know!"

Brock thought about all of the mistakes he'd made over the past year. Mistakes that someone as experienced as Kenny should have caught... and corrected. But the old guy hadn't seemed to notice.

Still, Kenny had given the diner a lot of years. He'd been like a grandfather when Brock was a kid.

For that reason, Brock felt obligated to let him down gently as he could. "And I know Mama really appreciated your help. But I'm making some big changes at the diner, Kenny. Things are going to be a lot different from here on out."

Kenny's lips pressed into a thin line. He frowned angrily up at Brock, unable to loom over him the way he used to before Brock hit his high school growth spurt.

"You *need* me," he repeated stubbornly. "Son, I've worked here longer than you've been alive."

"I'm sorry," Brock said. "But you're not coming back as manager. However, if you're willing to consider hosting, Terri and Katie could sure use some—"

"*Hosting?*" Kenny repeated in disbelief. "After everything I done for your mama? Kid, she would've *never*—"

"Maybe not," Brock snapped, angered that old guy was dragging his mother's name into it. "But Mama's not here anymore. *I* am."

"And I was the manager here long before she came around," Kenny shot back. His face flushed with anger. "Manager or nothin', kid. Because owner or not, if you think I'm gonna let Pamela's kid boss me around, think again."

"You're right," Brock said, crossing his arms. "I wouldn't dream of bossing you around, Kenny. Because you quit of your own free will. I'm just holding you to that decision." After a moment, Mama's ghost forced him to add. "I'm sorry, Kenny."

Kenny's eyes narrowed. He ducked around Brock and pointed at Summer. "Oh, so *that's* what's going on, huh?"

Brock glanced over his shoulder and saw that she'd twisted around her seat to watch the conversation.

Kenny continued, "I bet this is all *her* fault! Marlene said she was your new business partner. And now you're acting all crazy."

Great. Brock had known it wouldn't take long for Marlene to spread the word all over town. His assistant cook sure did love to gossip.

Summer's cornflower blue gaze flew to meet Brock's. His sudden surge of protectiveness took him by surprise.

"Summer had nothing to do with it," he growled. "You're the one who quit, Kenny. All I'm doin' is accepting your resignation."

Summer's eyes widened in surprise at his words.

What? She expected me to shove the blame onto her? Brock thought, irritated.

Sure, she could be annoying and high-and-mighty, but she had nothing to do with Kenny or the mess he'd created. And Brock wasn't the type to throw an innocent bystander under the bus.

"I've just spent the last three days fixing everything you fucked up," Brock told Kenny, returning the old guy's glare with one of his own. "The accounting, the invoices, you name it. And why the *hell* didn't you make our orders for stuff like potatoes and flour recurring on our supplier's website? There's no excuse for the diner running out of basic ingredients as often as we have."

"Website?" Kenny echoed. "Why the hell would I use a computer when I could just call someone at Robbie's Restaurant Supply? I've always done it that way, and the folks there know me." He shook his head disparagingly. "Website. Hah!"

Brock stared at him, momentarily speechless, then slowly shook his head. His mama's ghost would slap him silly if he cussed out the old guy like he deserved.

"Go home, Kenny," he said as calmly as he could. "We're done here."

"Just you wait, kid." Kenny's lips twisted in scorn. "You'll come crawling back soon enough, once you realize you don't know what the hell you're doin'. Pamela must be rolling in her grave right now!"

With that, Kenny turned on his heel and left.

"Poor guy. He probably doesn't know what to with himself now that he's not here all the time." Summer sounded sympathetic as she rose from her seat and came up next to Brock.

Brock sighed and shook his head before locking up. "Why can't he just enjoy his retirement? Most folks are counting down the days until they can stop working."

Together, they watched Kenny march across the street to the grassy town square. He made a beeline for the picnic tables under the trees where the town's retirees liked to hang out and play chess.

Brock became acutely aware of just how close Summer was standing. A wisp of fine golden hair had escaped from the confines of her black cap. His fingers itched to tuck it behind the delicate curve of her ear.

Then Summer turned to him. "Thanks for defending me just now."

She put her hand on his bare arm.

Brock didn't think, just reacted. He caught a flash of her startled expression before he pulled her into his arms and bent to kiss her. Her mouth was every bit as soft and hot as he'd been imagining.

His cock sprang to life, rising to the occasion after months of neglect, and pressed eagerly against the tight confines of his jeans.

She stiffened in his embrace, and he began to pull back.

Shit. That was stupid of me, he thought, unsuccessfully trying to summon up regret.

Even if she slapped him for it, he was still glad he'd finally done the thing he'd dreamed about but never dared back in high school.

Instead, her hands grabbed his shoulders, halting his retreat. She went up on tiptoes and kissed him right back.

Hallelujah! He wrapped his arms around her strong, curvy body, pulled her close, and devoured her lips like a starving man. He plunged his tongue into her wet, welcoming mouth and ground his aching hard-on against the soft curve of her belly.

He'd kissed a lot of women—his hated high school nickname had been "Brock the Cock"—but he'd never experienced anything like this before. Summer was heat and desire and pure magic in his arms.

Brock wanted more. A *lot* more.

Summer's hips thrust against him, creating delicious friction over his stiff length. Needy sounds rose from her throat, and he wanted to come on the spot.

Every nerve in his body screamed that he had to have her. *Now.*

He began walking her towards the back of the diner, where they wouldn't be on display to anyone walking by.

Then something abruptly began crowing loudly like a rooster and vibrating against his chest.

She immediately broke the kiss and shoved him away with surprising strength.

Startled, he let go of her. "What the fuck is that?"

"Oh, God," she panted, reaching into the breast pocket of her coat. "It's my phone. I'll turn it off."

She pulled out her cellphone and paused. Brock glimpsed "Grandma A" displayed on the Caller ID.

"Sorry, I have to take this." She threw him an apologetic glance.

Of all the fucking times for Mrs. S to call! Disappointment lanced through Brock. He'd gotten so close...

"Grandma!" Summer said into her phone. She sounded breathless. "Uh, how are you? Are you home yet?"

Brock's eyes never left her face. She was flushed, and her lips were swollen in the most enticing way. He pictured them wrapped around his stiff, aching cock, and groaned softly.

"Oh, that's great!" Summer was saying. "I'm so glad! And you're feeling better?"

There followed a minute or two of Summer repeatedly saying "Mm-hmm," then, "Are you *sure* you're up to it, so soon after your surgery?"

Another pause while she listened. Her brows went up in surprise at something her grandma said.

"Um, okay, sure, I'll ask him. He's right here—we're, uh, at the diner. Discussing some ideas." Summer's blush darkened a shade or two. It was fucking adorable. She glanced up at him. "Grandma Abigail wants to know if you'd like to have dinner with us at the ranch tonight. Six p.m.? Dad's making his famous bison and blue cheese burgers."

"Sure, that would be great," Brock replied. "Can I bring anything?"

Dinner with Summer and her family sounded more appealing than going home to his cottage and eating dinner while watching tonight's baseball game.

And if he played his cards right, maybe he'd get to kiss her again at the end of the evening.

"Oh, you heard that?" Summer said into the phone. "Yes, I'll tell him. I'll be leaving the diner in a few minutes—see you soon, Grandma."

She ended the call, and looked at him wryly. "Grandma said to just bring yourself."

Brock nodded, but decided that he'd cut another bouquet of roses from his garden when he went home to shower and change before dinner. Mama had taught him never to show up empty-handed to a dinner invitation. Plus, he wanted to keep making a good impression on Summer's folks.

"You know that Grandma and everyone else are going to be expecting a report on our diner project, right?" Summer asked.

"I figured." He grinned down at her. "We can tell them that the espresso maker is a 'go.'"

Chapter Eleven – Summer

Snowberry Springs Ranch
Wednesday, June 15

It had been two hours and seven minutes since that incredible, earth-shattering kiss, and Summer still felt the imprint of Brock's mouth against hers. Her chin still tingled with the tender scrape of his stubble. And her core still throbbed with unsatisfied need.

Kissing Brock was such a bad idea, she told herself, touching her lips. *He's already broken your heart once. Are you going to let him do it again?*

She'd driven back to the ranch in a daze, wondering what the heck had just happened. One minute, they'd been sparring over her proposed changes for the menu. He'd frustrated the hell out of her with his stubborn, defensive refusal to consider anything new for the diner.

And then he'd defended her against Kenny's accusations before kissing her into a frenzy of need.

The past few days had been a confusing seesaw between the same Brock the Jerk she remembered from their high school days a decade ago, and the gallant man who drove her to the hospital after she was stranded at his diner, and who made her laugh with his outrageous double-entendres.

In a daze, she helped Mom peel and cut potatoes into home fries. Then she harvested lettuce and the season's first tomatoes from the garden.

Now it was nearly six p.m. and Summer was up in her old bedroom in the ranch house's second story, trying to decide what to wear. Should she go with her usual cut-off jeans shorts and tank top, or something a little nicer? And should she unbraid her hair and wear it loose?

She dithered until she heard the crunching of gravel under tires drift through the open window.

Brock's here, and I'm still in my underwear. Crap!

She grabbed for her shorts, tank top, and a cute floral button-up blouse and scrambled to get dressed. No need to attract comments from her family by dressing up for Brock. And it was too late to do anything about her hair.

It's not like I'm embarrassed about kissing Brock, she told herself.

But she wasn't sure what to make of it, either. Was he finally interested in dating her? Or had the kiss just been a one-off thing, a way of blowing off stress after the tense encounter with Kenny?

Brock's truck pulled up in front of the house and parked. Summer headed downstairs.

Her older brother Spring had already opened the front door when Summer arrived at the foyer.

"—Diamondbacks versus the San Francisco Giants tonight," Spring said in his soft voice. "If they win this one, the Giants are headed for the playoffs."

It wasn't usual for Spring to chat like this. Her once-outgoing and confident older brother had turned into a silent, withdrawn man after returning from his deployments in Afghanistan.

Now, he turned at the sound of her step on the tiles. "Hey, Summer. Brock's here."

"Long time no see," she greeted her new business partner. She desperately tried for casual, but ended up sounding completely lame.

"Hey." Brock smiled at her from the wide verandah that wrapped around all four sides of the house.

She felt the heat of his gaze as it lingered on her bare legs. He wore his usual faded jeans, but had changed into a clean t-shirt. And he was holding a bouquet of perfumed roses and lilies.

"Well, come on in," Spring said, stepping aside. "It's such a nice evening that we'll be eating in the back yard."

"I could smell the barbecue as I drove up," Brock said to Summer as Spring led the way through the house. "And now I'm starving."

After pausing in the kitchen to grab a vase for the flowers, and to say hi to Mom and Autumn, who were busily toasting hamburger buns and keeping an eye on the oven fries, they exited the house via a pair of French doors at the back of the living room. They crossed the verandah, then went down the short flight of stairs to the large wooden deck built next to the house.

There, they found a long table, covered with a blue-and-white checked tablecloth, set with nine places. A wide oval platter of sliced tomatoes, fresh onions, and lettuce leaves stood in the middle of the table, along with pitchers of ice water and a collection of relish jars and ketchup and mustard squeeze bottles.

On the far corner of the deck, Dad was flipping thick burger patties on the huge gas grill he'd gotten for Christmas a couple of years ago. He wore his favorite cowboy hat, the really battered straw one that Mom called "Bob's Holey Hat."

A play set stood on the far end of the lawn, near the tall old fruit trees. Spring's two little girls, April and Abby, were busily clambering up the ladder to the old treehouse, while Autumn's son, seven-year-old Jayden, was working the swing, trying to see if he could go high enough to kick one of the apple tree's branches.

After driving from Bozeman because of Grandma's heart attack, Summer's younger sister Autumn had decided to stay at the ranch for the rest of the week. School was out for the summer, and her husband Phillip was away on another of his frequent business trips. He worked in pharmaceutical sales, and didn't seem to spend much at home.

Summer wondered what was going on. Autumn's social media feeds always showed happy photos of herself and her family, with tags like #happytogether and #blessed, but on this visit, she seemed wound so tightly that Summer feared her sister would snap at any moment.

When she'd asked what was wrong, Autumn had made it clear she didn't want to discuss whatever was going on in her life to make her so tense.

Dad turned and waved as the three of them came onto the deck.

"Glad you could make it, Brock," he said in a hearty tone. "Can I get you a beer?"

"No thanks, Mr. Snowberry," Brock said. "But if you have a can of Coke, I sure could use the caffeine right now. It's been a long day."

This refusal earned him a surprised look from Dad, but to Summer's relief he didn't push the issue.

Maybe he'd heard about Brock's dad, too. Knowing Snowberry Springs, he probably had.

"Sure, we have a whole cooler full of sodas and bottled water," he said, pointing at a large ice chest sitting nearby. "Help yourself."

Dad's bison burgers, made with his secret seasoning blend of Worcestershire sauce, herbs, and spices, and filled with rich blue cheese, were delicious as always.

Autumn and Mom brought out heaping trays of crisp, golden oven fries baked with minced garlic and Parmesan while Spring rounded up the kids and herded them inside to wash their hands.

Summer sat next to Brock on the long wooden bench. Despite being surrounded by family, it felt oddly intimate. His hard, jeans-clad thigh pressed steadily against her bare leg, and their hands occasionally touched as they passed around the burger toppings, fries, and condiments.

To her relief, no one interrogated her or Brock about The Yummy Cowboy Diner. Instead, the conversation revolved around Winnie's upcoming wedding and her successful transition from her business of restoring and reselling historic homes in Seattle to her hit show on HomeRenoTV.

"I don't begrudge Winnie her success, but it's such a pity she's too busy to spend much time here anymore," Grandma Abigail said. "The Snowberry Springs Inn, which started out as Frank's great-great-grandmother Caroline's mansion, is on the verge of falling down." She sighed. "It would be a pity if we lost it. It's a jewel of a house, with such an interesting past, too. Caroline Snowberry was one of the town's founders, you know." That last was directed at Brock.

He nodded, "I remember you mentioning it."

Grandma continued, "It would be a crying shame if this important piece of Snowberry Springs' history was lost. Frank's mother always talked about how Caroline arrived in the Montana Territory as a widow, with nothing but the clothes on her back. But she was enterprising and extremely hard-working, and twenty years later, she was the richest woman in town. She owned the water utility and most of the buildings on the town square."

"I've heard of her," Brock said politely. "My own great-great-grandpa came to Montana looking for gold, and decided it was easier and more profitable to sell beef and vegetables to the miners. Mama always told me that he was a city boy who didn't know how to ride a horse when he arrived."

"Speaking of horses," Dad said. "Autumn, your brother and I were talking about teaching his girls how to ride and fish. That got me thinking that maybe Jayden would like to learn, too. He could stay here with us on the ranch until school starts at the end of August."

Jayden bounced excitedly in his seat. "Ooh, yes! I want to be a cowboy like Uncle Spring! Can I, Mommy? Please?"

Autumn pressed her lips together. Once again, she looked tense, brittle. "I—I don't know honey." With a forced smile, she said, "Dad, thanks for the offer. I'll ask Phillip when he calls tonight."

Jayden abruptly stopped bouncing. "But Daddy *always* says no to everything fun!" he blurted. "He doesn't even let *you* do anything fun!"

Alarmed, Summer's gaze flew to her sister. Autumn shook her head. "Don't be silly, Jayden. Daddy is strict, but only because he's worried about spoiling you now that he's so successful."

Jayden pouted. "I hate Daddy's job! He's never home and he made you cry when he told you that you couldn't work for the marketing company anymore!"

"What?" Summer asked, horrified. "But you loved working there! And you're a genius when it comes to social media stuff!"

Autumn wouldn't meet her eyes. "Phillip's travel schedule—" she began. "We, ah, decided it would be best if I stayed home full time to take care of our son."

"But he's in school during the day. And why you can't just put Jayden in an afterschool program, or hire a nanny, Autumn?" Mom asked. "Surely you two earn enough to pay for child care."

Autumn shook her head, looking stressed and miserable. "Phillip strongly believes that children should be raised by their parents, not hired child care providers."

"Easy for *him* to say, sweetheart, since he's traveling all the time," Dad chimed in, with a look of concern. "It sounds like you're the one doing all of the parenting right now."

"Phillip says that it's a privilege to be part of Jayden's childhood. They grow up so fast, you know." She turned to her son. "I promise I'll ask Daddy about spending your summer vacation with Gramps and Nana." Then, signaling that she wanted to change the subject, Autumn asked, "So, Summer, Brock, I hear that Grandma Abigail made you two business partners. How are things are going at the diner?"

"Just fine," Summer said quickly. "Brock and I are discussing what changes we need to make. We've agreed that leasing an espresso machine and adding a coffee bar is a good first step."

Brock leaned into her, his warmth radiating through his clothing.

"And what about adding a dinner service, like you suggested, Summer?" asked Grandma Abigail.

"Well…" she began.

And just like that, Flirty Brock vanished, replaced by Stubborn Brock. He subtly eased himself away from her. She instantly missed the contact.

"We're still hashin' it out," he said flatly. "I'm not convinced we need dinner, especially when it means hiring more people when we're tryin' to cut overhead costs."

"And I think we should start slow, with a trial run," Summer countered. "The diner would be closed for breakfast, and open for lunch and dinner only on Friday. No need to hire extra staff right away."

"That sounds reasonable," Grandma Abigail said. "What were your thoughts on the dinner menu?"

Summer caught Brock's mutinous expression out of the corner of her eye.

"Farm-to-table New American," she said, promptly. "Upscale versions of familiar dishes, most items sourced locally. Small menu with three or four appetizers, four or five entrees, and a gourmet dessert menu with a selection of espresso drinks as an add-on."

"And you don't agree, Brock?" Grandma Abigail asked.

Brock sat ramrod-straight on the bench and crossed his impressively muscled arms. "Upscale's the wrong way to go. Maybe it would work in Bozeman, but the people here in Snowberry Springs like my food just the way it was. A menu filled with fancy and expensive dishes isn't gonna appeal to my customers."

"But what about the LVR? And all the people it's going to bring to town?" Grandma Abigail asked, clearly unhappy with his resistance.

"Mrs.—I mean, Abigail—you know as well as I do that tourists are only around for a few months a year. If you want the diner to be profitable all year round, then we need to stick with what works."

"You mean meatloaf? Chicken fried steak? Hamburgers?" Summer asked, not bothering to disguise her scorn.

"Better meatloaf than some vegan tofu dish topped with seaweed, or whatever the hell it is you cook in San Francisco," he shot back.

"New American cuisine is *not* tofu and seaweed." She turned her head to glare at him. "And you have no idea what kind of food I serve at SummerTime!"

He glared back. She saw a muscle in the corner of his jaw twitching.

Gah! He was a jerk, plain and simple. A willfully ignorant jerk.

She was sorry she'd let him kiss her. And even sorrier she'd kissed him back, no matter how good it felt at the time.

"Why don't you settle this dispute with a contest?" Grandma Abigail suggested.

Summer looked around and saw that everyone was staring at Brock and her with varying expressions of amusement and speculation. "What kind of contest?" she asked warily.

"Yeah," Brock added. "If it's arm-wrestling, I'm in."

And then he actually flexed his impressively thick arms.

Summer rolled her eyes. "Seriously?"

"I'd pay to see them mud-wrestle," Spring said, unexpectedly. "Especially since I know how my little sister hates to get dirty."

Grandma Abigail chuckled. "I propose that you do a trial dinner service as Summer suggested. Each of you puts your two or three best dishes on the new menu. At the end of the evening, we'll see which dishes prove the most popular—Summer's or Brock's."

"And what's the prize if I win?" Summer asked.

"How about the winner gets to create the entire menu for the next month?" asked Grandma Abigail. "Then, if you still can't agree, you can run another contest to see who creates the next monthly menu."

"That sounds fair," Mom said.

"And delicious," said Dad.

Summer pursed her lips, looking for a catch. But the proposal made sense. It would keep her and Brock from bogging down in endless arguments, and making no progress at the diner.

"Okay," Brock said to her relief. Then he added, "But I wanna up the stakes. The loser has to spend one whole day, twenty-four hours, doing whatever the winner says." He turned his head and grinned cockily at her.

"No way," Summer retorted. "You just want to reverse all the changes at the diner if you win."

"Oh, so you think I'm gonna win?" Brock's grin widened. "I mean, if you're scared of scared of going head to head with me, Ms. Fancy Pants Chef, then we stick to plain old homestyle cooking."

"Oh, heck no! I'm not backing down! You're on, Mr. Grumpy Pants." Summer shot back. "But I want two conditions. First, neither of us can change the winning menu until the month is up. And I want a—a safe word in case the 'do whatever I say' part is, um, too outrageous."

"They've already given each other nicknames. Isn't that sweet?" Mom stage-whispered to Dad.

Summer's face promptly heated. Brock turned red, too.

Brock scowled. "A safe word, huh? Well, that's no fun."

"Take it or leave it. We both know I'm going to win, Brock." Faking unconcern, Summer served herself another helping of the garlic-Parmesan fries.

"Huh, you really think that? What's that saying? 'Pride goes before a fall'?" Brock smirked at her.

"'Pride goeth before destruction, and a haughty spirit before a fall,'" Dad quoted with smile. "It's in the Bible. Which you should know, Summer," he added in gentle reprimand.

She smiled apologetically at him, all-too-aware that this past Sunday was the first time she'd been to church in a long while. Her busy work schedule in San Francisco made it impossible to take any time off on the weekends.

"I could create some social media accounts for the diner, and post about the contest," Autumn volunteered unexpectedly. "It would be a great way to spread the word about The Yummy Cowboy Diner. I'd need to take some photos of your contest dishes. Then I could tease the contest for a few days in advance, then update the contest results hourly on the night of."

"Oh, that would be great!" Summer exclaimed. "Thanks! The diner doesn't have a social media presence yet, but it's on my list."

"Again, with the lists," Brock muttered.

Summer couldn't resist smirking at him. "I love my lists," she agreed cheerfully.

In fact, she loved them even more now that she knew how much they irritated him.

"Why the photos?" he asked Autumn. "I mean, who the hell wants to look at pictures of food from some diner out in the middle of nowhere!" He gave Summer a baleful side-eye. "Besides, you were the one who told me no food photos in the menu."

"That was the menu. This is Instagram. It's different," Autumn explained with a laugh. Suddenly, she looked like her old self again, not the tense, unhappy woman she'd been since arriving at the ranch yesterday. "And you'd be surprised at how popular the #foodstagram tag is, Brock. Honestly, I'd love to help you guys out. Anything to support my family and my hometown."

"We'll all be there to try your food and cheer you on," Mom said. "As will everyone else in town, once they hear what's happening. Just let us know when."

"How about this Friday?" Brock said confidently. "Unless Ms. Fancy Pants Chef here doesn't think she can be ready by then."

"Bring it on," Summer said. "I'm looking forward to bossing you around for an entire day when I win." She gave him a saccharine smile. "But remember, you can always use your safe word, Mr. Grumpy Pants."

Chapter Twelve – Brock

T he Yummy Cowboy Diner
Thursday, June 16

"We need to close the diner for breakfast *and* lunch tomorrow," Summer announced in the middle of lunch prep.

"Are you crazy?" Brock spun around from where he was mixing up a batch of biscuit dough in the big Hobart mixer. "I already agreed to give up all of my breakfast checks. Now you want to take away all my lunch earnings as well?"

Predictably, Marlene spun around to watch the fireworks, turning her back on a batch of bacon and eggs sizzling on the flattop, courtesy of a late breakfast order.

On weekdays, breakfast rush typically ran from six a.m. until about eight-thirty. The diner always had a few latecomers trickle in between nine and ten-thirty, mostly retired folks wanting to enjoy a leisurely brunch over a friendly card game with their friends.

Without a pressing need to turn over tables, Brock didn't mind them hanging around, as long as they cleared out before lunch rush started around noon.

"I *told* you," Summer said, her condescending tone setting Brock's teeth on edge. "The dinner checks will more than make up for it, especially with the appetizers and desserts. You'll just have to trust me."

She gave him one of those superior "I'm a trained chef" smiles, and that did it.

"Trust you? Trust isn't gonna cover my bills!" Brock shouted. "Or anyone's paychecks."

"But—" Summer began.

"You don't seem to understand that *I'm* the one putting everything on the line here!"

"That's not true," she said, her quiet tone a rebuke to Brock's yelling.

It only made him angrier. He glared at her back with its thick braid of golden hair. "Oh yeah?"

She sighed loudly, put down the knife she'd been using to dice tomatoes for a test run of bruschetta, and peeled off her food service gloves before turning to face Brock.

"Look, we have a lot of prep for tomorrow evening. Not to mention, a bunch of new menu items that neither you nor Marlene have cooked before," she pointed out with maddening calm.

Dammit! He couldn't decide if he wanted to throw her and her smug attitude out of his kitchen—or just shut her up by kissing her again.

With her family there yesterday, he hadn't gotten the goodbye kiss he'd been hoping for. And it annoyed him she hadn't even tried to follow him out to his truck after dinner was over.

He hated the idea that he was the only one burning for a second round of tasting her sweet lips.

Fantasies about her hot, wet mouth wrapped around his cock had kept him awake for a long time last night, and even repeated sessions of jerking off had done little to relieve his desire.

He couldn't deny that he wanted her, and he resented the power that gave her over him, even if she didn't know what she did to him.

It was fucking unfair.

"We won't have time to learn everything we need to do if we're dealing with lunch orders tomorrow." Summer was still talking, oblivious to the turn his thoughts had taken.

She turned to Marlene. "Marlene, what do you think? How much time will you need to learn to make the appetizers, my seared bison filet, and the fish?"

"This isn't a fucking democracy!" Brock yelled. "Marlene doesn't get a vote! And for Pete's sake, don't burn the fucking bacon again!"

Marlene gave him a reproving look, but turned back to the flattop without comment.

"But as your business partner, *I* get a vote!" Summer finally lost her cool. "And do you always have to instantly veto *everything* I suggest? Can't you at least stop and think about it for a moment before you say no?"

"I do not veto everything you suggest!"

"Oh yeah?" Summer put her hands on her hips. "Name one thing that you agreed to without arguing about it first!"

"I—uh." Brock began to mention the bound menus, then remembered he'd pooh-poohed her critique before thinking it over and changing his mind. "Fuck."

She'd always driven him crazy. And he'd always reacted in exactly the wrong way.

"Mm-hm." Summer nodded. "I want us to kick butt tomorrow! Dinner service has to be flawless, and the only way that's going to happen is if we all have time to properly prepare!"

Day Two of their partnership and they were already fighting in front of Marlene and Austin. Everyone in town would know about it by dinnertime.

Just fucking awesome, he thought. Between her attitude and his aching cock, the next three months were going to be hell.

He looked at her flushed cheeks and the angry sparks flying from her eyes, drew breath to argue... and suddenly pictured her draped over his lap as he spanked her bare, deliciously round ass.

Holy shit! His cock instantly came to attention. And he abruptly lost his train of thought.

"She's got a point, young man," Marlene said, booting him back to reality. "I need to practice those dishes. And Summer's right— there's gonna be an awful lot of prep."

Desperate to conceal his sudden case of uncontrollable hard-on, he turned away from the two women. He reached blindly for his insulated bottle of ice water, hoping to quench the heat.

"Fine," he muttered, hoping desperately that the apron tied over his jeans hid the bulge at his crotch. "No breakfast, no lunch on Friday. Dammit. But it's your job to write up a sign, hang it on the door, and deal with the complaints."

He hated handing Summer a win, but she was right. It made sense to focus all their attention on dinner prep tomorrow. And if his regulars realized that the lack of lunch service tomorrow was her fault, win-win.

"Not a problem," she said with annoying cheerfulness. "With that settled, I'm going to walk over to Jenna's Java & Bakery in a bit and see about ordering desserts for tomorrow. Should I ask if her barista if they're willing to work for us tomorrow night, making the espresso drinks?"

Brock groaned. Summer was apparently unwilling to settle for an inch when she could grab the entire fucking mile. *Or my balls.*

Though not in the way he kept fantasizing about.

But if tomorrow evening went the way they hoped and prayed it would, then Terri and Katie would be too busy to make cappuccinos while he, Summer, and Marlene worked flat-out in the kitchen. "Fine," he growled.

"And you're okay with the dinner menu?" she asked, transferring the diced tomatoes from the cutting board to a bowl. She grabbed the bunch of fresh basil, harvested this morning at oh-dark-thirty from Brock's vegetable garden, rolled it, and began to chiffonade the flat leaves into thin strips. "We're done tinkering with it?"

"I am if you are," he said. He had to admit that the new menu looked damned good.

After a heated debate during breakfast prep this morning, they had finally agreed on a selection of two appetizers: a classic hot spinach and artichoke dip, served with tortilla chips; and Italian bruschetta, made from toasted slices of baguette from Jenna's Java & Bakery, topped with a mixture of fresh diced heirloom tomatoes and basil tossed with minced garlic, vinegar, and olive oil.

The new menu also offered a choice of three salads: a standard garden salad with a choice of dressings; his Caesar salad with house-made dressing; and Summer's brand-new and very fancy YC salad.

The YC salad comprised baby spinach tossed with a custom Dijon mustard and peach jam vinaigrette, and topped with toasted walnuts and crumbled goat cheese from the Ornelas Organic Dairy in Bearpaw Ridge, Idaho.

"Great! And no matter which entrée wins tomorrow, I think you're going to be happy with the profit margins," Summer pointed out. "The bruschetta, especially, costs almost nothing to make, but it's fresh, delicious, and seasonal. I'm really glad your tomatoes ripened early."

Brock shrugged, pleased despite himself that he'd been the one to provide an entire basket of vine-ripened heirloom tomatoes he'd grown himself, plus a dozen bunches of Genovese basil, which always grew like a weed as soon as the weather turned warm. "I've got a small greenhouse in my back yard. It helps my plants get a head start."

Her anger apparently forgotten, she looked up and gave him a smile that made his breath catch. "May the best entrée win tomorrow."

Brock nodded and immediately felt better. For his entrées, he'd selected the diner's two best-selling lunch items, the buttermilk fried chicken and the bison meatloaf with onion gravy, as his contest entrées. They were both damned tasty, and his customers loved them.

On Summer's advice, he'd costed out the old portion sizes and reduced them by half. The new portions still made a satisfying meal but reduced his food costs to about nineteen percent.

Summer had created a pan-seared bison filet sourced from her family's ranch as her first entrée. She topped the filet with sautéed mushrooms and placed it on top of a neat mound of mashed potatoes flavored with roasted mild green chiles.

She served the dish with a Scotch ale demi-glace. Brock declared it "that fucking delicious beer sauce" when she'd cooked a test dish for Marlene and him to sample after the breakfast rush ended.

Should he be worried about tomorrow night's contest? Sure, Summer's bison filet was damned good, but Brock assured himself that his bison meatloaf was better.

And Summer's high-falutin' writeup of her dish on the menu was bound to scare off anyone looking for steak with mushrooms-and-beer gravy.

Her second entrée was fresh Alaskan halibut with a honey soy glaze, placed on a bed of jasmine rice with grilled broccolini in a wasabi butter sauce.

Tasty but way too fancy for Snowberry Springs, he thought with glee. Like the bison filet, it was surprisingly easy to cook and plate, which would be a bonus if tomorrow's dinner rush was as hectic as he hoped.

Plus, they'd gotten a great deal on the halibut from Robbie's Restaurant Supply, with the promise to deliver more by tomorrow early afternoon.

Robbie's would deliver the fish whole, so they needed to butcher it into portions before dinner service started. Summer suggested reserving all the leftover parts and turning them into a seafood chowder for Saturday's Soup of the Day.

Summer assured them that butchering the fish could be done quickly, then demonstrated on the test fish.

The woman had crazy-good knife skills. It nearly killed Brock to admit it, but he *could* learn a few things from her.

Now, she finished with the basil, and quickly moved on to mincing garlic before she put them in the bowl with the tomatoes, added salt, pepper, olive oil, vinegar, and tossed the mixture. She covered the bowl and placed it one of the kitchen's low-boy fridges under the counter.

"Okay, I'm off to Jenna's," she announced, untying her apron, "to talk to her about the baguettes and the desserts for tomorrow."

Brock couldn't help following the sway of her hips and her sweetly-rounded ass in those checked pants as she left the kitchen. Then he caught Marlene watching him, and flushed at the older woman's knowing smile.

"She's good for you, you know," Marlene observed. "You should be nicer to her."

"You've gotta be kidding me," Brock snarled.

Marlene just shrugged. With one smooth motion, she put two plates of food on the pass, hit the call bell for the servers, and shouted, "Order up for table six! Two breakfast specials with French toast, bacon, and eggs sunny-side!"

Chapter Thirteen – Summer

Still fuming from her latest argument with Brock, Summer left the diner and cut across the town square. Downtown Snowberry Springs had changed little since she moved away.

The same old historic brick buildings surrounded three sides of the large, grassy square with the old train depot and tracks bringing up the fourth side. At the center of the square stood a simple, white-painted war memorial column surrounded by bronze plaques commemorating the men and women who had fallen in service to their country in every major conflict since the town's founding. The large roofed gazebo-style bandstand next to the memorial badly needed a fresh coat of paint, but the picnic tables under the stand of trees were still the hangout for the town's chess players.

As she walked over the springy grass, Summer tried to figure out Brock's problem. Alternating between Sweet Sexy Brock and Grumpy Mule-Headed Brock gave her whiplash. And she was so danged tired of his continual opposition to her perfectly reasonable ideas.

His problem is that he wants to be in charge all the time, she thought angrily. *He's such a control freak!*

What's he like in bed? Does he want to be in complete control there, too? The thought gave her a guilty shiver of pleasure.

Instead of Brock the Cock, she'd started thinking of him as Brock the Block. As in blocking every suggestion for improvement. As in completely block-headed. *Argh!*

Because from what she'd seen so far, he wasn't doing much partying these days.

No booze, no girlfriends texting or calling him, nothing but working at the diner... which isn't healthy, either.

With his seven-days-a-week work schedule, he was clearly heading for a burnout if he couldn't get some work/life balance.

Maybe getting laid would chill him out.

Too bad she absolutely hated the idea of Brock sleeping with anyone. *Except me.*

She touched her lips. It had been a long time since just a kiss had turned her on so quickly. *Oh, jeez, I can't be falling for him again, am I? Because that would be really stupid.*

Summer shook her head angrily to clear out the memory of his kiss. She walked even faster.

Her destination was a two-story beige brick building directly across the square from The Yummy Cowboy Diner. A sign embedded in the facade above the second-story windows said, **E.F. Forster & Sons, 1913.** Swags of red, white, and blue striped bunting hung over all the windows, including the large plate-glass store windows on the ground floor, and a large American flag flew beside the front door.

A large sign advertised **Jenna's Java & Bakery - Locally Owned & Operated - Fresh Daily - All Natural.**

Mom and Grandma Abigail had both raved about Jenna's pastries. Jenna and Summer had been friends all throughout middle school and high school. A few months after graduation, Jenna had married her longtime boyfriend, moved away from Snowberry Springs, and lost contact. By that time, Summer was in California, attending the Culinary Institute of America.

Now Jenna was back, and making a name for herself with coffee and sweet treats.

Summer entered the café and found the interior was bright and modern while still maintaining rustic charm. Which was more than she could say about The Yummy Cowboy Diner, whose current decor epitomized everything that sucked about the 1970s.

A large blackboard hung from the ceiling behind the register. It advertised salads, soups, and sandwiches in addition to a long list of coffee drinks. On either side of the register, clean, lighted display cases held a large selection of tempting pastries.

This could work, thought Summer. Whoever had baked these had to be a trained pastry chef. All of the cookies, éclairs, croissants, tartlets, Danishes, and pastel-colored macarons looked uniform, attractive, and utterly scrumptious. A set of shelves behind the counter held loaves of bread in all sizes and shapes, including the baguettes she sought.

"Hi there," the young man working behind the counter greeted her with a smile. His gaze landed on her chef's coat, and his eyes widened a fraction. "...Ms. Snowberry. How may I help you?"

"I'll take one of everything from the second shelf on down." She indicated the pastry selection, omitting the cookies on the top shelf. They looked great, but she needed to know if the upscale items tasted as good as they looked. "For here. Oh, and a baguette to go, please."

"Uh, sure," said the young man, clearly taken by surprise. Summer had to commend him for remembering to ask, "And would you like a cappuccino or latte to go with your order?"

"A latte would be great, thank you," she said. "Double shot, whole milk, one pump of vanilla syrup, please."

"You got it." He grabbed two white lunch plates from a stack on the backbar, and swiftly filled them with pastries. "No cookies?"

"Not today. Just the pastries."

While he began making her latte, Summer took the plates and found a table. The cafe was deserted at the moment, probably because it was halfway between breakfast and lunch.

She began sampling the pastries, and had to suppress a moan of pleasure. They were perfect—buttery, flaky, flavorful but not sickeningly sweet.

"How are the pastries?" The young man came around the counter and set her latte down on the table. He pointed at the glazed rectangle of flaky puff pastry sandwiching a thick layer of vanilla crème pâtissière. "The Napoleon is my favorite."

"It's all wonderful," Summer said around a mouthful of éclair. She swallowed and said, "I was wondering if I could talk to Jenna about a dessert catering opportunity."

"I'll go get her right away!" He vanished through a door at the back of the café.

A minute later, a woman Summer's age came in. She wore a flour-dusted, butter-stained apron over a black t-shirt. Her long black hair was pulled into a ponytail that stuck out from a baseball cap with her bakery's name. "Summer! I heard you were back."

"Thanks. And it's great to see you, Jenna. How are you?" Summer rose to exchange hugs with her old friend.

"Doing pretty well," Jenna replied. "I was so sorry to hear about your grandpa. He's the one who let me set up here, rent-free, for the first six months, and loaned me the money to buy all of the bakery equipment and furniture I needed. He said the huckleberry turnovers I brought him sealed the deal."

Summer chuckled. "He always did have a big sweet tooth. And how's Luis doing?"

Jenna's face fell. "We got divorced last year. He had another woman."

"Oh no!" Summer couldn't hide her shock. Jenna and Luis were supposed to be one of those forever couples who celebrated their fiftieth wedding anniversary together.

"I told him I'd give him another chance, but he had to choose: me or her. He chose *her*." Jenna's expression twisted.

"I'm so sorry."

Jenna shrugged. "So, I took the twins and moved back home." She pulled out the chair opposite Summer and sat. "Vince, *mijo*, could you pull me a latte, too?"

"Sure thing, Tia Jenna!" Vince replied.

"Hm, let me think...what else is new?" Jenna mused. "Did you hear that Evie is running the Tony Carter & Son Garage? It's called E.V. Carter Automotive now."

"Good for her!" exclaimed Summer. She'd always liked Emmaline Violet Carter, who hated both her first and middle names, and went by "Evie," for her initials. "She always loved cars, but last I heard, Mr. Carter was dead-set against letting her work as a mechanic. What changed?"

Jenna laughed. "The Heir Apparent got a job at a big gaming company in Silicon Valley instead of becoming a mechanic like Dad wanted."

The Heir Apparent was Tony Jr., Evie's younger brother. "At least Evie got what she wanted, and Junior is probably happier where he is," Summer said.

"So, I heard you own your restaurant now," Jenna said. "In San Francisco. But you're helping out at The Yummy Cowboy Diner?"

Summer nodded. She was tempted to confide in her old friend about what was happening with SummerTime. But she couldn't risk it. In Snowberry Springs, everyone knew everyone else's business.

Jenna immediately confirmed this by asking, "And what's the

deal with Kenny Stinson? He's been telling everyone that you convinced Brock to fire him out of the blue."

"Oh, jeez, *really*?" Summer shook her head. "I had nothing to do with it. Kenny quit a few days before I started working at The Yummy Cowboy Diner. Then he changed his mind and asked for his job back, but Brock said no, because Kenny really messed up the inventory and the bookkeeping."

"Brock, huh?" A dimple appeared in Jenna's smooth brown cheek. "What's the deal with you two? Why are you helping him? He was always horrible to you in high school, and I heard that you guys fight a lot when you're working at the diner."

Thanks, Marlene, Summer thought wryly.

"It's a favor to Grandma Abigail," she explained. "She asked me to partner with Brock for the next three months to give The Yummy Cowboy Diner a makeover in advance of the LVR service starting up next summer. Which is actually why I dropped by. We're starting a dinner service with a new menu. Would you be interested in creating some exclusive, high-end desserts for us?"

Jenna's face lit up. "Of *course* I'm interested, silly! What did you have in mind?"

"A separate dessert menu, with items that change from week to week. Maybe a couple of evergreen classics, like a crème brûlée or cheesecake, definitely a chocolate cake or torte of some kind, and then two seasonal items using locally-sourced ingredients."

"I'd love to do this!" Jenna said enthusiastically. "What's the timeline? And how many portions will you need?"

"That's the catch," Summer said. "How about tomorrow evening? We're doing a trial dinner service tomorrow night, and I'd really like to test the dessert menu concept if you can provide us three unique items on such short notice."

Jenna nodded, and Summer went on. "I'm estimating that we can turn the tables at least twice during dinner service, so, say about a hundred desserts total? Brock's agreed to make fifty strawberry shortcakes in addition to the hundred desserts you provide."

Jenna's dimple reappeared. "Oh, I've heard all about the contest! I hope you win, Summer... someone needs to put Brock in his place."

"Couldn't agree more." Summer tried to hide her smirk with a hasty sip of her latte.

"All right, for tomorrow, how does huckleberry cheesecake and my double-chocolate brownies with salted caramel topping sound?" asked Jenna. "I also make ice cream here... I could include a three-gallon tub of my vanilla bean ice cream, which proves about ninety-six half-cup portions. Your third dessert could be a hot fudge sundae or cherry sundae. I'll provide the hot fudge, chopped nuts, and a gallon of my own Flathead Lake cherries in spiced syrup."

"That all sounds great! And if tomorrow's dinner service goes as well as I hope, let's talk about setting up a contract for all of The Yummy Cowboy Diner's desserts."

"I'd be willing to offer you a ten percent discount if you and Brock give me credit on your menu," Jenna said.

"We can do that," Summer said without hesitating. "Then we have a deal?"

Jenna nodded. "I'll deliver the cheesecake, brownies, and ice cream with fixings by four p.m. tomorrow," she promised.

"Oh, there was one more thing," Summer said. "Do you mind if we borrow Vince to work as our barista tomorrow night? My coffee distributor is delivering a new espresso machine first thing in the morning."

"Let's ask him."

After hashing out the remaining details, including the price for the desserts and Vince's pay and working hours tomorrow,

Summer left Jenna's Java a half-hour later. She felt great about what she'd accomplished at the bakery. Plus, it was wonderful to see her old friend running her own business and thriving.

As she crossed back through the town square, Summer realized that she'd missed the connections and the ability to make handshake deals because everyone in Snowberry Springs knew everyone else. People here trusted each other in a way that San Franciscans didn't.

What if I stayed here instead of going home? I could sell SummerTime—what's left of it, anyway—and keep working with Brock at The Yummy Cowboy Diner. The thought snuck in like a ninja. With it came the ghostly imprint of his mouth on hers.

She immediately dismissed it. *That kiss meant nothing to him, or he would have asked me out on a date. Or at least tried to kiss me again!*

Besides, Brock had made it crystal-clear that he disliked all of her ideas and hated sharing control of his diner.

He's probably counting down the days until I leave.

And I should be, too. Relaunching SummerTime is the only thing that matters.

Chapter Fourteen – Brock

The Yummy Cowboy Diner
Friday, June 17, 8:45 p.m.

Katie popped her head into the kitchen. "You guys, come out!" she said in an excited tone. "Autumn's gonna announce the winner now."

Brock finished plating one last dessert order and slid the plate onto the pass. "Two strawberry shortcakes for table ten," he announced, then peeled off his gloves with a sigh of relief.

The Yummy Cowboy Diner's very first dinner service was over. And thanks to Autumn Snowberry's social media magic, Contest Night had been a colossal hit.

When five p.m. had rolled around and Brock unlocked the diner's front door, a line of customers already stretched down the street and halfway around the square. The diner was crowded to capacity during all four hours of dinner service.

"Got it, boss," Katie said, grabbing the plate and vanishing into the dining room.

The burden of worry that he'd been carrying all day about canceling breakfast and lunch service finally dissipated in the non-stop flood of orders pouring into the kitchen. All three of them had worked at a punishing pace, pushing out dishes in a steady stream.

He knew in his heart that he'd won tonight. Summer would have to follow his orders for the next twenty-four hours. He couldn't wait to have her at his beck and call.

Except that she'll probably use her damned safe word as soon as I try anything.

He blew out a frustrated breath.

All evening, he'd done his best to ignore her temptingly curvy figure. They moved around the kitchen in a fast but controlled dance, she cooking her entrées, he cooking his, and Marlene cooking the sides and plating for both of them.

Most of tonight's customers were locals, but Terri and Katie had popped into the kitchen a few times to announce that guests from Livingston, Ennis, and even Bozeman were among the diner's usual customers.

Now, sweaty and exhausted, but exhilarated by success, Brock emerged from the kitchen, followed closely by Summer and Marlene.

He was dying to hear the results. He'd tried keeping track of the incoming tickets while working, but it had proved impossible to figure out which of the dishes on the new dinner menu had taken the lead.

Did that mean it was going to be a close race? He'd hoped for an overwhelming victory. But he'd take what he could get, as long as he won.

As the three of them entered the dining room, he was astonished —and gratified—as all the guests broke into enthusiastic applause.

Autumn wove her way towards them. Terri tailed her, filming everything on Autumn's sparkling, rhinestone-studded phone for upload to social media.

Autumn grinned at Brock, Summer, and Marlene before turning to face the dining room. She waved for silence.

"Ladies and gentlemen," she announced. "Thank you so much

for coming and supporting The Yummy Cowboy Diner. As you know, the point of tonight's contest was to find the most popular dish on our new menu. What we *didn't* tell you is that Summer and Brock each created three dishes—a salad and two entrées—and are fighting it out for not only Best Dish of the Week, but Best Chef of the Week. Katie?"

Katie, having delivered the desserts to table ten, waved. "On it!" She pushed past them and went into the kitchen.

Autumn paused as Katie vanished into the kitchen. More clapping and cheering came from the crowd in the dining room. Brock spotted his firefighter buddies squeezed around two four-top tables that were shoved together.

Smiling broadly, Jason gave him a thumbs-up, and began leading a chant of "Brock! Brock! Brock!"

The Snowberry family, crowded into two booths on the other side of the diner, countered with, "Summer! Summer! Goooo, Summer!"

Brock looped his arm around Marlene's shoulders and squeezed. "You did a helluva job tonight, Marlene. Thanks." He hesitated an instant, then put his other arm around Summer. "You, too, Ms. Fancy Pants."

"We make a darned good team, Mr. Grumpy Pants," she said, sliding her arm around his waist in return. He pulled her close and enjoyed her soft curves pressing against his side.

She was right, despite their rocky start yesterday. She'd been right about a lot of things. *Dammit.*

Jenna's desserts, many of them ordered with cappuccinos, had been a hit with this crowd, increasing the value of each dinner check exactly the way Summer had promised.

"If you're grumpy and she's fancy, what kind of pants am I?" Marlene demanded. "I want a nickname, too!"

"How about Hot Pants or Sizzling Pants?" Summer suggested.

"Gossip Pants," Brock said in a teasing tone. "Or maybe Mama Pants?"

Marlene snorted. "Sizzling Pants." She bumped Brock playfully with her hip. "Because I still got plenty o' sizzle, young man."

He chuckled. "You sure do."

Katie reappeared, holding a pair of small whiteboards that she and Terri had used to keep track of the orders.

One board listed the salads and the other board the entrées, with a running total of orders next to each item. They had agreed in advance that the house salad and the desserts wouldn't be counted in the tally for most popular dish.

Holding the whiteboards carefully turned away from the dining room and angling them to hide the contents from Brock and Summer, Katie moved to stand next to Autumn.

Autumn raised her hand for silence, and the competing chants died away. "Now it's time to find out whose cuisine has reigned supreme in our culinary battle at The Yummy Cowboy Diner. Will it be our very own celebrity chef Summer Snowberry, owner of the renowned SummerTime restaurant in San Francisco—"

Cheers and whoops erupted from the Snowberry family contingent. She paused until they fell silent, then continued, "—or hometown favorite Brock Michaels?"

More applause, with piercing wolf whistles from Jason and Evie.

Brock held his breath.

But Autumn knew how to draw out the anticipation. "But before we reveal the winners, why don't Brock and Summer tell us which dishes belong to them? Brock, you first."

"I, uh..." *Fuck*. He hated being put on the spot like this! "Caesar salad, bison meatloaf, and the fried chicken."

Summer removed her arm from Brock's waist and stepped

forward. Looking poised and confident, she said, "YC Salad, seared bison filet, and the soy-glazed halibut."

As if everyone here hadn't already guessed which dishes were hers!

"You go, baby girl!" Priscilla shouted, and everyone laughed while Summer turned beet red.

"Thanks a lot, Mom," she muttered, retreating. Brock couldn't suppress his smirk.

"Katie, show us the salad board!" Autumn ordered, smiling widely.

Kate struck a Vanna White pose, slowly lifting and turning the board to show it to the dining room. Brock craned his neck, but couldn't read it from where he stood.

"And the winner in the salad category is... the YC salad, everyone!" Autumn declared. "Edging out the Caesar salad by only three points."

Summer whooped. Grinning, she pumped her fist in the air. "Yes!"

Brock's heart sank as she reached across him to high-five Marlene. He'd been *positive* that the diner's beloved Caesar would triumph over a concoction made with ingredients like goat cheese and peach jam!

Not wanting to look like a sore loser, he forced himself to smile and high-five Summer in turn.

At least three points aren't an insurmountable lead, he told himself. If his entrées won, then the salad loss wouldn't mean losing the contest.

"Now, on to the entrées. Remember, the chef with the highest number of total orders this evening wins."

With agonizing slowness, and clearly playing to the crowd, Katie lifted and rotated the second whiteboard.

"In first place, with thirty-three orders… the bison filet!" Autumn announced. "In second place, the bison meatloaf! And tied for third place, the fried chicken and the halibut."

Brock stared in disbelief at the totals written on the whiteboard. *That can't be right!*

"Ladies and gentlemen, it was a close race, but tonight's winner is Summer Snowberry! Summer, would you like to say a few words?"

Everyone clapped and cheered as Brock gritted his teeth and tried to keep smiling.

"First of all, I'd like to thank our line cook, Marlene Wittenmeyer. Without her, Brock and I couldn't have prepared all those dishes for you tonight."

Summer turned and hugged Marlene briefly before continuing.

"My good friend Jenna Gomez of Jenna's Java & Bakery provided most of this evening's scrumptious desserts. And finally, I'd like to thank my new business partner, Brock Michaels, for being a good sport about letting me invade his kitchen, and for making all those fabulous strawberry shortcakes. They sold out tonight."

To another round of applause, she went up tiptoes and hugged him, too. But even the delightful sensation of her breasts, round and firm against his chest, couldn't distract him from the bitterness of defeat.

He'd been wrong. About everything. The dinner service, the popularity of the espresso drinks, and worst of all, the food. He'd been so sure that he knew what the people of Snowberry Springs wanted and liked.

In reality, he hadn't known shit.

The realization burned his gut like acid.

But he liked to think that he wasn't an idiot. The truth hurt, but he was a big boy. He could take it… especially if it meant that his diner would be profitable by Abigail's deadline.

He hugged her back, then straightened up and raised one hand. "Folks, thanks so much for coming out tonight and supporting my—*our* diner. Your support means everything to us."

∞∞∞

"Hah! I was right! We *killed* it tonight!" Summer crowed, leaning over Brock's shoulder to peer at the computer screen. "That's, what, triple the amount of yesterday's sales?"

"You don't have to rub it in," Brock grumbled. The heat of her hand soaking through his t-shirt distracted him from the numbers.

It was late, and the two of them were alone in the diner. After cleanup, everyone else had clocked out. Summer and Brock had retreated to the office to review tonight's receipts and enter them into the bookkeeping program.

Summer chuckled, her breath warm on the back of his neck. "Just this one time, admit I was right about adding dinner service. And about closing for breakfast and lunch today. In return, I promise I'll never mention it again."

He blew out a breath and scowled at the screen. But the numbers in the accounting software didn't lie. They'd made a shitload of money tonight.

But what came out of his mouth was, "You won the contest, didn't you? Go ahead, lord it over me. I lost, fair and square."

Her touch vanished. She straightened up. "Jeez, Brock. You really can't do it, can you? Can't admit I actually I know what I'm doing!"

She sounded hurt.

Then she spun on her heel and strode out of the cramped office.

He heard her footsteps in the tiled hallway. And he was suddenly, absolutely certain that if he didn't stop her now, she wasn't coming back.

She drove him crazy in more ways than one, but if she left, Abigail Snowberry's deal was history and he'd be royally screwed.

"Summer, wait." The ancient office chair creaked loudly as he pushed his way up and out of it.

Soft clattering and scraping sounds led him to the kitchen.

She stood at the kitchen's prep counter, gathering up her knives and peelers and thermometers, and packing them in her well-worn canvas knife roll. *Shit.*

"What are you doing?" he said, coming up behind her.

She slid her wickedly-sharp, very high-end chef's knife into the pocket made for it, and kept her back to him. "Trying to decide whether my half of the diner is worth dealing with *you*."

He froze.

"Answer me this: are you willing to institute Friday and Saturday night dinner service, even if it means hiring more staff?"

"Why do you care?" he shot back. "You won the fucking contest, Summer. You're the boss for the next twenty-four hours. You want dinner service, you've got dinner service."

"For crying out loud, Brock!" She slammed her hands down on the spotless stainless-steel counter. "Tonight wasn't about winning—though I won't lie, it felt good to beat a worthy opponent. It was about making changes to this place that *work*. And to do that, we both have to be willing to try something new. Not just when there's a stupid contest!"

"It wasn't a stupid contest!" he retorted, stung. "And even if it was, look me in the face and tell me you didn't enjoy it."

She stared at him, her cornflower eyes wide. And all he could think about was pulling her close and getting his hands on her round, perfect ass.

"Admit it," he urged. "Wasn't tonight the most fun you've had in a while?"

"Fun?" She looked at him like he was crazy. "*That's* your idea of fun? I can think of at least ten things I'd rather do on a Friday night than working."

"Okay, name one," he challenged her. "A fun thing you enjoy doing. And, no, cooking doesn't count."

"Well…" She bit her plump lower lip, and suddenly all Brock could think about was kissing her again. Her mouth had been so soft and hot. "You first."

A faint spatter of freckles ran across the bridge of her adorable little nose and over her cheeks under her light tan. Brock was exhausted, annoyed with the whole situation, but suddenly obsessed with tasting and touching her everywhere.

"Okay," he said, moving in closer. He couldn't help himself. She drew him in like a summer moth circling a porch light. "I enjoy doing *this*."

He grabbed her shoulders and pulled her against him, then bent to claim her mouth.

His world instantly shrank down to her skin, her hair, her scent. His cock stirred and swelled to hungry life.

She made an incoherent sound and melted against him. Her lips devoured his, and her arms wound around his shoulders. Her fingers felt like steel against the back of his neck, keeping him from escaping.

As if he was going to stop now! He'd been dreaming about this for days. Years.

She tasted like sun-warmed strawberries and melted chocolate, sweet and hot. He needed more from her. He needed it all.

He backed her against the counter, plundering her mouth, grinding his aching hard-on against her soft belly.

Brock ran his hands over her magnificent ass, squeezing as he plundered the depths of her mouth with his tongue. He grabbed one of her legs, brought her knee up to his hip, and molded himself between her thighs. She fit against him so damned perfectly, like they were made for each other.

This time, when he thrust against her, feeling her heat through his jeans and her loose pants, she moaned loudly and thrust back.

Then she grabbed his t-shirt, her fingers scraping across the cloth and over the small of his back, and yanked the hem out of his jeans. Her hands feverishly stroked his back, his waist, his torso, and she pushed his shirt up over his chest.

Brock was in fucking heaven. She wanted him, too! Maybe even as badly as he wanted her.

He tore his mouth free of hers long enough to ask, "Like what you see, Ms. Fancy Pants?"

"You are *such* a jerk!" Summer's mouth was swollen from kissing and unbearably sexy.

"But I'm *your* jerk, Summer Snowberry," he said before he could stop himself. "And you can't deny we've got some serious chemistry."

He reached out and pushed her knife roll out of the danger zone. His hands closed on her rounded hips. He lifted her and set her on the counter.

She stiffened. "Hold on! I am *not* screwing you in a kitchen. On a surface where we're prepping food tomorrow." Her tone was weirdly prim for someone who'd just yanked his shirt half-off.

She hopped right back down, sliding down Brock's front with

teasing friction.

Dammit. Another fantasy destroyed.

"It's not like the boss is going to find out and fire us," he said hoarsely. He hung on to her hips. She wasn't getting away. Not this time. "Besides, I know where the cleaning supplies are."

She giggled but stayed put, both feet planted firmly on the kitchen's tiled floor.

He pulled up the hem of her chef's coat and stroked the smooth, warm skin beneath. His brain was fogged with her scent and the velvety slide of her skin beneath his palms. He slipped his hand under the elastic waistband of her checked pants, seeking the prize.

His fingertips encountered damp cotton panties, then slid down further, to cup her mound. She was hot and soft and deliciously plump against his hand. "I want you, Summer."

To make his point, he stroked one finger over the taut fabric, tracing her slit.

She whimpered with need. He stroked her again, teasing the barely perceptible bud of her clit this time while kissing the long line of her throat. He licked and nipped the tender skin ravenously.

Desperate to taste her pussy, he began to push down her pants.

She grabbed his wrist.

"Stop. Please." Her cheeks and throat were flushed. Wisps of sweat-darkened hair had escaped her cap and clung to her temples and cheeks. She was the most beautiful woman he'd ever seen.

"Shit," he groaned. He couldn't fucking believe it. Neither could his poor deprived cock. He wanted her so badly he could hardly think straight.

She grinned at him, an unexpectedly wicked glint in her

cornflower-blue eyes. "I'm the boss, remember? The boss wants you, but she needs a shower first. I *reek*." She took a deep, ostentatious sniff. "And so do you."

A shower meant that they'd both be getting naked. Preferably together.

"Fine," Brock growled. "Your place or mine?"

"Are you *kidding* me?" she asked.

The lust of fog momentarily parted, and he remembered that she was staying out at the ranch. With her parents, sister, and nephew in the house.

"Yeah, bad joke," he said, backpedaling like crazy. "My place, of course. I've got clean towels. And condoms." He only hoped they hadn't expired during his long dry spell. "Let's go and get naked and clean before we get naked and dirty, Ms. Fancy Pants."

Oh please, oh God, don't let her change her mind on the drive over to my place.

Chapter Fifteen – Summer

"**Y**ou've got to be kidding me," Summer said, squeezed back to front against Brock's hard chest as warm water poured over them both.

The hard ridge of flesh poking her lower back reminded her why his nickname was The Cock. He was *huge*. The thought of taking him inside her made her knees go weak.

After a brief but heated make-out session at his front door, they'd left a trail of clothing leading from the living room of his cottage to his bathroom. Stumbling and laughing between kisses and frantic caresses, they peeled out of their sweaty, food-stained clothing.

All the smells from dinner service—seared meat, garlic, onions, and vanilla—revived in the clouds of steam billowing around their naked bodies. The heat felt good, loosening the tension and easing the fatigue from a long day on her feet, first powering through the mountain of prep and then cooking on the line.

They'd all worked their butts off tonight, pleased a crowd by feeding them good food, and earned a nice profit to boot.

Even better, a decade after the hopeless crush that never quite went away, Brock was *finally* treating her like a desirable woman. Happiness fizzed like Champagne bubbles through Summer's chest.

"Hey, you're the one who dropped the soap," Brock pointed out. "But I'm willing to work around that."

His shower was old, built into his clean but dated bathroom like a tiny closet. It was barely big enough for one person to move without bumping elbows against the vintage mint green tiles.

"How?" she challenged.

Two people crammed here could barely move, much less bend over. She bent her head and studied the bar of soap now resting against the side of her foot. So close, yet so far out of reach. The whole situation was ridiculous.

But so much fun.

"Like this." Brock's arms came around her, and his sinewy hands, white with suds, cupped her breasts.

His thumbs swept boldly over her nipples.

Summer gasped as pleasure ran like an electric current straight down to the place between her legs already swollen and aching with desire.

"You are so fucking gorgeous, Ms. Fancy Pants." Brock's teeth nipped lightly, branding a path down the side of her neck. His hands continued to work magic on her breasts, his touch firm but slippery. "I'm gonna touch and taste every inch of you tonight. I'm gonna lick your pussy until you're screaming my name."

Dirty talk wasn't normally Summer's thing—one of the men she'd dated briefly in San Francisco had accused her of being a prude after a failed attempt at sexting, and promptly ghosted her.

But it felt different when *Brock* talked to her like this.

Maybe it was the way his voice rasped in her ear, hoarse with need. Or how he interspersed words with action, his hands and lips discovering every sensitive spot on her upper body and lingering over each of them, whipping her senses into an inferno of burning need.

She was panting and arching against him when he finally left her breasts and skated lower. He took his time, smoothing his hands over her stomach and tracing the dip of her waist before his fingers pushed between her thighs, urging them apart. "Open up for me, sweetness."

"What—?" she gasped. He wasn't seriously thinking about screwing her in the cramped confines of his shower stall, was he?

How would that even work when he barely had enough room to get his arms around her?

I'm up for it if he is. The thought made her giggle, because the pressure against her backside informed her he was definitely up for *anything* right now.

Then she felt the teasing stroke of his fingertip against her folds. When he brushed over her clit and circled it, Summer was ready to come on the spot. She heard herself make a noise somewhere between a cry and a whimper.

"Yeah, that's what I want to hear," Brock said. "I want you to come on my hand."

He stroked her again. Simultaneously, the fingers of his other hand pinched her nipple. He bit the side of her neck.

Summer moaned. Loudly.

"Oh, yeah. Just like that," Brock encouraged her.

He kept torturing her breast while stroking her. She writhed against the hard length trapped between them, and he groaned.

"Stop that," he ordered.

"Why?"

"Because right now, it's taking every ounce of self-control I have not to haul you out of this shower, push you up against the nearest wall and fuck your brains out."

"That sounds like—*oh!*—a pretty good plan to me!"

"Don't worry, it's on the agenda, but later. Right now, I wanna see and hear you come for me."

He circled her sensitive bud, teasing it with his fingertip, and she moaned again.

Then he slid his finger inside her. She clenched around him, all heat and slick need. She was so close now. Everything he was doing was driving her crazy in the best possible way.

"Are you ready to come for me, Ms. Fancy Pants?" he ordered.

"Yes," she panted. "Oh, yes!"

He thrust in and out of her with a quick, steady rhythm, teasing her bud with the heel of his hand on every stroke while continuing to caress her breast with his other hand.

She went up on tiptoes and tilted her hips to give him better access in the tight quarters, letting her head fall back against his shoulder.

Her release gathered rapidly inside her belly, rising like an ocean swell about to crest into a wave. She was panting now, needy whimpers escaping her throat.

"Yeah, just like that," he urged her. "Let me hear you, Summer."

The wave surged and broke over her senses with crashing pleasure.

He held her, supporting her as her climax throbbed and pulsed through her in waves, his fingers continuing to move inside her, prolonging her release.

"Holy crap," she said finally, sagging back against him, feeling utterly boneless. "That was amazing."

He chuckled, and the vibrations from his chest passed through her skin like a caress. "That's my girl."

When she could stand on her own again, she said, "My turn. But first, let me get that soap before it dissolves into nothing."

She slid out of his embrace and stepped out of the shower. Before bending to retrieve the soap, she took a moment to admire his muscled chest with its furring of dark hair, sculpted torso, and the magnificent cock jutting out from the dark thatch at his groin.

"Now I get to soap you down," she said, grinning up at him. "Remember, I want you clean before you get dirty with me."

"Ms. Fancy Pants, I've already gotten dirty with you," he pointed out.

"Don't get hung up on details." She squeezed back inside the shower stall, facing him this time. Then she lathered up, careful not to drop the slippery rectangle of soap again. She explored his hard body, learning what he liked and where his ticklish areas were.

Finally, she took his stiff length in her hand, fisting his thick shaft. She pumped him, swirling her thumb over the broad head at the top of each stroke, until he grabbed her wrist in steely fingers.

"Stop," he ordered. "Or I'm gonna come. And as nice as this is, I wanna come inside you… and I want you to come again, this time on my cock."

"Promises, promises," she teased, but released her hold on him.

A few moments of comic contortions followed as they tried to rinse off without bruising their elbows against the unyielding tiles… or giving the other person a black eye by mistake.

When they emerged from the cramped shower stall, they dried each other with the soft, clean towels that sat folded on the counter. They both used the opportunity to grope each other under the excuse of toweling off.

While he rubbed her down, Brock described exactly what he wanted to do to her and what he wanted her to do to him.

"—and that sweet mouth of yours wrapped around my cock, swallowing me as far as you take me, while I lick your pussy and fuck you with my tongue—"

Her arousal blossomed again with urgent, throbbing heat. It was as though she'd never climaxed. She wanted more of him. A lot more.

He unexpectedly lifted her and slung over his shoulder, caveman-style. She shrieked with laughter, pounding his damp back weakly with her fists as he carried her into his bedroom.

Brock dropped her on his bed and yanked away the towel. "Get ready, Summer. I'm gonna fuck your brains out tonight."

She giggled and stretched, liking the way he devoured her with his hot brown gaze. "Is that a threat—or a promise?"

"Take it whichever way turns you on more." Brock joined her on the mattress. He straddled her legs, then leaned forward and put his palms on either side of her head. His heated cock dragged along the inside of her thigh, rigid and heavy. He lowered himself to kiss her.

She panted and squirmed against him, rubbing herself against his hard length while he plundered her mouth with his wickedly skilled tongue.

"I wanted to take my time and enjoy this," he said. "But I can't wait much longer."

"Then don't," she urged. "I'm more than ready for you."

He laid a line of hard, sucking kisses over her jaw and down her throat, then cupped her breasts and closed his lips around one nipple while he teased the other with his thumb.

She opened her legs and raised her hips, then suddenly remembered something very important. "Condoms," she gasped.

"Fuck. I nearly forgot." He moved off her and reached out to yank open his nightstand drawer.

A moment later, a square plastic condom packet landed on her stomach. "Your mission, should you choose to accept it..." he quoted solemnly.

"Is to wrap up your manly member?" she finished, bubbles of laughter rising in her throat. She couldn't remember having sex this lighthearted before, with the unexpected bonus that she'd already climaxed.

Most of the time, she didn't come at all. Once her dates reached the finish line, they lost interest in helping her cross it, too. They'd gotten off, so as far as they were concerned, the date was over. Time to get dressed and head out.

She tore open the packet and rolled the condom down his shaft, turning the task into a long, stroking caress.

"Ms. Fancy Pants, you're going to kill me," Brock declared, his face flushed and his eyes squeezed shut in what looked like pain.

"Come here, big guy, and die happy," she responded, urging him on top of her.

She was more than ready for him.

"You're fucking gorgeous, you know that, right?" he said, panting, as he lowered himself onto her.

"So are you, when you're not frowning all the time and shooting death rays out of your eyes," she said.

He chuckled. "Hell, most of the time, I really wish they *were* death rays. It would take care of the people giving me shit all the time."

"People like me?" She prevented him from answering by pulling down his head to kiss him.

She devoured every inch of skin she could—his mouth, his chin, the side of his neck—as he settled on top of her, pushing her into the mattress as she wrapped her legs around his hips.

"No death rays for you." He moved his hips until the blunt head of his cock nudged her entrance. "I'm just going to pound you into submission."

Then he pushed into her, slowly but inexorably. He felt even bigger than he looked.

"Oh. My. God," she gasped, arching beneath him.

"You okay?" He stopped moving, and his quivering muscles betrayed just how that cost him.

"Just need a minute." Her passage burned as it stretched around the huge object now impaling her.

She lay beneath him, breathing as her body adjusted to the invasion. He filled every inch of her, and she loved it. "Holy crap, you're armed and dangerous with that thing. No wonder they call you Brock the Cock!"

He stiffened and scowled down at her. "Don't call me that. I fucking *hate* that nickname."

She nodded. "Okay. Sorry."

He grunted, then said, "You feel fucking awesome. How're *you* doing?"

She wriggled experimentally, touched that he cared enough to ask. "All systems 'go.' You may proceed with the pounding, good sir."

A laugh exploded out of him. Then he set to work.

He took her fast and hard. His mouth covered hers, muffling her moans as he moved against her, angling his thrusts. His shaft caressed her clit with every long, sliding movement. She hooked her heels around the backs of his knees and hung on for the ride.

Summer wound her arms around him, and kissed him hard as a fresh coil of pleasure began winding tight in the pit of her belly, surprising her.

Twice on the same date? That's a new personal best for me.

"You getting close?"

She nodded. "I can't believe it, but yes."

"Good." His hand dove between their bodies. She gasped as he found her bud and began stroking it in time with his pistoning cock. "Come for me again, Summer," he commanded. "I'm so close to the edge. I want us to come together while I'm balls-deep inside you."

Her climax blossomed like a rose made of flame as her release exploded and consumed her in an inferno of pleasure.

She cried out his name as sweet shudders wracked her for long moments, and clutched at his shoulders. Her short nails dug into his skin as he continued to work magic between her legs.

Brock groaned loudly. He buried his face against her neck as his thrusts faltered and lost their rhythm. Then he stiffened against her, swearing loudly, and found her mouth in a deep, hard kiss.

And that was only the beginning.

Brock was insatiable... and so was she. Two more rounds of urgent, extremely satisfying sex followed.

Round two began with her on her knees next to the bed, his cock in her mouth and her hands braced against his powerful thighs as she licked, sucked, and swirled her tongue around him like a Popsicle. It ended with her on his lap, impaled on him as his mouth did wicked, wonderful things to her breasts.

During round three, he rolled her over, pulled her hips up and took her from behind, each powerful thrust hitting a place inside her that made her see stars.

She bit down on his pillow to muffle her screams of pleasure as she crested yet again, this time even more powerfully than before. She'd never suspected that she could climax so many times in a row.

All those years spent having mediocre sex with guys who didn't care if she got off as long as they did! What a waste... except without them as a baseline, she wouldn't have been able to appreciate Brock's awesome skill set as much as she did at this moment. He sure as heck knew what he was doing with his fingers, tongue, and amazing cock.

Panting and sweaty, she lay draped limply over him, feeling completely relaxed for the first time in years. *Guess Brock pounded all the stress right out of me, complete with multiple happy endings.*

He was the first lover who made sure that she came first, every single time. As she cuddled up against him, she tried to figure out what this night meant for their partnership.

Was it only a one-night stand? A way for each of them to relieve stress and frustration? Friends with benefits?

Or something more?

She grimaced at that. She didn't consider him a friend. He behaved like a jerk most of the time. A stubborn, opinionated, short-tempered jerk. Last night, she'd been ready to walk away from their partnership because of his refusal to cooperate with her.

So, what on earth am I doing in bed with him? Is this what's meant by "hate sex"?

If so, maybe she needed to hate more men. Because, hands-down, this was the best she'd ever had in her life.

He didn't need to know that, though. His ego was already the size of the town square.

Plus, he still hadn't apologized for fighting her on every single decision that turned out to be the right thing to do.

Who knows, maybe getting laid will sweeten his attitude a little. But she wasn't pinning her hopes on it.

He might be Sweet, Thoughtful Sex God Brock right now, but come morning, was she going to wake up to Brock the Block Everything?

Now he stroked her butt and pulled her on top of him. He was clearly interested in round four, and unmistakable evidence of that interest pressed eagerly against her mound.

She was tired and more than a little sore. But no lie, round four sounded extremely appealing.

Then her stomach growled. Loudly.

Neither of them had had any time to eat dinner. After working her butt off in the kitchen all day, she'd gotten an extra-energetic workout riding her very own yummy cowboy. Suddenly, she was ravenous and ready to launch a raid on his fridge.

And if he has ice cream, it won't be pretty.

"Was that *you*, Ms. Fancy Pants?" Brock asked, his tone incredulous. He stopped squeezing her butt cheeks.

"You know what? I think it's time I ordered you around a little. As your boss for the next, uh," she glanced at the digital alarm clock on his nightstand, "nineteen hours."

"An order, huh?" His dark brows shot up. His lips stretched in a smirk.

She sat up, straddling his narrow hips. "I feel like I should enjoy my power over you before any more time slips away."

He chuckled and folded his arms behind his head. "I'm not worried. I have a safe word. What do you want, boss lady?"

Chapter Sixteen – Brock

"**F**ood," she said. "Because I'm starving."

Well, damn. He'd been hoping that for their next go-around, she'd ride his cock while he lay back, watching her gorgeous tits jiggle as she bounced her way to a happy ending for them both.

Hell, she could tie him up and he wouldn't object, as long as she was naked and touching him.

"I can do that," he replied. Now that he thought about it, he was pretty hungry himself. They'd take a snack break, then get back to enjoying themselves.

And damned if he wasn't having a great time with her. Maybe it was just the effects of his long dry spell, but Summer was sexy, responsive, and gorgeous as fuck. Or maybe their endless arguments had been foreplay.

Lord knew he was having a grand time pounding away his frustration... and hers, too, he hoped.

"And what does the boss lady want?"

"I'm pretty sure that Snowberry Springs doesn't have an all-night pizza place yet, so what can you offer me?" She grinned down at him. "I'm good with peanut butter and jelly, or ham and cheese."

A sandwich? He stared incredulously at her. Ms. Fancy Pants had nineteen hours left to order him around, and all she expected from him was a fucking *sandwich?*

He could do better than that. A *lot* better.

He fucking loved to cook for people. That was how his mama had shown how much she cared. His gran, too. *Guess it runs in the family.*

Besides, this was his golden opportunity to show her he knew how to make more than just eggs, waffles, and meatloaf.

"How about I make you my favorite dish? I have all the ingredients in my fridge, and it only takes about twenty minutes to prepare."

He braced himself for a flood of questions and critique. Instead, she beamed and said, "Sounds great."

She swung one long, lovely leg over him, and rolled gracefully off his bed and onto her feet. He stayed put, admiring the view.

"Well, don't just lie there!" She put her hands on her hips and tossed her long, tangled golden hair. "Into the kitchen with you, Mr. Grumpy Pants!"

"Ma'am!" He saluted her from his place on the bed. "Yes, ma'am!"

That got him another smile.

He chuckled and heaved himself to his feet, then went to pull a clean pair of boxers out of his chest of drawers.

He couldn't resist adding, "I love me a bossy woman, but don't get *too* bossy. Or I'll put you over my knee and spank you."

"Could be fun," she said, surprising him. Then she vanished into his bathroom.

When Summer wandered out of his bedroom a short time later,

she wore one of Brock's clean t-shirts, which hung to mid-thigh.

He found he liked seeing her in his clothes.

Actually—and this was kinda hard to admit—he liked *her*. She was beautiful, sassy, and confident, and extremely good at what she did. Best of all, she seemed willing to teach him what she knew.

When they weren't butting heads—and that wasn't *all* him, she was plenty feisty and every bit as stubborn as he was—they actually worked really well together.

Never in a million years could his seventeen-year-old self have predicted that he'd end up with a naked and very enthusiastic Summer Snowberry in his bed. And his shower. And now, in his kitchen.

At the end of their senior year of high school, he'd been sick with jealousy when he heard Summer was heading to the Culinary Institute of America after graduation. It wasn't fair that her grandparents were rich.

Meanwhile, his mama had been working herself to death at The Yummy Cowboy Diner, and Brock had been stuck working there every day after school, and most weekends, too. He'd lusted after Summer and resented her in equal measures.

He knew she had a thing for him. He also knew that she was way out of his league, and he'd only make a fool of himself if he ran panting after her. So, he'd been a real dick to her whenever she tried being nice to him.

Now, as he assembled the ingredients he'd need and hauled his gran's cast-iron skillet out of the cabinet, he stole glances at her.

Summer was giving herself the tour of his cottage. He didn't mind. He kept his place neat, so he wasn't worried about scaring her off.

He stole glances at her bare legs and fine ass every time she bent to gather up their scattered clothing from the hallway, living room, and mudroom.

"This is a cute place," Summer said, wandering back into the kitchen. "But if you don't mind me saying this..." She paused, as if trying to think of what to say next. "Um, it looks like your mom still lives here. Except for your clothes, I don't see anything that belongs to you."

He shrugged, but Summer was right.

Brock might be the only one living here now, but this was still Mama's house. Her presence still permeated the cottage, from the framed prints and family photos on the vintage flowered wallpaper, to the vases and knickknacks on the bookshelves. He hadn't changed the furnishings or decor since his mother's death.

"I keep meaning to get to it," he said, "But I've been too damned busy to sort through Mama and Gran's belongings and figure out what to donate or sell. Plus, I'm basically only here to sleep and cook, so cleaning out the place is at the bottom of my priority list."

"I understand," she said. "Plus, it would probably stir up a bunch of grief and feelings of loss. Autumn is the one who cleaned out Grandpa's side of the closet in Grandma Abigail and Grandpa Frank's house on our ranch, because Grandma just couldn't face going through all of his stuff. But it has to be done, eventually, or it's never really going to feel like *your* place."

He blew out a breath. Summer's words scraped against a still-raw spot. "I'm... not ready yet," he confessed. "But soon."

"Okay. I'll help sort and haul if you want me to."

"Thanks for the offer, but aren't you going back to San Francisco in September?" he asked, trying to ignore the rush of warmth ignited by her offer. She understood what it felt like to lose someone she loved.

"Yeah, but there are daily flights to Bozeman. I could come out for a few days, if you, um, wanted me to." She bit her lower lip and looked around the kitchen. Her expression betrayed that she'd said more than she wanted to. Transparently changing the subject, she asked, "So, what are you cooking me?"

She studied the items laid out on his counter. He had chicken breasts, flour, butter, a bulb of garlic, and a package of dry spaghetti, along with a couple of lemons, a jar of capers, a carton of chicken broth, a container of salt, and a tall pepper grinder.

He grinned at her. "I'm making you my gran's special lemon chicken."

"Yum!"

"That's right," he said, pleased by her reaction. "Prepare to be impressed, Ms. Fancy Pants."

"Can I help with anything?" she asked. "I really didn't want to put you to any trouble. I was hoping you'd slap together a sandwich or pour me a bowl of cereal." Her smile made his breath catch. "But I love it when someone cooks for me. You would *not* believe how weird my friends get about preparing a home-cooked meal for me, because I'm a professional chef. It's like they expect me to go all Gordon Ramsay on them, but really, I'm in heaven when someone else is cooking for a change."

"Sounds like I need to cook for you more often, then," he said. "And I'm sure Mr. Ramsay wouldn't turn his nose up at a home-cooked meal, either. My gran loved watching his shows, though she never allowed *me* to swear."

He tried to remember the last time he'd eaten a meal someone else had made for him, other than the staff meals at the diner, when it was Marlene's turn to cook.

Two years, at least. Before Mama's cancer ate her alive.

Renewed pain and grief ambushed him. Brock forced down the surge of pain. He pointed at a medium sized stainless-steel mixing bowl standing next to a flashlight on his small breakfast table. "If you wanna help, go out and pick some green beans and parsley from my garden."

"I'd love to."

She opened the back door, letting in the sounds of a Montana summer night. Crickets and frogs chirped and croaked love songs. A distant spark of lightning lit the clouds piled over the mountains on the west side of the valley. A soft rumble of thunder followed a few seconds later.

Cool air wafted into the kitchen, perfumed with Mama's heirloom roses that grew against the walls of the cottage.

Brock watched as Summer descended three wooden steps to his large vegetable and herb garden.

"Wow, this is amazing." She swept the flashlight beam around, illuminating his carefully-tended raised beds and trellises, then lingered on his small greenhouse and the row of mature fruit trees—cherry, plum, apple, and pear—planted in a row at the back of the garden. "Where do you find the time to take care of all this?"

"There are usually a few hours of daylight left by the time I leave the diner," he replied. "It helps me unwind."

He turned his attention back to preparing the meal.

When she came back inside a few minutes later, her basket was mounded with the requested green beans and parsley, plus fresh lettuce, tomatoes, and a couple of carrots.

"Thought I'd make a salad," she said, coming up next to him. She put the bowl in the sink and turned the faucet on.

Brock gave her an amused glance as she began scrubbing the carrots. "So, you're appointing yourself my sous-chef?"

She fluttered her eyelashes at him with comic exaggeration. "Why, Mr. Grumpy Pants, I didn't expect you to be using those fancy French terms."

He suppressed a laugh and began pounding the chicken breasts flat with a wooden rolling pin, just like his gran had taught him.

"Working off your frustrations?" she teased.

He couldn't keep his eyes off her slender fingers, which were now lovingly washing the tomatoes.

Even after all of the sex they'd had, his cock stirred. It wanted to feel her touching him like that.

He grinned. "Pounding *chicken* isn't what relieved my stress, Ms. Fancy Pants. Your sweet pussy, though…" He looked her up and down. "And don't think we're done yet," he added. "Not by a long shot. You'll be walking funny tomorrow."

"I accept your challenge," she answered. "Even if it means we're both going to be dead on our feet for breakfast service." She sneaked a glance up at the clock over his oven. "Crap! It's *way* past my bedtime."

"Nothing a pot of coffee and a good breakfast won't cure in the morning," he declared. Then he smirked. "Tell me this isn't worth losing sleep over."

"What, and inflate your already massive ego, Mr. Grumpy Pants?" she asked, reaching for a knife and one of the cutting boards stored on a countertop rack. "Where do you keep your olive oil and vinegar?"

∞∞∞

"Ooh, I love chicken piccata!" Summer exclaimed fifteen minutes later, when he brought a pair of plates to the table.

She had set the table for two, placed the salad bowl between them, and poured them both glasses of ice water garnished with leftover slices of lemon.

"Piccata? Well, aren't you all high-falutin'?" he joked as he put

146

the plates down on the table. "Why, this here's my Grandma Russo's lemon chicken with capers over spaghetti, and a side of fresh garden vegetables in garlic butter."

"Well, it looks delicious." She handed him the bowl of salad. "And there's nothing as good as lettuce and tomatoes fresh from the garden."

They sat down and dug in.

Pleasantly relaxed from several bouts of great sex, he'd had time to do some thinking while he dredged the flattened, seasoned chicken breasts in flour, then fried them up. And he'd come to some conclusions. Now it was time to man up, and say his piece.

"Look," he began, after a few mouthfuls. "I wanted to tell you were right about the diner."

Her eyes widened in surprise. She stopped with her fork halfway to her mouth. "What part? I thought you hated every item on my list."

He winced. But, yeah, he deserved that. "Yeah, well, everything you've told me to do has worked out okay. *Better* than okay," he amended. The next part was even harder to say. "I'm sorry I've been such an asshole about, well, everything."

There. He'd managed to get the words out without choking on them.

Summer lowered her silverware and studied him, her cornflower-blue eyes serious. "Brock, help me understand why you're hell-bent on keeping everything at the diner the way it's always been."

He stared back at her. He didn't like the turn the conversation was taking. Why couldn't she just accept his apology and move on with finishing dinner and then going back to bed?

She added, "I want to help you turn the place around, but I also don't want to keep stepping on your toes."

He bit back his first, sarcastic reply. *Not the way to go after you just apologized*, he told himself.

Especially since she sounded sincere about wanting to help him, not just because her grandmother had a cut a deal with her.

Plus, she'd worked her ass off over the past couple of days. He owed her the truth.

"I don't know how much you've heard, but my dad walked out on us when I was in the fourth grade. We didn't hear from him for years, and Mama never got a cent in child support. He was a drunk and a total deadbeat." Brock blew out his breath. It wasn't easy talking about this stuff. "Mama was always at the diner, so Gran was the one who raised me. She loved watching cooking shows and competitions, and she was a damned fine cook herself. She's the one who taught me. When I got older, I started working at the diner, too. I did a little bit of everything— waited tables, washed dishes, swept floors, prepped ingredients, even cooked. I pitched in whenever and wherever we were short-handed."

"So, you basically grew up at the diner?" Summer asked. "It was your second home?"

"Yeah. It was Mama's place... like this house," he said. Realization dawned. "Maybe that's why making changes feels, well, *wrong*. Like I'm trying to erase her."

A sympathetic expression on her face, Summer reached across the table and put her hand over his. "I'm sorry. I didn't know. And I love this chicken dish."

"Thanks."

Then she said, "I really do think we need to give the diner a facelift, though."

Brock tensed. Hadn't she understood what he was trying to tell her?

His expression must have given him away, because she added,

"What if we put this lemon chicken on next Friday's dinner menu? It's quick, delicious, and doesn't use any expensive ingredients. The profit margin would be good."

"That sounds like a great idea. Gran would be tickled to know that her lemon chicken was good enough to serve in a restaurant."

Summer nodded. "And if you have any other favorite recipes from your gran or your mom, maybe we could feature those as well, on a rotating basis." She smiled at him. "It would be a way to keep their memories alive at The Yummy Cowboy Diner."

"But I thought you only wanted upscale dishes on our dinner menu," he said. Was she serious about wanting to serve Gran's recipes, or just trying to make him feel better? "I mean, everyone went nuts for your goat cheese and peach jam salad, and the bison filet with the fucking delicious beer sauce… oh, excuse me, the *demi-glace*."

"Brock," she said, frustration sharpening her tone.

"What?" Why was she riled up now? He'd just complimented her cooking, hadn't he?

She sighed. "Tonight was a special occasion. You get that, right? We primed our guests to want to try something new and different."

"Yeah. Wasn't that the whole idea? Get people to show up?"

"It also means tonight's sales aren't an accurate prediction about how my salad and the bison filet will sell on a daily basis." Summer leaned back and took a long sip of her ice water. "We don't have enough data yet. But I *do* feel comfortable predicting that during our next dinner service, a lot of our guests will be craving comfort food and classic American dishes."

He wasn't sure what she was getting at. At least she didn't look mad anymore.

She continued, "That's why I think our tonight's dinner menu hit a nice balance. We had two fancy entrées, and two comfort food entrées. There was something for everyone."

He thought about that for a long moment, then nodded. "So, do you think my gran's lemon chicken counts as a fancy entrée or comfort food?"

He couldn't help poking at her a bit. She was fun when she got feisty.

It won him a smile. "Depends on how we describe and plate it. It's all in the marketing. We could put it on the menu as Grandma Russo's Lemon Chicken with spaghetti and mixed garden vegetables in garlic butter, and describe it as your favorite meal when you were a kid, lovingly cooked by your gran. Or I could list it as Classic Italian Chicken Piccata in a tangy lemon and caper sauce over pasta *al dente*, served with *verdure miste dell'orto*."

Wow. She really did have the gift for fancy descriptions. "And I'm guessing that the Chicken Piccata would cost more than Grandma Russo's Lemon Chicken?"

"You got it, padawan," she said, still smiling.

That made him laugh.

"And just for that," he told her, "I'm gonna give you a brand-new toothbrush and ask you to stay the night. I'll even run a load of laundry now, so that you'll have clean clothes for breakfast service tomorrow."

"Deal," she responded. "Let me just text Mom and let her know I won't be coming home tonight."

He'd forgotten that if she stayed over, there would be questions from her family. Probably a lot of them. And how would Summer's brother react to the news that Brock was fucking Summer?

But if she didn't care, neither did he. Right now, he was looking forward to more sex, and then falling asleep with an armful of cuddly naked woman.

He wondered if she'd be willing to repeat the sleepover tomorrow night.

Whoa there, cowboy, he told himself. *Don't get ahead of yourself. And whatever you do, don't spook her.*

Chapter Seventeen – Summer

Saturday, June 18

Autumn: Sis, I noticed you didn't come home last night. What happened?? Details!

Summer: I stayed out late celebrating the successful launch of YC's dinner service. Like I texted Mom, I crashed at a friend's house in town because I have to be at the diner at oh-dark-thirty this morning.

Summer: I am so tired right now. I would kill for a nap.

Autumn: A friend, huh? Is your friend named Brock the Cock, by any chance? ::eggplant emoji::

Summer: Taking the Fifth. He hates that nickname, BTW.

Summer: Also, those eggplant emojis you're sending make me want baba ganoush. I wonder if I can get some eggplant and tahini at the market here in town.

Autumn: So you don't want to tell me about your sleepover at Brock's, excuse me, your "friend's" place?

Summer: What sleepover? ::angelic face::

∞∞∞

"*Someone's* in an awfully good mood this morning," Marlene said, tilting her head in Brock's direction.

Summer's face heated. "Weird, isn't it? He really doesn't seem to mind me bossing him around for another—" She checked the clock on the kitchen wall, "—fifteen-and-a-half-hours."

"I'm just happy we turned a big profit yesterday."

She turned from the prep counter, where she was assembling the ingredients for today's lunch special of bison chili, and eyed Brock's broad back. He stood at the mixer, making his pancake batter, resolutely keeping his back to them.

No one should sound that chipper at five-thirty in the morning. And especially not after only getting three-and-a-half hours of sleep. "Who are you and what have done with Mr. Grumpy Pants?" she demanded.

He snorted. "I could yell at you if you want me to, Ms. Bossy Pants-for-another-fifteen-and-a-half hours."

"Nah, I'm good," she retorted. "But maybe we need to change your nickname to Mr. Sunshine."

Marlene chuckled at this. "Not so fast. Whatever's making him so chirpy, I don't think it's gonna last."

"You might be surprised, Sizzle Pants," Brock said, reaching for a bottle of vanilla standing on the counter.

Summer noted the flush rising from the collar of his t-shirt to his nape and wondered whether his cryptic comment was a hint.

Is he interested in a replay of last night's action?

She could be persuaded into extending their one-night stand into a weekend fling.

Because Marlene was only half-right. *Two* people in the diner's kitchen were in extremely good moods this morning.

Even if one of them was sore in unmentionable places.

Summer had started morning prep hobbling around stiffly while *certain* muscles protested loudly about the vigorous workout they'd gotten.

She'd had fallen asleep in Brock's arms late last night.

At dawn, she'd awakened to find his face between her thighs, enthusiastically licking and sucking her to a climax.

Wow. She could *definitely* get used to waking up like this. It beat any regular alarm clock all to heck.

Then he handed her a strong, freshly brewed mug of coffee with a big glug of milk but no sugar, just the way she liked it. She was ready to marry him on the spot. Caffeine delivery in bed forgave any amount of stubborn and grumpy.

Once she came to full consciousness, she'd discovered her chef's coat, pants, socks, and underwear, laundered and neatly folded in a stack.

No Walk of Shame for me this morning, yay! Not that she had anything to be ashamed about. She was an adult and single, and Brock was the same.

She still didn't know if last night had been a onetime thing. When they left his cottage and got in their separate vehicles, Brock hadn't mentioned he was interested in continuing whatever-it-was that they had started yesterday.

Summer tried to quash her disappointment. She'd had truly amazing sex last night. Plus, they'd worked out some of their issues. That was pretty amazing for a one-night stand. No need to make things weird and awkward if he wasn't interested in a repeat.

Disappointing, though.

"So, are we doing dinner-only again next Friday?" Marlene asked. "Gotta say, it was nice to sleep in for a change and only have to show up here after lunch."

"I vote yes," Summer said.

"But what if no one shows up next Friday?" Brock countered. "I mean, you're the one who said that most of the people last night were there because of your sister's contest hype."

"Even if that's true, I think they'll come back for the food," Marlene predicted confidently. "Austin and Katie both told me we got nice reviews last night on Yelp. And from people in Bozeman and Livingston, too!"

"I'll think about it," Brock hedged.

"And I'm making an executive decision. Yes, on canceling Friday breakfast and lunch in favor of dinner," Summer said firmly.

"But—" Brock began, his shoulders tense.

"Just for next week," Summer interrupted. "If things go well again then let's discuss how we can make Friday dinners a regular thing, and add Saturday night dinner, too."

"Now, just wait a min—" Brock's voice had descended into his sexy growl.

Not that she was ever going to tell him she found it arousing rather than intimidating.

"I'm the boss for another fifteen hours," Summer reminded him.

"And twenty minutes," added Marlene.

He groaned loudly, but didn't protest further.

∞ ∞ ∞

Brock: Hey. Got any plans for after work today?

Summer: Not really.

Summer: Why are you texting me from the walk-in?

Brock: Because if Marlene finds out about us, she'll tell everyone in town.

Summer: Us? There's an 'us'? It wasn't just a one-night stand?

Brock: It was. And now I want another one. I'll cook you dinner. You like lasagna?

Summer: I *love* lasagna! Another one of your gran's recipes?

Brock: Yup. Made with Italian sausage and ricotta. You'll fucking love it.

Summer: Sounds delicious but fattening.

Brock: Yeah, well, I'll help you work off the calories.

Brock: So, that's a yes?

Summer: Yes. Should I plan to stay the night?

Brock: Definitely.

Summer: Okay, I'll swing by the ranch after work and pack an overnight bag. I'll pick up a loaf at Jenna's for garlic bread, too.

Brock: Sounds great. Okay, I'm heading back into the kitchen. My balls are getting frostbite in here.

∞∞∞

The lasagna was delicious. So were the garlic bread and garden salad with a balsamic vinaigrette that Summer whisked up. The only thing missing from a perfect comfort food dinner was a glass of hearty red Sangiovese.

But in keeping with his vehement refusal to consider a liquor license for the diner, Brock kept no alcoholic beverages in his house. Now that she knew why, Summer didn't mention it.

Later, after ice cream and dishes, she realized he was a cuddler.

They were in his bed, breath slowing and sweat drying after some extremely satisfying sex. Brock pillowed his head on her breast, one ridiculously muscled arm flung over her belly. Eyes closed, he stroked the curve of her hip as if he couldn't get enough of touching her.

By this point, he'd thoroughly explored every inch of her… and she had the beard burn to prove it on her breasts, stomach, and the tender skin on the inside of her thighs. She didn't mind— the scrape of his dark stubble had the ability to send darts of pleasure shooting along her spine.

In return, Summer ran her fingers through Brock's short hair, letting her fingernails scratch lightly across his scalp.

He groaned with pleasure and snuggled closer. "Don't stop. That feels fucking amazing."

"Then I won't stop." She kept up the steady rhythm for a while, as her pulse slowed and lingering ripples of pleasure from a truly amazing climax slowly faded into a satisfied glow.

So what if she couldn't walk tomorrow?

This morning, her legs and belly muscles had been stiff and sore for the first hour or two, before she warmed up and stretched. Tomorrow morning, she was going to be *epically* sore. She was going to need a hot shower and a handful of Advil with breakfast.

Then she remembered that tomorrow was Sunday. *Oh crap.*

Her parents would definitely notice something was up if she ghosted Sunday morning services at church. They knew perfectly well that the diner didn't open until 9:30 a.m. on Sundays.

If they haven't figured it out already. Mom had certainly given her overnight bag a Look when Summer encountered her on the way out of the ranch house a couple of hours ago.

But at least Mom hadn't *said* anything, so Summer could keep on pretending that her mother didn't know her daughter had spent last night having lots of fun naked time with Brock. And was planning to do the same tonight.

They'd sure gotten off to a good start.

This morning, she had rated last night's sex as her best ever. Brock had just surpassed that. Her bones felt like melting butter, and his warm breath tickled her nipple in just the right way.

"So, I was thinking…" she began.

Brock groaned. The vibration teased her breast, making her shiver with pleasure. "If you're still thinking right now, then I'm doing something wrong."

Summer laughed. "This is actually something that's been in my head for a few days now."

"Okay. Shoot." But before she could launch into her spiel, he licked her nipple.

"No fair!"

"I'm listening," he said in a deceptively mild tone. But then he moved the arm slung across her hips and began teasing the tip of her other breast with a deliciously callused thumb.

A familiar warm pulse rekindled between her legs. "You're evil. You know that, right?"

She tried to corral her thoughts. Thanks to his fresh assault on her senses, they ran every which way, like geese being chased by a determined toddler. "It's about The Yummy Cowboy Diner makeover. I've been thinking about what you told me. I'm going to contact Geoff and see if he can come up with some low-cost design ideas that'll refresh the dining room but not destroy the spirit of the place."

"Who the fuck is Geoff?" Brock's tone was suddenly hostile. He stopped his sensual tease. "Someone back in San Francisco? Your *boyfriend?*"

Good grief, is Brock actually jealous?

"No, Geoff Schaefer. My sister Winnie's fiancé. You know, the guy who designs all of the interiors on her show?"

"Oh. Yeah. Okay. I've never seen her show. But it sounds good to me."

"Happy to hear it," Summer retorted. "Because, according to your alarm clock, I still have an hour left of being the boss." She hesitated. "But you're really okay with renovating the dining room?"

"Yeah, I'm fine with it. And thanks for not trying to turn my diner into an expensive, white tablecloths, big-city kind of restaurant."

"You're *fine* with it?" she echoed in disbelief. "Brock Michaels, you realize this is the first time you haven't given me a knee-jerk no when I make a suggestion?"

"Can't sass the boss lady *too* much," he murmured, resuming his delightful toying with her breasts. "At least not until nine p.m. rolls around." Another slow, sensuous lick. "And I've been doing some thinking of my own."

"Oh?" Her breath was coming faster now. It was taking effort to continue his scalp massage.

"Yeah. Hey, if the next few weeks of dinner service go well, what do you think about expanding the dining room? I'm thinking of buying the old Cooperman's Hardware & Ranch Supply building next door. It's been vacant for a while. If we knocked a few walls down and fixed up the space, we could double our current seating capacity. More customers, more money."

"That sounds interesting," she ventured. "I like that you're looking ahead to the future. With any luck, Grandma Abigail will forgive your mortgage and loans when September rolls around."

"Great. Glad you agree. My buddy Dave, the one who works at the Ranchers Federated credit union, told me last week that they're offering business loans at really good rates. What do you say we look into it sooner than September? If we buy the Cooperman building before anyone else snaps it up, it could be a really good investment."

Crap. Her heart began pounding. She hadn't expected this turn in the conversation.

Should I tell him that I can't apply for any loans because things went horribly wrong at SummerTime? Her debt/income ratio was appalling right now. Even if she somehow managed to get a loan, the interest rates would be sky-high.

But then she'd have to tell him about Greg Brandywine. And she could imagine Brock's reaction to hearing that she was on the verge of bankruptcy. *Ack.*

"I think it's a great idea for the future," she managed. "But whoa there, cowboy, let's not get carried away! We should wait to make any big changes like that until the diner has a consistent positive cash flow. It's only been one dinner service so far."

He didn't say anything, but skin to skin, she sensed he wasn't happy with her pushback.

She added, "I mean, I'm confident that The Yummy Cowboy Diner is headed in the right direction, but let's wait to see what happens between now and September."

"I guess that makes sense." He sounded crestfallen. To her relief, he didn't push the idea.

Suddenly he's the one proposing a sweeping change and I'm the one who's stepping on the brakes. Ironic, huh?

"If we're going to reinvest the diner's profits," she said, "we should post job listings for a new general manager, line cooks, servers, and a second dishwasher. I'm confident that the extra income from our new dinner service will offset the extra payroll expenses."

He didn't respond right away. She hoped he was thinking it over. It was better than his previous instant refusals.

"Plus," she added in her most persuasive tone, "if we hire additional staff, then the diner can support breakfast and lunch service on Fridays and Saturdays, as well as dinner. And you could schedule at least one day off a week."

Brock stopped his delicious torture of her breasts. "I don't want to—"

"You can't work non-stop every day of the year. That's a recipe for burnout," she interrupted. "How long has it been since you took a day off?"

He heaved a sigh. "Mama's funeral. I closed the diner for five days after she passed so that I could make all of the arrangements."

Summer dipped her head and kissed his temple. "Tell you what, Brock. Once we've hired those extra cooks and servers, let's promote Marlene to general manager, if she's interested. She's competent and hard-working, and I could train her in the stuff she doesn't know how to do, like inventory management and front-of-house."

"I'll think about it." She saw his mouth twist in a wry smile. "Not sure what I'd do with myself on my days off."

"Sleep in? Watch baseball? Get some sunshine and fresh air?" she suggested. "In fact, I'd love to show you my favorite place on my parents' ranch. We could pack a picnic lunch and go for a ride…" A thought occurred to her. She'd grown up on the ranch, with a stable of working horses to herd the cattle and bison, but Brock had been raised in town. "Have you ever been horseback riding?"

"Yeah, but it's been a while. Uh, like, years."

"Well, it's time to refresh your skills, big guy."

"And right now, you can ride *me*," he said, rolling onto his back and tugging her on top of him.

Working *with* Brock instead of butting heads with him all the time was nice.

As she swung her leg over him, wincing as her overused inner thigh muscles complained at the stretch, she realized she was eager to see what they could accomplish between now and

September.

∞ ∞ ∞

Monday, June 20

Jenna: So, I hear that you and Brock are a thing now.

Summer: What? Who told you that?

Jenna: It's all over town. Apparently, your car was parked in front of Brock's house every night this weekend.

Jenna: Spill.

Summer: Sheesh. I'd forgotten how nosy people are here. In San Francisco, no one pays attention to that kind of stuff.

Jenna: Yeah, well you're not in SanFran anymore, chica.

Jenna: So? Are you guys dating or what? Is it serious?

Summer: Nope and nope. We have this weird FWB thing going on, except we're not really friends and we argue all the time, so it's more like Enemies with Benefits.

Jenna: EWB? Gotcha. But is the hate sex good?

Summer: The best. But for God's sake, don't tell anyone that. Especially not B.

Chapter Eighteen – Brock

Snowberry Springs Ranch
Monday, July 19 (One month later)

"I forgot to tell you while we were saddling up," Summer said as they rode away from the Snowberry Springs Ranch stables. "I heard from Geoff this morning. He sent me three different concepts for the dining room renovation."

It was a beautiful summer morning with cloudless blue skies, and Brock was looking forward to this horseback outing.

After many busy weeks of work, Summer was finally taking him to the place she described as her favorite place on her family's ranch. Their saddlebags bulged with the fixings for a generous picnic lunch, plus drinks, a large picnic blanket, and beach towels.

On either side of the dirt road that led up into the hills, cattle and bison grazed in wide green pastures that were slowly turning to golden hay under the summer sun. Ahead of them, forested mountain peaks rose, their tops still snow-capped despite the recent hot weather.

As he'd told Summer when she first mentioned the outing last month, it had been years since he'd ridden a horse. She'd picked out Scout for him, describing him as the calmest horse on the ranch.

Like all the horses on the Snowberry Springs Ranch, Scout was a Painted Horse, his coat a pattern of bold black blotches on white.

He was a stocky, powerfully muscled gelding used for herding cattle and bison on the ranch's most rugged upland pastures, where even ATVs couldn't compete with a trained cow horse.

Summer rode alongside Brock on a lively white-and-chestnut Painted Horse mare named Ranger. She looked like a real cowgirl in her long-sleeved blue cotton shirt, faded jeans, and riding boots, a tan-colored cowboy hat perched on her head and a colorful bandanna tied around her neck.

It had been a busy month, with lots of changes at the diner, but things were finally settling into a routine.

Encouraged by the continuing popularity of the diner's Friday night dinner service, Brock and Summer had added Saturday dinner.

Brock then promoted Marlene to general manager and gave her a raise. Summer was currently training her to fill the position Kenny had vacated.

Marlene was ecstatic about not having to be on her feet all day in the kitchen anymore. And despite Brock's initial worry that her easily distracted nature might lead to another Kenny-sized mess, she was reliably managing the diner's inventory and supplier orders, and providing calm but firm management to the wait staff and new barista.

After hiring and training, two new cooks were now running Sunday and Monday breakfast and lunch services.

At Summer's urging, Brock took those days off, though he was always reachable by phone or text.

His relationship—or whatever it was—with Summer hadn't stayed a secret for very long.

"So… you're dating Summer?" Jason asked over pizza on Brock's first Monday off.

Brock had to think about his answer. Dating to him meant something more serious, like auditioning for marriage. What he and Summer shared felt totally different. He shook his head. "Nah. It's more like we're having a series of one-night stands."

Jason laughed. "Dude," he said in a tone that combined disbelief and admiration.

But it was true. Brock and Summer continued to butt heads over changing things at the diner, and yelled at each other a lot. Lately, their biggest bone of contention was an automated point-of-sale system that would print tickets directly to the kitchen and also tie into an online inventory and accounting system. Summer just wouldn't let it go, and Brock considered it overkill... especially when he looked at the price tag.

They didn't do any of the conventionally lovey-dovey stuff, not even when they were alone at Brock's place. They hung out, cooked together and talked, and then had great sex. But there wasn't anything particularly romantic about it, though he *was* beginning to think of Summer as a friend.

Then Summer's parents invited Brock to join the Snowberry family at their 4th of July barbecue on the ranch. It made Brock wonder what Summer had told them about him. Everyone in her family accepted his appearance as Summer's date with only mild surprise, even Spring.

It had been a fun and relaxing day, which concluded by watching Bob, Priscilla, Spring, and Summer serve as flag-bearers on horseback in the town's traditional Independence Day Parade. After sunset, they all enjoyed live music and the fireworks display in the town square park before going their separate ways.

Since then, Bob and Priscilla had invited Brock over for dinner every Sunday. He and Summer generally went back to his place for the night, then spent the day together on Mondays.

Spending time with the Snowberry family made Brock realize how much he had missed being part of a family. Gran had passed away two years after he graduated from high school, and all of his uncles, aunts, and cousins lived in other parts of the state.

Now, Brock looked forward to having Summer all to himself for an entire day. "Did Geoff send you an estimate for how much his plans would cost?"

"Just a rough one," she replied, and urged her horse alongside his. "He wrote that none of his proposed designs will cost much if we do the work ourselves."

"I can get some of my buddies to help," he said confidently. "Jason is a carpenter, and he owes me for helping him move house in a snowstorm last April. Rick's a plumber. And Evie's a genius when it comes to using power tools."

"And I'm sure I can rope in my brother and a few cousins to help paint and lay new flooring," Summer said. "I'd call Winnie to help with this project, but she and Geoff are working all-out right now to wrap up the Dream House renovation project before their wedding in November. Apparently, all kinds of problems have cropped up. Last I heard, all of their interior doors and kitchen cabinets are back-ordered and might not arrive before the scheduled reveal."

"Sounds like a real nightmare," Brock commented. "Are they really gonna live in that house, or is it just some fake TV bullshit?"

"They're planning to live there," Summer confirmed. She offered Brock her phone. "Here, take a look at the designs. I sent Geoff the measurements and photos of the dining room interior, and he created three different computer-generated mock-ups. What do you think?"

As the two horses walked sedately side by side, Brock swiped through the mock-ups, expecting the worst. Out of the corner of his eye, he saw Summer watching him closely, as if she were worried about his reaction.

But what he saw surprised him in a good way. As Summer had promised, all three designs maintained the spirit of the current diner.

"Hey," he commented out loud. "These are pretty good."

Summer beamed at him. "I thought so, too. Which one's your favorite?"

He swiped back through the designs, studying them.

Then her phone buzzed. A text message preview from someone named Maggie popped up.

Hey. You alive? Just checking to see if you've nailed down the reopening date for ST yet.

Well, damn. He'd nearly forgotten that Summer was heading back to San Francisco in a few weeks.

Last month, he couldn't wait to get rid of her pushy ass.

Now he looked forward to their daily arguments. He enjoyed working with her. And doing other things. He wasn't ready for their string of one-night stands to end so soon.

He handed back her phone. "I like this one."

Mock-up #2 showed the dining room with pale green walls and floors that looked like weather-beaten wood planks. The breakfast counter was now marble-topped, and the booths had been transformed into high-backed padded benches built against the dining wall. All of the seating was upholstered in dark green. The backbar and breakfast counter were both paneled with reclaimed wood, and vintage barn lamps hung on long cables from a ceiling covered in old-fashioned whitewashed tin tiles stamped with a pattern of leaves and squares.

The mock-up even retained the diner's current cowboy-themed memorabilia, just a lot less of it and neatly organized on the dining room's walls and open shelving.

"Oh, that's the one I liked best, too!" she exclaimed. "So, we're agreed?"

Brock nodded. "Yeah. There's a lot of wood, which is great, but isn't the reclaimed stuff expensive?"

Summer shrugged. "There's an old barn here on the ranch that looks about ready to fall over. I'm sure Dad wouldn't mind if we salvaged wood from there."

She swiped again, and Brock saw a bulleted list appear on her phone. "Looks like everything else is doable, too. A few gallons of interior paint. Geoff is recommending vinyl plank flooring, which is half the cost of hardwood, and a lot easier to install. Hm... let me see... Lighting—I'll bet you that Autumn knows a place in Bozeman where we can find vintage lamps with the right look, and really cheap. White quartz or natural stone for the countertops—Geoff suggests asking around if anyone has any remnants from a finished project that they'd be willing to give us for free or next to free. And Winnie will know where we can order upholstery fabric for the best price."

"Sounds like you have it all figured out," Brock commented. "Since you're the brains, I guess I'm the brawn?"

She shot him a flirtatious glance. "You *know* how much I like your brawn."

They continued discussing the renovation project as they began the ascent into the hills. Then the dirt road narrowed into a path, forcing them to ride single-file.

Forty-five minutes later, they arrived in a small, beautiful hollow tucked away behind the first line of hills. A small lake sat in the center of the hollow like a sparkling gem, with a hot spring unfurling long banners of steam from a rocky outcropping on the shore.

Brock spotted a single-room log cabin surrounded by cherry trees heavy with fruit a few yards from the lake shore. A rough-hewn table stood on the cabin's roofed porch, along with a collection of five or six rickety-looking chairs.

"Wow," Brock commented as Scout made his way towards the cabin. "This is really nice. Ever spend the weekend out here?"

"Yes," Summer replied. "I'd really love if Winnie renovated that cabin before it falls down. We used to ride out here for sleepovers when we were in high school." She smiled and added wistfully, "But of course, Winnie's really busy these days. She hardly ever leaves Seattle anymore."

"So, picnic, or do you want to go for a swim first?" Brock asked. "Doesn't look like there's anyone around to catch us skinny-dipping."

"Let's go for a swim. The lake's really cold on this end, but it's nice near the spring. Someone dug out a hot tub and lined it with rocks. It's over there." She pointed in the direction of the spring, and Brock saw a semi-circular depression where the spring's steaming water flowed into the lake.

While Brock unpacked the picnic supplies and set up their lunch on the porch table, Summer produced several coiled ropes from her saddlebag. She strung a highline between two of the gnarled cherry trees, then used the other two ropes to tie the horses' halters to the highline, so that Scout and Ranger could graze while still being safely restrained.

Then it was time to swim. He and Summer stripped down to bare skin.

Summer yelled, "Race you to the water!" and instantly launched into motion. Her long, muscled legs ate up the distance to the lake.

Brock's first impulse was to sprint ahead of her and win. Then he saw the mouthwatering collection of boobs and ass on display, and decide to slow down and enjoy the jiggling, bouncing, all-around sexy view.

Summer didn't slow down when she reached the lake's edge. Her feet raised miniature geysers for another few steps, then she dove cleanly into the clear water. She swam underwater for several yards before surfacing, her golden hair as dark with moisture and sleek as a seal's fur.

Brock dove in after her. The water was cool and refreshing after the warm, dusty trail ride. He came up next to her, then took her into his arms and kissed her. Half-floating together, he grabbed her gorgeous rounded ass cheeks and squeezed them before pulling her forward and sliding his half-hard cock against her pussy. She closed her legs, cradling him, and they kissed and groped each other for a while before she slipped free.

Then she splashed him, sweeping her hand along the surface to raise a small tidal wave that hit him full in the face.

She giggled, then tried to escape when he came after her for payback.

An all-out splashing war ensued, punctuated by shouts and laughter and gleeful shrieks.

Brock finally forced her out of the lake. Laughing breathlessly, she sprinted for the cabin, presumably hoping to find refuge inside and lock him out.

"Oh, no, you don't!" he roared.

He came after her, pouring on every ounce of speed he could, and caught her ten feet from the cabin.

His hands closed around her waist, stopping her in her tracks. She tried to break free, though not very hard. He locked his arms around her and covered her breasts with his hands. Her small stiff nipples poked at the center of his palms.

"Caught you," he panted in her ear. "Now you're my prisoner. Do you know what happens to prisoners? Especially bad little girls who splash me and then try to run away?"

She shivered. "Is there pillaging and plundering involved?" Then she ground her ass deliberately against his cock.

"I should spank you," Brock threatened. He was enjoying this game. So was his cock, which was stiff and aching now. "But we have a long ride back and I'm not a monster."

"Thank you, Dread Pirate Brock. Saddles and spanked bottoms are *not* a fun combination." She continued to squirm and grind against him.

He turned her to face him, and wrapped her braid around his fist. He kissed her, hard, then closed his teeth on her plump lower lip, running his tongue along it before releasing her mouth.

"On your knees, prisoner," he ordered. "Demonstrate how grateful you are."

Her cheeks flushed, Summer sank to the grass, deliberately sliding the length of her body against him. He kept hold of her hair.

Brock looked down, watching her delicious mouth fall open. Her warm breath caressed his cock, and he almost came on the spot.

Summer took her sweet time, teasing him with her lips and tongue before taking him deep into her hot, wet mouth. Then she set to work with enthusiasm that made his knees turn to jelly.

As nice as this was, he preferred to take her along for the ride.

"Stop!" he ordered, and pulled on her braid.

Summer released him with a long slide against her tongue and a pop of suction that made his breath jolt. He dropped to join her in the grass, parting her thighs to lie between them.

He dipped his head and licked her sweet pussy in a long stroke that ended at her clit. She moaned and filled his mouth with the taste of tangy honey. He loved her taste and the sweet sounds she made when he gave her oral.

"What turned you on?" he asked, resting his chin on her thigh. "Was it when I threatened to spank you, or when I ordered you to suck my cock?"

"Pretty much everything you do turns me on," she confessed. "You're is the best sex I've ever had." Her blue eyes widened.

"Crap. I wasn't supposed to say that part out loud."

He laughed, the compliment radiating warmth through his chest as though a tiny sun had lodged there. "And just for that, you get to come first."

He dove back in with enthusiasm.

Chapter Nineteen – Brock

A long time later, they finally got around to eating the chicken, mint, and lettuce wraps with Thai peanut sauce packed in the picnic basket along with a salad of shredded carrots and radishes in sweet vinegar flavored with fish sauce, and apple turnovers.

"It's a shame to leave all those cherries to the birds and squirrels," Summer said, studying the trees laden with ripe red fruit while licking pastry crumbs from her fingers. "And I've got a great recipe for a pie that you can make with either sweet or tart fresh cherries."

"Cherry pie's my favorite," said Brock. "Let's do it. We can bundle the cherries in the picnic blanket and tie up the edges."

Back at the ranch house, the horses unsaddled, rubbed down, and back in their stalls, Brock and Summer sat on the ranch house's wide verandah, and began pitting their haul of cherries.

The text message he'd accidentally read on her phone this morning lingered in his thoughts. "So, what are you planning to do once our ninety days are up?"

He knew it was stupid, but he hoped she wanted to stay, at least a little longer.

Summer's face lit up. "I'm looking forward to reopening

SummerTime in San Francisco with a new look and a completely revamped menu. In fact, I've been working on the menu in my free time." She shot him a wry smile. "Mom's been letting me test recipes in her kitchen. Her oven *sucks*."

Brock's stomach dropped. *She's been cooking without me?*

It was stupid, but the news that she was working on her own private menu felt like a betrayal somehow. He fought not to let his feelings show. "Uh, what type of dishes are you putting on your new menu?" He forced a smile. "I've got a killer chicken piccata recipe, if you're interested."

She grinned at that, dumped a handful of pits into the tin waste bucket at her feet, and reached for more cherries. "I'm completely reworking my restaurant concept. I want to move away from a traditional lunch and dinner service, and switch SummerTime over to an upscale small plates and signature cocktails place. Not only are the profit margins great, especially on the cocktails, but the tables turn over a lot more quickly, too."

She sounded really excited.

I should be overjoyed that she's leaving me to run The Yummy Cowboy Diner my way, without having to argue over every damned thing with her.

But he wasn't happy. Not at all.

Today had been perfect, and he wanted more days like that with her.

Well, I've always been a greedy bastard.

His expression must've betrayed him.

"Look, Brock," she said, her expression somewhere between apologetic and defiant. "You're a great guy and a talented cook. And despite what you might think, I really enjoy working with you. And our, um, fling, has been a lot of fun." She looked down, her tanned cheeks flushing.

She was so damned adorable that it almost made him forget she was delivering bad news about their newly forged partnership. "But the only reason I've stayed this long in Snowberry Springs was because Grandma asked for help."

Something about the way she said that tipped him off that there was stuff she wasn't telling him. *Like developing a new menu and not mentioning anything about it until now?*

But before he could probe further, she said, "Speaking of working on projects, have you thought about putting together a book of your gran's recipes?"

He blinked at her, thrown off by the sudden shift in the conversation. "Uh, no."

"You should do it," she urged. "Then you could publish it and sell it at The Yummy Cowboy Diner, along with branded merchandise like t-shirts and caps, once the LVR brings tourists to town."

"It sounds like a project for the winter months," he replied.

That was when it got dark early, when his garden went into hibernation, and when it was too fucking cold to spend much time outdoors.

And from the sounds of it, he'd be spending his indoor time alone again this winter, instead of snuggled up with her. *Dammit.*

They continued pitting cherries in silence for a while. Then Summer began talking about the benefits of that damned POS system again. Ms. Fancy Pants was every bit as stubborn as he was. She still hadn't given up trying to convince him the diner needed it.

Later, when the cherry pies were in the oven and filling the ranch house with the mouthwatering fragrances of browning pastry, cinnamon, and hot cherry juice, he asked, "So, do you want to come back to the cottage when these pies are done?"

She'd started spending three or four nights a week over at his place, so it dismayed him when she shook her head. "I'm sorry, I can't. April has a dance recital over at the Masonic Hall after dinner and I promised I'd be there."

"Oh," he said, fighting yet another surge of disappointment.

Unlike him, Summer had a big, close-knit family. Of course they wanted to spend time with her when she wasn't at the diner.

Brock left shortly after the pies came out of the oven, deep crimson filling bubbling between the sugared, perfectly browned strips of pastry crisscrossed over the tops of the pies.

Summer gave him a lingering kiss and two of the six still-steaming pies to take with him, neatly packed in a flat box with a dishtowel to keep them from sliding around on the drive home.

As soon as he arrived, he went straight to the kitchen and cut himself a big slice of warm pie. Then he sat at his table and felt the silence close in around him.

He'd spent a year living completely alone, devoting himself to working at the diner and his garden. Now Summer had ruined solitude for him. She was as fiery as a ghost pepper, sweet as the honey from his backyard beehive, and rich as cream.

The sex was great, but even more, he enjoyed cooking with her after the diner closed and waking up with her in the mornings.

Hell, he even got a kick out of seeing her bottles of shampoo and grapefruit-scented conditioner in his bathroom, and her pink razor sitting in the shower's soap niche. He couldn't imagine anyone else sharing this house with him.

Except she wasn't staying.

And he wanted her to. His mama's voice echoed in his head. *She's a keeper, that one.*

Yeah, she was. And he needed to keep her right here, with him.

First, he had to figure out how to transform their series of one-

stands into something more. And then, convince Summer to change her mind about leaving Snowberry Springs.

Monday, July 25 (One week later)

The Elk's Head Tavern, located on the side of the highway about twenty minutes north of town, next to Fred Mason's gas station, was a dive, no two ways about it. But they had pool tables and served decent food.

More importantly, Brock's friends liked to meet there for beer and pizza once a month. Since Summer had made lunch plans with her old friend Jenna for today, Brock decided to join his buddies and catch up. Between all the changes happening at the diner, and his relationship with Summer, he hadn't seen anyone but Jason lately.

As Brock came through the door, he spotted the group sitting in the back corner of the mostly-empty tavern.

Evie caught sight of him first. "Oh my God, look who's here. I thought he was missing in action!"

Everyone looked up.

"Hey, Brock!" Rick Stinson waved at him.

As usual, he wore his dark blue Stinson and Sons Plumbing & Electrical trucker's cap. He was sensitive about the fact that his short, light brown hair was balding prematurely on top, so he rarely took off his hat in public.

"Dude! Glad you finally decided to join us," Jason called, grinning. "We've already ordered pizza. Grab a drink and come on over."

Brock raised his hand to acknowledge them, and detoured over to the bar.

"Root beer, please." The female bartender, a woman with graying dark hair pulled into a loose bun, looked surprised at his request, but didn't comment. She even poured it into one of the chilled glass beer steins before handing it to him.

"So, you finally got a day off," Jason commented as Brock approached them. "Heard you hired a bunch of new people at the diner. Things are going well, huh?"

"Can't complain," Brock replied, pulling up a chair and squeezing between Rick and Jason. "It's been busy, though. Lots of projects going on right now."

"We heard," Rick said. "You ever gonna have time to rejoin the Fire Department?"

"Hoping to," Brock replied. "Maybe this winter, when things calm down some."

Like most small towns, the Snowberry Springs Fire Department was an all-volunteer organization. During his previous volunteer stint, he'd enjoyed the firefighting training and the adrenaline rush whenever a call came in. Not to mention the respect he got as a firefighter.

"So, what's going on?" Jason asked. "Any more cooking contests planned?"

"On tonight's episode of *Iron Chef: Montana*," Rick intoned in his best television announcer voice. "It's Round Two of Small-Town Chef versus Big-City Chef in Battle Huckleberry!"

Everyone laughed.

"I'll drink to that," Brock said, grinning. He raised his mug of root beer in salute. "To Round Two. And may Small-Town Chef triumph this time."

"Hell, yeah!" They all drank.

A server delivered two large everything pizzas to the table, loaded with sliced ham, pepperoni, nuggets of Italian sausage, ground beef, onion, bell pepper, mushrooms, and olives. They smelled heavenly.

"Is there going to be another contest?" asked Jason as they all dug in. "The one last month was a blast."

"We're talking about it," Brock confirmed. "I need the chance to redeem myself after tanking in Round One. Maybe after we finish re-doing the dining room."

"You're finally updating the place? Hallelujah!" Evie asked. "I bet that was Summer's doing."

"Yeah," Brock admitted. "She got her future brother-in-law, the one who works with Winnie on that TV show, to send us some design ideas. I won't lie, I was worried, but I think it's gonna look great when we're done. It's still going to be homey and welcoming, just not as, well, *brown*."

"Or dingy," Evie suggested. "Or dusty?" She shook her head. "The food's great, Brock, but your place is a shrine to everything bad from 1972."

Brock glared at her. "Funny, that's what Summer said."

Everyone laughed.

"Anyhow, we're trying to save money by doing the work ourselves," Brock continued. He hoped his friends would catch the hint.

"Sounds great!" Evie said. "What kinds of changes are you guys going to be making?"

Brock briefly described the items on the to-do list that Geoff had sent along with the mockups. "…it's a lot to get done," he concluded, "but we're hoping that we'll only have to close the diner for a couple of days." Now came the hard part. He swallowed his pride, and added, "I could really use a hand next week, if anyone has time."

"Of course," said Jason. "I can help you reconfigure your booths and turn them into banquettes. Plus, figure out the reclaimed wood wainscoting and breakfast counter siding."

"I drove out to the Snowberry ranch yesterday," Brock said. "There's an old barn that Mr. Snowberry said I could scavenge. Spring and I loaded up my truck and his with a ton of old boards. There's a towering pile of them in the diner's parking lot."

"Cool! I'll bring my table saw!" said Evie. "And my staple guns. You're gonna need a few of those if you're reupholstering all the stools and benches, too."

"And I'll rope my dad and brothers into coming with me," added Rick. "If you're putting in a bunch of pendant lights to replace your fluorescents, you're gonna need some help with wiring the new lamps."

Relieved, Brock released a pent-up breath. "Thanks, guys. I really appreciate it. This makeover is a big job."

"Since we're discussing changes at the diner," said Jason, "I heard you promoted Auntie Marlene to manager. What happened to Mr. Stinson? I've been hearing all kinds of rumors flying around."

Rumors? Shit. "Oh yeah?" asked Brock.

"My great-uncle Kenny is spitting mad about losing his job," Rick said. "He blames Summer. He says she badmouthed him and got you to fire him."

"What the actual fuck?" Brock snapped. "None of that's true."

Rick shrugged. "You know Uncle Kenny. He likes to stir up shit. I figured there was more to the story than he's telling."

"First of all, Summer had nothing to do whatsoever to do with Kenny leaving the diner," Brock said vehemently. "And I didn't fire Kenny."

Rick looked surprised. "You didn't?"

"Hell, no. He quit in a huff after I called him out for fucking up the supplier orders for the third week in a row. A few days later, he asked for his job back. I said no because of the mess he made of the inventory system and bookkeeping software." Brock shook his head. "Jesus. It's so fucking unfair for him to blame Summer when all this happened before she even showed up. I swear to you—what happened was all on Kenny."

He slammed down his mug of root beer and noticed that his friends were all grinning at him.

Even Rick. "I believe you," he said. "Uncle Kenny always tries to blame someone else when he messes up."

"Brock, buddy," crowed Evie, her gray eyes sparkling. "You've got it *bad* for Summer, don't you? How long have you two been sneaking around, anyway?"

"We haven't been *sneaking* around at all," Brock defended himself. "And we've been seeing each other for about a month. It's, uh, been fun."

"I think she's perfect for you, dude," volunteered Jason. "I remember you've had a thing for her during senior year."

"Yeah, well, she's heading back to San Francisco in September." Brock stared glumly down into the depths of his mug. "It fucking sucks."

He hadn't intended to say that much. The last part just slipped out on its own.

Over the past week, Brock had done an awful lot of thinking about Summer and her impending departure. And he still hadn't come up with a good plan to make her change her mind.

"Have you asked her to stay?" Evie had both elbows propped on the table, and was leaning forward, apparently fascinated by his love life.

He sighed. "Nope. I mean, she owns a fucking restaurant in city, and from I saw online, it's the kind of high-class place where bankers and stockbrokers hang out. Why would she want to stay here to run a fucking *diner?* Even a really good one," he added, because he had his pride.

"Dude. You're talking like she's out of your league," Jason said. "Don't give up, man. I mean, she's hooking up with you, right? She obviously thinks you're a sexy beast. She might even like you as a person and shit."

"Yeah, thanks." Brock rolled his shoulders, trying to ease some of the tension gathering at the base of his neck. He'd come here for pizza and to catch up with his friends, not a fucking relationship counseling session. "Look, I don't wanna turn into some kind of pathetic, creepy stalker after we hit our expiration date."

"Expiration date? Seriously?" Evie rolled her eyes. "With an attitude like that, she's got no reason to hang around. If you want her to stay, you'll need to work a little harder. I mean, have you noticed the way she looks at you? I think she's fallen for you just as hard as you've fallen for her."

Brock shrugged, but couldn't deny the spark of hope suddenly careening around his insides like a firefly on speed. "Well, I'm working on a strategy. Anyhow, I really appreciate you guys agreeing to lend us a hand at the diner next Monday and Tuesday. I promise that we'll feed you, and it won't just be the usual pizza and beer Moving Day Special."

Chapter Twenty – Summer

Summer: Hey, Mags, sorry for the delay in getting back to you. I was out of cellphone range when you texted me, and didn't notice I had a message until this morning.

Maggie: Out of cellphone range? Where the hell are you, anyway? Haven't seen you around lately.

Summer: I'm still in Montana.

Maggie: What the fuck are you doing in Montana? The funeral was WEEKS ago. I thought you were ghosting me because you were working on the restaurant revamp.

Summer: I *am* working on it, I swear. New small plates menu is almost done. Just putting the final touches on my Thai fish tacos with curry sauce and shredded green papaya salad. They're killer, but I want to tweak them just a little.

Maggie: Okay. But again, why the fuck are you doing that in Montana? And when are you coming home?

Summer: Soon, I promise. I've been dealing with some family stuff since my grandpa died, and it's taking longer than I thought. I should be back in six weeks.

Maggie: Six WEEKS? What happened? Did the family farm burn down or something?

Maggie: No, wait. There's a man involved, isn't there?

Summer: It's a long story. TLDR; my grandma needs help with this diner she co-owns. I'm a chef, so...

Maggie: Oh, okay. I get it. It's like that in Chinese families, too. The oldies ask you for a favor, you do it. Or major bad karma ensues.

Summer: And yes, there's a man, too. Long story. I'll tell you all about it over cocktails when I'm back in the city.

L ivingston, Montana
Monday, July 25

"I can't believe the guy at the Junk & Disorderly cut you such a good deal on those old barn lamps," Jenna said as she and Summer seated themselves at Fiesta En Jalisco, a popular Mexican restaurant in downtown Livingston.

"Probably because I agreed to take all of them, even the dented and rusty ones," Summer said.

She smiled at the host and accepted a menu before continuing, "But yes, it was a lucky find. I was planning to spray-paint any vintage lights I found, but since these are all the same color, I'm thinking I'll just leave them as-is, to add character."

Jenna's Java was closed on Mondays, so Summer and Jenna had driven up to Livingston to hit the antique stores and have lunch while Brock met up with his buddies over at the Elk's Head.

Summer was glad that he was finally taking some time for himself. But also felt strange to be away from him. They'd spent almost every day of the past month together, and she'd gotten used to having him around all the time. Even on the nights when she slept at the ranch rather than his place, they still spent all day together at The Yummy Cowboy Diner.

"And that old pharmacy counter is cool, especially with all of those drawers," Jenna said proudly. She was the one who had spotted the long, dark-oak counter hidden away in the back of the store.

After measuring it, Summer realized it would be a perfect replacement for the diner's plywood and Formica backbar. She'd purchased it on the spot, glad that she had borrowed Dad's big Ford pickup instead of taking her own Subaru station wagon.

Dad had promised to phone his old friend Kevin Aberdeen at Aberdeen Kitchen & Bath Works, and ask if Kevin had any remnants left over from other jobs that he could sell Summer and Brock at a discount. Hopefully, there would be enough stone or quartz to top the new backbar with the same material as the breakfast counter.

"We scored big on our antique-hunting expedition," Summer agreed. "I think that calls for a margarita!"

"I agree," Jenna said. "And tacos, too."

Their drinks and complimentary chips and salsa arrived. Summer raised her salt-rimmed goblet. "Here's to hoping all the pieces actually fall into place for next week's dining room renovation!"

"Hear, hear!" Jenna lifted her mango margarita and saluted Summer with it.

They drank.

"So, how *are* things going at the diner?" Jenna asked, dipping a tortilla chip into the bowl of salsa. "I hear you guys have been making a ton of changes. Everyone's still talking about the contest last month, and wondering if you're planning another one soon."

"Autumn's been asking about that, too," Summer said. "Maybe next month. Business has been great since she created those social media accounts for the diner. We're getting guests from all over. Last week, we had a family drive all the way from Butte just for dinner. They weren't visiting Yellowstone or anything."

Jenna took another sip of her margarita. "And what about you and Brock? Still doing the EWB thing?"

Summer laughed. "I think we may have actually crossed over to Friends with Benefits territory. I have to tell you, when Grandma Abigail asked me to work with him, I was convinced we'd kill each other within a week."

Jenna snorted. "You're not the only one. Jason and Evie were actually taking bets on how long your partnership would last after Marlene told everyone about how you guys were always yelling at each other in the kitchen."

"Marlene is really nice, but jeez, she loves to gossip." Summer shook her head. "Brock's actually a pretty cool guy, now that he's adjusted his attitude. I mean, we still argue about stuff all the time, but he's not mean or an asshole. Just *extremely* opinionated." She grinned at Jenna. "But I can usually change his mind if I work at it."

No need to mention that the "working at it" part usually happened while she and Brock were naked.

Jenna nodded. "It's nice to see that he's come out of his shell since you showed up. After his mom died..." She frowned. "Well, he just kind of disappeared. He used to stop in for coffee and a cookie after the diner closed, but after the funeral, he never came by again. Evie says he stopped showing up at Pizza and Beer Mondays over at The Elk's Head, too."

"His mom's death really knocked the wind out of him," Summer replied. Sudden sympathy for him burned in her chest.

"Yeah, and you've been great for him."

"He's been good for me, too." It was true. Over the past month, their dinner-and-sex sleepovers had slowly turned into something resembling actual dates. That point had been driven home last week, after their outing to Hot Springs Lake.

Their conversation over the cherries—and his reaction to finding out about her plans for SummerTime—had laid a real guilt trip on her, even though she'd never hidden her intention of leaving as soon as their ninety days were up.

As if reading Summer's mind, Jenna asked, "And how does he feel about you leaving in September? Hell, how do *you* feel about it?"

Summer took a long pull from her drink while she considered how much to tell Jenna. "I won't lie. I've had… uh… some thoughts about returning to Snowberry Springs for good."

Jenna brightened. "That would be awesome!"

"But it's just not workable right now," Summer continued with a sigh. "Believe me, I've been thinking really hard about how I could make it work… and I can't. I committed to being in San Francisco for the long run when I invested all of my savings and partnered up with Greg to open SummerTime."

Jenna's eyes widened. "Greg? Who's Greg?" Before Summer could answer, she went on, "You have a *boyfriend* in San Francisco? Does Brock know?"

"No, not a boyfriend!" Summer shook her head. "Greg and I are —were—strictly business partners. We never dated or anything like that. He founded a software startup in the city, and he used to eat at Il Giardino Segreto all the time when I was the executive chef there. He was a big fan of my food. Eighteen months ago, he asked me if I'd be interested in opening my own place."

Jenna's dark eyes grew wide. "Wow! He must have really believed in you!"

"I thought he did," Summer said.

Maybe it was the margarita, but she was so tempted to spill the beans about Greg and the disaster he'd left for her. But she couldn't take the risk. It wasn't that she didn't trust Jenna, but

Snowberry Springs was a small town, and the only way to keep a secret was to keep silent.

She settled on the truth, minus the most important details. "We aren't partners anymore, but I'm still committed to SummerTime. It's closed temporarily while I make some big changes, but I'll be relaunching it before the end of the year."

If she kept repeating that like a magic spell, then she could make it true, right?

Even though Greg had screwed her over big time, she wasn't willing to walk away from SummerTime while there was still a chance she could turn things around. It was *her* place. Her baby.

Besides, her parents had taught her that running away from her problems never solved them. Heck, she might be in Montana right now and not California, but that was only because of Grandma Abigail and her offer.

It definitely *wasn't* because she'd run away from her problems in San Francisco.

Besides, I'm handling the situation, she told herself. Most of her remaining savings, including her retirement account, had gone to convince the most obnoxious of her investors that she wasn't defaulting, just regrouping.

She was keeping the rest of the group at bay with daily texts and emails describing her plans for SummerTime's relaunch and new profit model. Walking this tightrope was exhausting, but if she could just keep from falling for the next six weeks, she'd have the money she needed.

Her phone chimed softly. She glanced down to see a text from Brock.

Mission accomplished. Friends recruited to help paint & saw. Rick said he'll wire up the barn lights, if you find any. How's it going on your end?

She chuckled and told Jenna, "Brock wanted me to know that his

Pizza and Beer Gang is going to help with the reno next week. He wants to know whether we accomplished our mission, as well."

Jenna giggled. "Tell him that we're having margaritas to celebrate our success."

Summer grinned. "He's been stressing about closing the diner for two days in a row while we reno the dining room next week. And when he gets stressed, he gets bossy."

She turned her attention back to her phone, and snapped a photo of their half-empty goblets.

She sent it to Brock, then followed up with a text message.

One dozen barn lights acquired. Also, margaritas and tacos. And I found something really cool for the diner. Planning to pick up Spring on the way back to help us unload it from the truck.

He replied almost instantly. **It's gonna take 3 of us to unload? What the fuck did you buy, Ms. Fancy Pants?**

Wait and see, she typed, then set aside her phone to let him stew.

Their tacos arrived at the table. Summer had gotten three different kinds—shrimp, al pastor, and carne asada. Jenna had gone for chicken, fish, and shrimp.

"Hey, do you guys need any extra help for your reno?" asked Jenna when her first taco had vanished. "The café's closed on Mondays, so I could help you lay flooring. Thanks to all the work I did turning the old Phillips & Son store into my café and bakery space, I have a *lot* of experience laying tile and gluing down flooring."

"That would be great!" Summer replied. "We found a great deal on vinyl plank flooring, and it's the peel-and-stick kind that's super easy to install. We could really use some extra hands with that."

"I'll ask Vince if he can help, too. He did a good job with the floor tiles last summer."

"Thanks, Jenna. You're the best! I really appreciate it. There's a lot of flooring to install. If you and Vince help out, then we'll be able to reopen by Wednesday morning for sure. And Brock won't stroke out from a stress attack."

Jenna waved off her thanks. "Hey, that the way things work around here, remember? We help each other out, and what goes around, comes around. For good *and* bad." She grinned at Summer. "Promise you'll text me with Brock's reaction to that pharmacy counter."

Chapter Twenty-One – Brock

[Unknown Number]: Hi, Autumn. I need to ask for a favor.

Autumn: Who's this? I don't recognize your number.

[Unknown Number]: Sorry, it's Brock. Your grandma gave me your number. Hope you don't mind.

Autumn: Oh, hi, Brock! I don't mind. I thought you might be another Nigerian prince texting me about a surprise inheritance. ::money mouth face emoji::

Autumn: What kind of favor?

Brock: I just found out that Summer's birthday is on Sunday. I want to get her a gift. Abigail said you know the stuff Summer likes.

Autumn: What kind of gift? Cute & funny? A friend-type gift? Or a romantic gift?

Brock. Romantic. Definitely romantic.

Autumn: Oh, goody. I was hoping you would say that. Give me a few minutes and I'll text you some links.

∞ ∞ ∞

S nowberry Springs Ranch
Sunday, August 1

Brock sang "Happy Birthday" along with the Snowberry family as Priscilla returned from the kitchen with a tall chocolate cake in her hands. She'd stuck a pair of number-shaped candles—a 2 and a 9—in the dark swirls of fudgy frosting, and lit them.

"I made your favorite devil's food cake, baby girl," Priscilla said to Summer as she set the cake down in front of her daughter. "Don't forget to make a wish!"

Brock, sitting next to Summer, saw multi-colored sprinkles scattered over the top of the cake around the candles.

A pang of wistful nostalgia stirred up memories of Gran's special birthday treat, a yellow cake topped with a layer of chocolate pudding and whipped cream. It was the only thing she ever made from boxed mixes, and only because he begged for it.

I know what I'd wish for, he thought, and reached for Summer's knee under the table, squeezing it gently. *More family dinners like this, because you decided to stay.*

It wasn't only the great food served at Priscilla and Bob's home, though Summer's birthday dinner had been outstanding. Her parents had made barbecued pork spareribs, baked mac-and-cheese, and a fresh garden salad topped with freshly picked sweet yellow grape tomatoes.

All the Snowberrys, except for Winnie and her fiancé, were gathered around the long farmhouse table.

Autumn and Jayden had driven from Bozeman. Spring sat across the table from Brock and Summer, his two little girls on either side of him. Abigail, looking fully recovered from her heart attack six weeks ago, held court at the head of the table, beaming at everyone like a queen.

"When's *your* birthday, Brock?" asked Autumn after Summer had leaned forward and extinguished both candles with a single puff of air.

"March fifteenth," Brock replied.

"The Ides of March? Cool!" Jayden exclaimed. "That's when Julius Caesar was assassinated."

Brock couldn't help smiling. "Was that before or after Caesar salad was invented?" he joked.

"Uh." The kid looked flummoxed. "I have no idea." He pulled out his phone, presumably to Google the answer.

Autumn reached out to stop him. "You know the rule. No devices at the table unless it's an emergency. And no, the history of Caesar salad is *not* an emergency."

Priscilla had surprised Brock with an invitation to this birthday dinner. Did that mean his status had changed to "boyfriend" in the Snowberry family's eyes?

Was Summer on board with that change?

He sure hoped so. As promised, Autumn had sent him links to a few different things, but only one of her suggestions jumped out at him. He hoped to God Summer would like his gift, because he'd spent the week practicing what he was going to say to her tonight once they were alone.

Summer pulled the pair of candles out of the cake and handed them across the table to April and Abby so that they could take care of the frosting. Then she quickly and efficiently sliced the cake and began handing around plates.

The cake was delicious. And watching Summer lick the last bits of dark chocolate goodness from her fork gave Brock a few highly inappropriate thoughts about what *else* he wanted to lick tonight.

When only a few crumbs and smears of frosting remained on the cake plates, the kids cleared the dishes from the table. The adults took their coffee cups and went into the living room.

Then it was time for Summer to open her birthday presents. Brock sat next to her on the sofa as the kids eagerly carted a pile of gifts from the next room and piled them at Summer's feet.

As expected, she received all kinds of cooking-related items from her family: a "Kiss the Cook" apron from Jayden; a maple cutting board laser-engraved with Priscilla's apple pie recipe from Spring; a new canvas knife roll with leather handles from Bob and Priscilla; a mushroom farm in a box, courtesy of April and Abby; a set of Japanese paring knives with handles and protective sheaths in every color of the rainbow from Autumn; and a large gift box of assorted gourmet finishing vinegars and truffle oils from Winnie and Geoff.

Summer saved Brock's gift for last. He held his breath as she lifted the small, flat box and untied the ribbon. Alone among all the presents, his gift had nothing to do with cooking.

"Oh," breathed Summer as she removed the lid from the box. She stared down at for a long moment.

Brock saw her bite her lower lip. Doubts suddenly swooped in like hawks stooping on prey. *Fuck. I got it wrong.*

Then Summer looked at him. "It's perfect. Thank you." And then, right in front of her family, she leaned in to kiss him.

When she drew back, little April demanded, "But what did she get?" And Abby chimed in, "I wanna see!"

Summer's face lit up with the most beautiful smile he'd ever seen on her. It made her eyes glow like sapphires.

Brock let out a breath of relief. Autumn hadn't steered him wrong, after all.

Summer lifted the slender gold chain from the box and showed his gift to the family. It was a pendant set with a faceted, heart-shaped pale green peridot, her birthstone, framed in a gold band set with tiny diamonds.

An elegant swirl of gold topped the pendant and formed a loop for the chain.

It was the sort of gift you gave a girlfriend, not a "friend with benefits," and that was why it had been risky.

"It's gorgeous!" Priscilla exclaimed. "Brock, how very thoughtful." She shot him an approving look.

From the other side of the living room, Autumn gave him the thumbs-up.

They spent the rest of the evening playing board games. Brock and Summer teamed up for a round of *Settlers of Catan*, and lost to Spring and Autumn's team by huge margin.

After the kids were put to bed, Bob and Spring began to wash the pots and pans and the non-dishwasher safe items.

Brock followed them into the kitchen and grabbed a dish towel, preparing to do his part in drying the dishes.

But Bob turned from his place at the sink, and made a shooing gesture. "Kind of you to offer, but don't you and Summer have somewhere to be?"

Summer, who'd followed Brock as far as the doorway separating the kitchen from the living room, raised her hand to touch the pendant now hanging from her throat. "Do we, Brock?"

"Yeah. There's a special dessert with your name on it at my place." Fuck. He couldn't believe he'd just said that in front of Summer's dad.

But Bob only chuckled. "Have fun, you two."

"Summer, will you be home for dinner tomorrow?" asked Priscilla, who was on the other of the kitchen, busily packing away the leftovers in plastic containers of various sizes.

"I don't think so," Summer replied. "Tomorrow's when we start the big renovation at the diner. We're hoping to finish up by Tuesday night, so that we can reopen for business on Wednesday morning."

"Oh, that's right!" Priscilla said. "Your dad and I will be there as soon as morning chores are done, paintbrushes in hand. Have a good night, and happy birthday, baby girl."

She turned from the counter and gave Summer a long hug. Then, to Brock's surprise, Priscilla hugged him, too.

He and Summer left the house hand in hand. As they walked to his truck, he swallowed hard, silently rehearsing the words he wanted to say to her once they arrived at his cottage.

Chapter Twenty-Two – Summer

Summer had barely closed the cottage door behind her when Brock seized her and pushed her up against the living room wall.

He pinned her there with his hips, hands tangled in her loose hair, and bent to capture her mouth in a heated kiss. It was passionate, a little rough, and totally hot.

She made a noise of pure need deep in her throat and arched against him, grinding herself against the ridge of his erection, encased in denim.

Under the sensual assault of his mouth, her fingers scrabbled against the fabric of his shirt. She tugged it out of his jeans, craving his bare skin against her palms, taut and warm over hard muscle.

Brock drew back a little, his breath coming fast. "So, you liked your birthday present?"

"Loved it. It's very... romantic." She hoped she hadn't misinterpreted his intentions in choosing it.

On previous occasions when Mom and Dad invited him over, Summer and Brock had been careful to behave as if they were just friends. Tonight had been different. He'd entwined his fingers with hers before they sat down to dinner. Then he'd spent the rest of the evening with his hand on her shoulder or resting against the small of her back.

It had felt good. And very right. But confusing.

They'd never talked about what their evolving relationship should be called. *Is this still just a fling? Or am I his girlfriend now?*

Maybe I'm overthinking it?

Then Brock cupped her breasts through her cute summer top, and drove all the questions out of her mind when he caressed her sensitive nipples with his thumbs. They stiffened, and her desire flared.

Desperate to get him naked as quickly as possible, she yanked the rest of his shirt up and began pulling at the buttons. It was tricky, because he was trying to undress her at the same time and with the same single-minded speed.

Both of them quickly became tangled up in sleeves and necklines.

Laughing, Summer flattened her hands against his half-bared chest. "Wait—wait—" she protested breathlessly. "Let me do you first."

"But the birthday girl always comes first," he responded in a sultry tone that made a fresh set of giggles bubble up like Champagne.

"Well, *this* birthday girl wants to undress you and put her hands all over your body," she shot back.

"Your wish is my command." He took a half-step back and held his arms out to the side.

It was all she could do not to tear the pearl buttons off his nice cowboy shirt as she fumbled them. Why? Why were there so many of them? And why were they so darned slippery?

Finally, she got his shirt all the way open. She pushed it off his wide shoulders and tossed it onto the floor. Then she ran her hands reverently over his broad chest and muscled abs.

"You're beautiful," she said fervently.

He grinned, a flush rising from his collarbones. "Shouldn't I be saying that to *you?*"

"Sure," she responded, fluttering her eyelashes at him. "Let's start a mutual admiration society."

He laughed, then froze as she put her hands on his belt buckle. It was surprisingly fancy, a silver oval engraved with traditional scrollwork surrounding a gold "B."

"Admire me all you like, as long as you keep touching me like that," he replied, grinning. His brown eyes glowed with amusement and desire. "And if you remove my jeans, there's even more to admire."

She grinned at him, moved her hands to his hips, and slowly sank down to her knees.

"Boots first," she said primly. He was wearing new-looking leather cowboy boots today.

Brock groaned but let her pull them off before she reached up to deal with his belt.

She pulled his jeans and boxers down to his ankles. His cock sprang free, thick and fully erect.

Summer licked her lips before leaning in to place a playful kiss on the broad tip. The soft skin was smooth and hot against her mouth. "Hello there, my friend. You look ready for action."

Brock growled and pulled her up to her feet.

He stripped off her blouse and bra in a jiffy and tossed them to the living room floor. Then he put the brakes on and slowly kissed his way down her throat to her bare breasts, paying loving attention to each one as she squirmed with impatience and rising heat.

The combination of slow kisses, his tongue, and the scrape from his stubble drove her crazy with need. And he knew it.

When he finally slid her shorts and panties down her legs, he urged to step out of them. Then he draped one of her legs over his shoulder, leaned in, and blew a teasing puff of air over her folds before licking her slit, a slow, wet drag of his tongue over her most sensitive place that finished with a leisurely swirl around her bud.

She moaned, and he repeated the caress until she was teetering on the knife edge of her climax. Shaking with desire, she clung to his head, her fingers curled into his short hair, trying to pull him closer, craving just a little more to push her over into her release.

"Brock," she begged. "Please. I can't wait. I need you inside me now."

"Oh fuck, yeah!" He released her leg. As she sagged against the wall, needing the support, he surged to his feet. "Screw the bed. I'm gonna fuck you right here."

That sounded like the best idea ever. "Yes, please!"

An empty condom wrapper floated down and landed on the carpet next to her foot. He finished rolling the latex over his rigid length. Then, his hands under her butt, he lifted her effortlessly and wrapped her legs around his waist. The wall pressed hard against her shoulder blades.

The blunt head of his cock nudged against her aching, swollen entrance. He squeezed his eyes shut as if in pain, and groaned. "Fuck, Summer. I love how hot and wet and tight you are for me."

Then he entered her with one powerful thrust, filling her completely.

"Oh. My. God," she gasped, relishing the way he stretched her.

She clenched her thighs around him as he began to move. He took her fast and hard, pounding her against the wall. His mouth covering hers, kissing her ravenously, muffling her moans as he moved against her, his stiff length caressing her clit with every long thrust.

Summer clawed at his back and feverishly returned his kisses. Electric jolts of pleasure shot along every nerve in her body. She cried out and clung to him, biting his shoulder as the deep, powerful pulses of her climax began shaking her.

Brock's thrusts sped up, a sign that he was close to his own release. Her release went on and on without dying away, lifting her on waves as if she were floating in a vast sea of pleasure.

He growled against her lips, and shuddered hard. Every muscle in his body tensed as he came, his thrusts faltering and losing their rhythm.

When he was done, he shifted his grip and stepped back from the wall, holding her still firmly joined to him. "We're not done yet, birthday girl. I want to see you come at least twice more. It's my other present to you."

"I like the way you think," she said as he staggered in the direction of his bedroom.

They fell on his bed together. There, he proceeded to kiss and caress every inch of her until she was hovering on the brink of another climax.

Then he moved over her, his big, hard body pushing her down into the mattress as he entered her again. Summer wrapped her arms and legs around him, enjoying the weight and solid strength of him as he moved on top of her.

This time, his movements were slow and deep as he drove her to a second climax before coming himself.

"That's two," he said smugly, then he collapsed on top of her.

"I love your birthday presents," she agreed.

She received a breathtakingly sweet smile in return. He left the bed briefly to dispose of the condom, then returned to curl himself around her.

I'm going to miss this, she thought, as he rested his head on her breast. She began to run her fingers through his hair, running her nails lightly over his scalp the way he liked. *And I'm going to miss him so much.*

As if reading her thoughts, Brock wrapped his arm around her waist. "I don't want this to end. Stay with me, Summer." He paused, "Fuck, I'll even say yes to that fucking POS system if you give us a chance."

Her throat went dry at his declaration. Since her conversation with Jenna, she'd been thinking a lot about their relationship. She'd already acknowledged that leaving him was going to be harder than she ever expected.

In the warm darkness, lying with him skin to skin, surrounded by his scent and his touch imprinted everywhere on her body, she tried to imagine returning to her old life and her old routines without him.

Spending all day at her restaurant, then spending the evening alone in her hideously expensive, shoebox-sized apartment. Falling asleep, still alone, to the sounds of sirens and incoherent shouting drifting up from the streets. Waking up alone, with no one to bring her a mug of coffee, made just the way she liked.

She'd worked all of her waking hours in San Francisco so that she wouldn't have to stop and realize how lonely she was there.

She was just as busy in Snowberry Springs, but the difference was that she wasn't alone here. She had her parents, her brother and sisters, old friends willing to drop everything to pick up a paintbrush and help out... and Brock.

But returning to San Francisco is the smart thing to do, she argued with herself. *It's the only way I can dig myself out of the mess I'm in.*

Just a few short weeks ago, she'd dreaded working with him,

because she thought he was cocky and obnoxious. Since then, he'd revealed his thoughtful, softer side. He was everything she wanted in a man... and he even loved cooking as much as she did.

But if I stay in Snowberry Springs, I'll have to confess the truth about SummerTime. And then he'll know what colossal failure I am.

"Summer?" he asked.

She heard the pain and yearning in his voice, and it echoed the emotions ripping through her soul.

Despite the debate raging in her head, her heart knew there was only one right answer. She would just have to find a way to deal with everything else.

"I don't want this to end, either, Brock." She blew out a breath.

"Oh, thank God." His breath gusted against her neck. He kissed the top of her breast.

Suddenly, she felt lighter, as if a weight around her heart had fallen away. "God, I've got so much stuff I need to take care of in San Francisco, and I don't know how the heck I'm going to run SummerTime from Montana... but, yes, I want to stay here. With you."

"I'll do whatever I can to help you work out the details." His fingers stroked over the curve of her hip. "In case you haven't already guessed... I'm head over heels in love with you, Summer Snowberry."

She put her hand on his stubbled cheek, then drew his face up to kiss him. "You drive me crazy half the time, but I'm in love with you, too." She laughed shakily. "I've loved you for years, even though all that time, I've been trying to pretend I didn't, so that you wouldn't break my heart."

He kissed her back, deep and achingly tender.

"I won't break your heart, Summer. I promise. We're meant to be, and that means everything will work out okay. We'll make it happen. And now, there's something I need to take care of." His mouth traveled her jaw, then laid a line of kisses down the side of her neck. His fingers stroked the tip of her breast into yearning hardness. "I promised I'd make you come at least one more time, didn't I?"

Chapter Twenty-Three – Brock

The Yummy Cowboy Diner
Monday, August 2

"Wow, look at that crowd!" Summer exclaimed as she and Brock emerged from the diner's kitchen. "I thought we let everyone know we're closed today."

Brock blinked at the large group gathered outside at the front of the diner. "Uh, they don't look like customers."

He squeezed her hand as they walked through the deserted dining room. He'd laced his fingers through hers on the drive over from his cottage. Since then, he hadn't let go unless absolutely necessary.

He'd woken up smiling this morning. The diner was finally earning money. Summer loved him and wanted to stay with him. He couldn't remember the last time he'd felt this happy.

It was only seven-thirty a.m., but how could this day possibly get any better?

Then Rick, Jason and Evie spotted them through the big plate-glass windows, and waved.

Summer's parents and brother stood next to them, along with Marlene and her husband, Chris, who both wore tool belts.

Marlene had tucked her bleached blonde hair under a baseball cap embroidered with the Montana State Bobcats logo, and her usual bright red lipstick outlined her mouth.

Behind them stood more familiar faces—Jenna and her nieces and nephews; Rick's dad and brothers; plus, a bunch of people he barely knew, all of them holding hammers, drills, or paintbrushes.

He grinned like an idiot. Hard to believe, but his day had officially gotten better.

"I don't think they're here for breakfast, Ms. Fancy Pants," he said, striding forward to unlock the front door.

Summer, following on his heels, tapped his shoulder and pointed. "Holy crap."

That was when Brock noticed that someone had blocked off a large section of the street in front of the diner. An outdoor workshop was now set up there, complete with a generator, Evie's table saw, the two construction dumpsters he'd ordered, and several workbenches improvised from sheets of plywood set up on sawhorses. Long boxes of flooring material stood stacked on the sidewalk, paint cans formed a pyramid, and several ladders leaned against the brick front of the Cooperman building next door.

"Hey, sweetie," Bob Snowberry called as they emerged from the diner. "We rustled up a few extra helping hands for you."

Deputy sheriff Matt Parker, one of the town's two cops, grinned at him. In high school, he and Brock had been on the football team together.

"We got permission from the Department of Public Works—" Matt jerked a thumb in Chris Wittenmeyer's direction. "—to close this section of the street until midnight tomorrow."

"Thanks." Brock's throat tightened with emotion as he scanned the crowd.

For a kid who'd literally grown on the wrong side of the tracks, this display of support felt overwhelming. The people of Snowberry Springs not only enjoyed eating at his diner, but they apparently liked and respected *him* enough to volunteer their time and labor.

It was truly humbling.

He choked out, "Thanks so much, everyone. You have no idea how much I appreciate everyone showing up."

Chris shrugged and spread his hands. "Not much happening downtown on Mondays and Tuesdays," he rumbled.

Summer gripped Brock's hand tightly. "I'm overwhelmed, you guys." Her voice shook, and she sounded as stunned as Brock felt. "We never expected... thank you. Thank you so much! Most of you already know that I'm not very handy," she continued. A soft ripple of laughter moved through the onlookers. "But I promise you I will cook you a *great* lunch and dinner."

Everyone clapped and cheered.

"I guess we should go unload the lamps from the back of your truck," Summer suggested to Brock. "Then I'll check the walk-in to make sure we have enough supplies to feed everyone."

$$\infty \infty \infty$$

The next few hours flew by. Autumn, with Jayden in tow, showed up to take photos and film video snippets of the renovation work for the diner's social media feeds.

"Given our connections to *Restoring Seattle*, I'm planning to hashtag the heck out of these renovation postings," Brock overheard her promising Summer.

As promised, Summer spent most of the day working in the kitchen, with Marlene's son Austin helping her prep the fixings for lunch and dinner.

Brock and a few others, including Summer's dad, set to work under Jason's guidance, installing the barn wood wainscoting along the walls and on the front of the breakfast counter.

The loud whir of the saw from outside and the machine-gun rapid tat-tat-tat of multiple nail guns provided a constant level of background noise in the crowded dining room, interspersed with bursts of country music blaring tinnily from someone's boombox.

Mid-morning, Summer emerged briefly from the kitchen to supervise the removal of the junky cowboy memorabilia from the dining room walls. She'd warned Brock beforehand that she intended to whittle the current collection down to a few, carefully selected pieces.

He was on his knees, wielding a nail gun as he fastened vertical strips of barn wood to the front of the breakfast counter. He stopped what he was doing to admire Summer's sweet ass in her jeans as she went up on a ladder.

With an air of satisfaction, she hauled down the bison head mount from its longstanding place over the kitchen door. When she descended, the huge, shaggy, dusty head cradled in her arms, she began marching towards the front door. Brock got a bad feeling.

"Hey, wait a minute, Ms. Fancy Pants. Where are you taking that?" he demanded. "You're not seriously gonna throw it away, are you?"

"I'm taking it out to the dumpster, where it belongs." Summer replied, confirming his fears. "Unless it has some kind of sentimental value?"

Brock scowled, fighting the temptation to tell her it belonged to his grandfather.

Bob Snowberry, who was working nearby, laughed. "Don't let him fool you, Summer. That old thing was already here when Brock's mother Pamela bought the diner from Jack Peterson's grandpa."

"Thanks, Dad." Summer gave him a brilliant smile. "And now it's gone."

Brock sighed loudly. "Great. Thanks for the support, Mr. S."

Bob only chuckled and went back to nailing wood strips against the diner's wall.

By the time lunchtime rolled around and Summer began setting up a taco bar buffet on the breakfast counter, the dining room already looked dramatically different.

Half of the barn wood wainscoting was now installed, and the upper part of the walls had been painted a soft sage color. And the bison head over the kitchen door had been replaced with a stenciled image of The Yummy Cowboy Diner's new logo.

Autumn had created the logo, and Brock loved it. It was the stylized silhouette of a cowboy kneeling next to a campfire, coffee mug in hand, and an old-fashioned coffee pot hung over the flames.

Meanwhile, Jenna and Vince were leading the efforts to lay the vinyl plank flooring. It had the same weathered look as the salvaged barn wood, but it provided a non-slip, easy-to-mop surface. By lunchtime, they were nearly finished with the flooring, which meant that Jason and his team could install the new banquettes as soon as Brock, Bob, and the others finished the wainscoting.

Rick, his dad, and his two brothers were perched at the top of ladders, busily removing the old ceiling fluorescent lights and hanging the barn lights from long cables.

Outside on the street, Jason directed the reconfiguration of the diner's booths into long banquettes that would line the dining room's walls.

Staple gun in hand, Summer's mom Priscilla had taken charge of reupholstering the banquettes, chairs, and stools with new vinyl fabric in a darker shade of green that complemented the wall color.

Marlene, Katie, Terri, and Autumn were busy covering the Formica tabletops with the custom wallpaper Autumn had designed and printed using a collage of old Snowberry Springs newspaper clippings and advertisements.

Spring finished off each table by cutting thin Plexiglas sheets to protect the refurbished table tops from spills and stains, and to make cleanup easy.

It was hard work but fun, with music blaring and everyone joking around as they worked their asses off.

Most of the lunchtime taco fixings had vanished by the time Bob's old friend Kevin Aberdeen arrived in a large, flat-bed truck loaded up with two pieces of a white quartz slab with gray veining.

Kevin had phoned Summer a few days ago to offer her a deep discount on a large slab that had cracked in half during shipping. Despite Kevin's assurances that he could fix the damage with an invisible seam of epoxy, the customer had refused to take delivery and insisted on a replacement slab.

Not only had Kevin offered to drive down from Livingston to deliver the damaged slab, he'd offered to cut it to fit the breakfast counter and the antique backbar Summer had bought.

As expected, Brock had grumbled at first about the additional expense of the old pharmacy counter. But he eventually admitted that it added old-fashioned character to the diner, and would be the crowning touch on a great new dining room.

To Brock's amazement, all of the extra helping hands meant that all of renovations wrapped up by the end of the first day. The dining room was completely transformed, and it looked great.

When all of the tables, chairs, and stools had been carried back inside, Brock tapped a glass with a knife to get everyone's attention.

He reached for Summer's hand. "Thank you all so much for coming out to help us today," he began.

"I've cooked a special dinner for you, if you'd like to seat yourselves," Summer added. "But before that, I'd like to add one final touch to this beautiful new dining room. Autumn?"

Summer's sister approached Brock, carrying two large flat rectangles wrapped in brown paper. To Brock's surprise, Autumn presented the items to him.

"We've made a lot of big changes today, but we also wanted to pay homage to the diner's history," she said. "Go ahead, unwrap them."

Wondering what she and Summer had cooked up behind his back, he ripped away the paper. And then stopped in shock.

Unaccustomed tears stung his eyes as he gazed down at the two large matted and framed photos in his hands.

The first photo was of Mama at work in the diner, standing behind the breakfast counter and smiling at the camera while refilling a customer's coffee cup. The second photo showed Mama, a very young Brock, and Gran, all dressed in their Sunday best and posing in front of The Yummy Cowboy Diner.

"How…?" he asked in a choked voice.

Summer smiled shyly up at him. "I noticed you had a bunch of photo albums on your living room bookshelves," she said. "I went through them last week, while you were out picking some stuff in the garden for our dinner. Do you like them?"

In reply, he bent and kissed her, a long, sweet meeting of their lips as their friends and Summer's family whooped and clapped.

"I love them," he whispered. "Thank you, Summer."

She blushed. "Why don't we hang them over our new backbar?" she suggested, pointing at an empty patch of wall over the espresso station. The rest of the wall was lined with open shelving intended to hold cups, glasses, and plates.

Speechless and fighting his tears of gratitude and happiness, Brock nodded.

"Good," she said. She gently tugged the picture frames out of his grip and handed them to Jason.

"If you'll do the honors?" she asked him.

"Of course."

While Jason hammered in a couple of picture hooks and hung the photos, Austin, Brock and Summer went into the kitchen.

There, they rapidly plated and served a dinner of Brock's buttermilk fried chicken with macaroni and cheese made from Priscilla Snowberry's recipe, and fresh steamed corn on the cob.

Then he and Summer seated themselves at the Snowberry family table, and dug in. It felt incredibly good to share this meal with all of their helpers in this beautiful new dining room.

They were in the middle of dessert—Summer had whipped up a batch of Grandma Russo's strawberry shortcakes—and debating the merits of huckleberry pie versus cherry and apple pies, when the shopkeeper's bell installed over the front door tinkled.

Brock looked up to see Abigail enter the diner. Frowning, she peered around the crowded dining room, then made a beeline for the Snowberry table.

From the grim set of Abigail's mouth, Brock guessed that whatever had happened, it must be bad.

Did she get more bad news about her health? he wondered.

Then, without acknowledging anyone else at the table, she

marched straight to where Summer sat, next to Brock.

"Summer. I need to speak with you," she said, her words clipped. "Right now, and in private."

Brock saw the color drain out of Summer's face and felt a mule-kick of apprehension in his gut. Everyone stared at them.

Without a word, Summer rose and led her grandmother to the back of the diner. They vanished through the kitchen door.

"Do you have any idea what this is about?" Priscilla asked Brock, looking after them with a worried expression.

Brock shook his head. "No, but I'm gonna find out. Excuse me."

He shoved his chair back, got to his feet, and went to find some answers.

Slipping quietly through the kitchen door, he lingered just out of sight, eavesdropping shamelessly.

Abigail was speaking, her voice tight and angry.

"—Kenny told me he discovered that your restaurant is closed because you're *bankrupt,* Summer. Not because you're renovating, like you told me and everyone else. At first, I thought he was just bitter about losing his job at the diner."

Fucking Kenny! Brock thought angrily. His fists clenched. *I'm gonna have words with him. No more of this badmouthing Summer shit from him!*

"I'm *not* bankrupt," Summer protested. Her voice sounded shockingly thin and reedy.

It made Brock itch to charge in and enfold her in a protective embrace.

"No?" Abigail asked sharply. "Because just now, some of your creditors contacted me. I don't know how on earth they got my phone number, but they confirmed that you're in big financial trouble, young lady. Now, what do you have to say for yourself?"

Brock froze in shock. Summer had lied to him and everyone, including her grandmother about what was going on with her restaurant in San Francisco?

No wonder she didn't want us to apply for that business loan!

Chapter Twenty-Four – Summer

Summer's stomach twisted as she saw the hurt, bewildered look on her grandma's face. It took all of her self-control not to throw up.

Of all the awful, stressful things she'd been dealing with since Greg took the money and disappeared, this was the one she'd feared the most. The intense pressure of her shame squeezed the breath out of her like the remorseless coils of a hungry anaconda.

"I had faith in you, Summer," Grandma Abigail said. "Because I thought you were better than *this*." Her expression sharpened. Suddenly, she wasn't the sweet grandmother, but the savvy businesswoman. "How long have you been hiding this from everyone?"

"My business partner looted SummerTime's accounts and disappeared just before Grandpa Frank passed away."

Grandma Abigail's lips thinned even further. "And you didn't think to mention it when I asked you to help me make this diner profitable?"

This was Summer's worst nightmare. *I'm a failure and a fraud, and now even my family knows it. I was a fool to think San Francisco was far enough away that no one would find out before I could fix things.*

Summer couldn't deal with the disappointment and betrayal on Grandma Abigail's face any longer. She turned away.

And caught sight of Brock, watching them from the kitchen doorway.

Oh, God. Just when I thought things couldn't get any worse!

"Summer, what the hell is going on?" he asked. He looked shocked, and she knew that anger would follow in another minute.

She rarely cried. But she'd kept all of her fear and stress bottled up for weeks because she had to keep the disaster in the city under control while she focused on fixing the diner.

Now, that bottle shattered, loosing a flood of tears. Wiping angrily at her eyes, she tried to fight back the sobs, but found it impossible. Her vision blurred and fiery trails of tears stung her cheeks.

"I'm sorry. I'm so sorry!" she sobbed.

It was over. Everything she'd hoped to accomplish had just vanished. Worse, Brock was going to hate her now.

"What happened to your restaurant?" he demanded.

"Yes. Tell us, Summer. Thing were going so well," Grandma Abigail demanded coldly. "What went wrong? How was your partner able to steal from you?"

Trying to get hold of herself, Summer kept trying to wipe her tears away. It was useless. She was overflowing with salt water and snot. Someone—Brock—handed her a clean dishtowel, and she buried her face in it.

His hand landed on her shoulder, the warm weight anchoring her.

Why is he being so nice to me? I've just ruined everything for him! she thought, but she was still pathetically grateful for the comfort.

He and Grandma Abigail both waited in silence while Summer clawed at the scraps of her tattered self-control and gathered them back around herself.

When she could speak, she told them the same story she'd told Jenna about Greg Brandywine and his proposal that they open a restaurant together. He'd founded a successful software startup, he was rich, and he loved her food. She'd been ecstatic at his proposal to become partners, and she had eagerly invested her savings in the venture.

Then came the hard part. "Everything was great at first," she continued. "The restaurant reviewer at *The San Francisco Chronicle* gave SummerTime a glowing review, the foodies on Yelp loved us, and the restaurant had a long waiting list for tables every night of the week. I was so happy—I had a great staff and complete creative control over the menus."

"So, what happened?" Brock rasped. His hand was still on his shoulder, and she felt tension vibrating through him like a live wire.

"Greg's company went public in April and immediately tanked. I—I don't know why or what happened. I was busy at the restaurant and didn't really follow high tech news. Three weeks later, he embezzled all the money from the restaurant's business account and disappeared, leaving me holding the bag for everything. He didn't put his name on the title or mortgage, just the partnership agreement and our joint business account. I thought it was because he trusted me and he was being generous, ensuring that SummerTime was all mine..." She inhaled a shaking breath. "But it means I'm responsible for everything. I've been working to make it right. While the restaurant was doing well, I started saving up for a down payment on a home. Well, that's gone now, and I've drained my retirement savings, too."

"Your retirement savings?" asked Grandma Abigail, her tone heavy with condemnation. "Oh, Summer. You *never* touch your retirement!"

Summer shook her head. "I know the situation sounds terrible. But I can still turn things around! I mean, look at how well The Yummy Cowboy Diner is doing after just a few weeks. I'm going to do the same thing for SummerTime, too."

"How? By finding more investors and lying to them?" Grandma Abigail asked harshly.

Summer recoiled. She felt as if Grandma had physically slapped her.

Grandma Abigail continued remorselessly. "If you lied to your own grandmother about being successful in SF, what *else* have you been lying about, young lady?"

Summer's head snapped up. "I've *never* lied to you. I just didn't tell you everything that was happening. As far as the diner goes, well, I've done everything you asked for, haven't I? The business has been profitable for the past month... not hugely, but we're not losing money right now."

Grandma Abigail's gaze shifted to Brock. "Is that true?"

"Yeah," he said. "Summer and I have been running the numbers every day after the diner closes. We're in the black. Barely, but yeah."

"And what about the expansion we discussed?" Grandma Abigail asked. "Will you still be able to add the extra seating capacity before the LVR begins operation?"

Summer shrank in on herself. *The loan to buy the Cooperman building!* she thought in despair.

"I don't know," Brock said. "Maybe after September." He didn't say the words out loud, but Summer heard them loud and clear. *When The Yummy Cowboy Diner is all mine again.*

Grandma Abigail sighed heavily. "I just don't know what to do, Summer. I thought I could trust my flesh and blood to help me in my time of need. Now, I just don't know what to do about this diner."

The situation was getting worse by the minute.

How much of Grandma Abigail's plans for the diner depended on Brock being able to qualify for a new mortgage on the Cooperman building? By keeping silent about her own financial difficulties, had Summer just tanked the deal and screwed him over?

"Grandma, please don't punish Brock for my mistake," she begged. "If you have to, you can keep the half of the diner you promised me. But please, honor your promise to clear the diner's mortgage and Brock's loans. He's worked so hard—he *deserves* this!"

And he deserves it much more than me. Especially now that I've screwed up everything.

"I—I need time to think about everything I've learned today," Grandma Abigail said sadly. She turned and left the kitchen.

Brock's fingers tightened on Summer's shoulders. He tried to pull her into an embrace. "Hey, I'm sure we can—"

"Didn't you *hear* what I just told you?" Summer tore herself out of his grasp. "I'm a failure and a fraud, Brock, not the expert everyone thought I was! And if Grandma cancels the deal, it'll be my fault."

He stared at her, his eyes burning with some emotion she couldn't interpret. He opened his mouth as if to speak, but nothing came out.

"I'm so sorry. I never meant to hurt you. I was just trying to make things right!" Then she couldn't take it anymore. She turned on her heel and dashed for the diner's back door. Thank God she'd left her car parked there!

Back at the ranch house, Summer holed up in her childhood bedroom. Calls and text messages chimed non-stop on her phone. She turned it off.

She couldn't deal with anyone's sympathy or anger right now. Not when the enormity of her failure was crashing down on her like a brick wall collapsing in an earthquake. Without Grandma Abigail's deal and the money from cashing out her half of the diner, there was no way Summer could reopen SummerTime.

She couldn't even run back to San Francisco because she'd sublet her apartment until the middle of next month.

And Brock probably hated her for sabotaging his plans, as well.

She'd tried so hard. Worked her butt off. And all her plans had still failed.

Summer hadn't cried this hard since Brock broke her heart and shattered her hopes during their senior year of high school. She'd learned back then that tears changed nothing. Crying didn't get you anywhere. Only hard work and perseverance did.

Except they didn't.

So why not curl up on her bed and let all of her pain pour out of her?

Summer didn't know how long she lay there, sobbing, a flood of tears pouring from her eyes. Long enough to dampen the dusty old teddy bear she clutched to her chest and leave a clammy wet stain on her pillow.

She was distantly aware when her family arrived home in a crunch of gravel under truck tires, followed by the muffled sounds of conversation.

Are they talking about me? About all the trouble I caused?

Summer rolled over, curled into a miserable ball, and cried some more.

When a brisk knock sounded on her door sometime later,

she'd finally stopped sobbing and was lying on her bed in numb misery, watching the last rays of sunshine from the long summer evening spear through the window and land in a pool of golden light on her rug.

"Summer?" Autumn asked. "Can I come in?"

She didn't wait for an answer, but turned the doorknob and entered, carrying a box of Kleenex and a steaming mug. The delicate scent of fresh peppermint drifted into the bedroom.

Summer sniffled and pushed herself upright. "What do you want?" she asked hoarsely.

"I wanted to see how you were doing. Grandma said you'd gotten some bad news. She looked pretty upset, too." Autumn crossed the room and sat down on the bed next to Summer. "Mom and Dad are talking to her right now, so I thought I'd come up here and check on you."

She pulled a tissue out of the box and handed it to Summer. "Here. Blow."

Despite her utter misery, a ghost of a laugh moved through Summer. "You sound just like Mom."

Autumn smiled gently at her. "I've had some practice with being a mom."

When Summer had finished blowing her nose, her sister gave her the mug of peppermint tea. Growing up, there had always been a large patch of mint growing next to the back porch. A hot infusion of the fresh leaves heavily sweetened with honey had been Mom's remedy for everything from sore throats to heartache.

Autumn waited until Summer had finished half the mug before asking, "Do you want to talk about it?"

Summer shook her head. "Whatever Grandma Abigail told you... she's right."

Autumn sighed heavily. "I'm sorry about everything that happened to you in San Francisco. It wasn't your fault, and Grandma needs to get over it." She shook her head and handed Summer another tissue. "You know how she gets when she makes a Grand Plan and things don't work out exactly the way she envisioned."

Summer nodded. "It wouldn't be so bad... except I'm not the only one who's in trouble now."

"Well, that's why I'm here," Autumn said. "I mean, I came up here to deliver tea and sympathy, but I've got some actual good news for you, as well."

Her head clouded with misery and emotional fatigue, Summer couldn't imagine what kind of good news her sister could possibly offer her. "What?"

"I just heard from a food blogger friend of mine. Apparently, a well-known restaurant critic from a big national newspaper is planning to visit The Yummy Cowboy Diner later in the week, as part of an article they're writing about the best restaurants in the Yellowstone area." Autumn grinned at her. "This could be a huge break for The Yummy Cowboy Diner, especially once all those tourists come next year. And if you'd actually looked at your phone at any point in the past three hours, you'd have seen my messages."

"I turned it off when I got home," Summer confessed. "After what happened at the diner, I knew it would blow up with text messages and emails. I wasn't ready to deal with the fallout." She blew her nose again.

The strong, sweet tea was making her feel better. So was Autumn's sympathy and apparent unwillingness to judge Summer on her screw-ups.

She finished the mug and blew her nose one last time. "Thanks, sis. I needed that."

"And it looks like you needed to get a bunch of stuff out of your system." Autumn looked her over with a critical eye.

Summer's face was burning and her eyes were sore and itchy, which meant her face was probably red and blotchy and swollen. Crying always made her look like a swarm of angry bees had attacked her.

"So, are you ready to return to the diner tomorrow?" Autumn continued, her tone brisk now.

"What?" Summer couldn't believe what her sister was asking.

"C'mon Summer. Isn't this the big break you and Brock need? Especially after working so hard?"

Summer shook her head. "Yes, but... how can I face Brock now? How can I face *anyone* in this town? I'm sure word's already gotten out that I'm not the success they all thought I was. And if Brock's smart, he'll break up with me because I screwed up his big chance."

"Are you in love with him?" Autumn demanded.

"Yes, but—" Summer began.

Autumn took her by the shoulders. "Then *help* him. He needs you at the diner tomorrow morning, and every day that you're here, to make sure that you wow the *America Today* food critic when they show up."

"But—" Summer tried again.

"No 'buts,'" Autumn said firmly. "If you love him, put on your big girl panties and go clear the air. Don't you *dare* ghost him, not with an opportunity like this!"

Summer nodded. *Maybe I can't fix what I did, but I owe Brock the chance to make it on his own.* Out loud, she said, "You're right. I need to help him in any way that he'll allow me to."

"Good." Autumn rose to her feet. "Go wash your face in some cold water, and I'll give you some of my firming moisturizer."

A half hour later, Summer stood on Brock's porch. The sky overhead had darkened to cobalt blue and the first couple of stars had appeared, though a broad band of fiery red, orange, and gold still lingered over the mountains to the west.

She took a deep breath and went over her game plan. *Start with a sincere apology and end with the good news. If I'm lucky, he won't slam the door in my face before I get to the good news part.*

She raised her hand to knock. But before her knuckles connected with the painted wood, he yanked the door open. "Thought I heard you drive up," he growled, glaring at her.

Summer swallowed hard, resisting the urge to turn tail and run back to her car. "Brock, I'm so sorry—" she began.

He reached out, grabbed her upper arm, and hauled her inside his cottage. "Just shut up, Fancy Pants, and listen to what I have to say."

Chapter Twenty-Five – Brock

Summer wasn't answering her text messages. Or her phone. Brock endured the rest of dinner, doing his best to be nice to the people who'd given him so much help today. But he couldn't get over what he'd just witnessed.

How dare Kenny stir up shit like that! And how dare Abigail Snowberry blame Summer for something that sounded like it had been completely out of her control!

Summer's tears and the utter despair on her face had absolutely gutted him. She'd always appeared so strong and confident. After hearing what had happened to *her* dream restaurant, he understood why she'd been so fierce about her ideas for improving his place.

Most of all, he wanted to take her in his arms and comfort her.

Why didn't she tell me? Let me help her?

He loved her with all his heart. And she loved him. They were in the middle of trying to figure out a future together, and yet he hadn't guessed that there was a shitstorm of this magnitude blowing through her life. She had shut him out. And he wasn't happy about it.

What if she packed up and left? Ran back to San Francisco?

I can't let Summer leave. I'll do whatever it takes to get her to stay... even beg.

Because no matter what had happened in San Francisco, he

couldn't deny that Summer had put The Yummy Cowboy Diner on the path to success.

More than that, she'd given him back his life. He actually had time to date her, and watch baseball, and get together with his friends again.

When he hadn't heard from her after four hours, he decided he'd waited long enough. He wasn't just going to sit around here and let her hightail it out of town.

He changed into clean clothes and was picking up his wallet and car keys when saw her station wagon pull up and park in front of his house.

His heart leaped as he watched her get out of the car and walk up to his front door. She looked awful.

He waited impatiently for her to knock. When she didn't, he suspected she'd changed her mind about seeing him.

I can't let her go without talking to her!

He tore open his front door and met her startled gaze. It was obvious she'd been crying.

Dammit, Abigail! How could you do this to my girl?

Summer began apologizing as he pulled her inside. He stopped her.

"Just shut up, Fancy Pants, and listen to what I have to say."

Looking pitiful enough to break his heart, she pressed her lips together and nodded. She hadn't met his eyes since he opened the door, and at the moment, she was studying his feet.

"First of all," he said sternly. "You are *not* a failure or a fraud just because you trusted the wrong person. In fact, your restaurant really was the smash hit you said it was. *You* didn't tank the business. Your asshole partner did."

"You—you're not mad at me?" she asked, as if she couldn't

believe it. She met his gaze at last. Her eyes were red, her lids puffy and swollen.

"Oh, I'm plenty mad at you," he answered honestly. She flinched, and he continued, "I'm mad because you didn't ask me for help."

"But—"

"Let me finish. Didn't you teach me I couldn't run a successful restaurant as a one-man show?"

She nodded.

"So, why are you trying to pretend that Greg stealing the money was all your fault?" he asked. "And even if you made a mistake by trusting him... well, I've made plenty of dumb mistakes myself. Including how I treated you our senior year of high school."

"I remember," she said in a small voice. "You always hated me. And I totally humiliated myself by asking you to go to the prom."

"I never hated you," he told her. "In fact, I had a huge crush on you. But I was an insecure little asshole. I thought that if anyone found out I wanted to date the richest girl in town, the one with the perfect family, they'd laugh at me." He snorted at the memory.

"So... the prom?" she asked, eyes wide.

"Yeah, I couldn't afford to go. So, I kept up the asshole act so everyone would think I was too cool for the prom and not figure out that I was broke." He put both hands on her shoulders and looked her in the eyes. "I was a real dumbass, Summer, and I hurt you. I'm sorry."

He bent to kiss her. She responded, hot and sweet as always. "But what if Grandma Abigail reneges on her deal with you?"

"If that happens, you've given me the tools I need to stay profitable," Brock answered firmly. "I'll pay off my debts a bit more slowly, but it'll happen. And then I'll do what I can to help you with the Greg situation." He kissed away her protest. "After all the work you've done for the diner, it's the least I can do."

"I love you," she said, and finally smiled.

"I love you, too, and I'm not about to let you get away. If it takes putting Marlene in charge of the diner and following you to San Francisco, that's what I'll do."

She laughed. "I don't deserve you, Brock, but thank you for being on my side. For everything, really." Then she blinked. "Oh! I almost forgot. I have some great news!"

He drew her into his arms and listened as she told him about the newspaper and the restaurant reviewer. She finished with, "... and that's why I came here. I wanted to tell you I'll do everything I can to make sure we get a five-star review. *If* you want to keep working with me, that is."

"I do. And I want more. I want you to move in with me. No more overnight bags. No more sneaking around. I want to wake up next to you every morning. And think I'm ready to clear out Mama's stuff. We could go furniture shopping together and find something new, something we both like."

"Yes," she said, and his heart warmed at her enthusiasm. "I decided I want to stay in Snowberry Springs. I loved living in San Francisco, but coming home reminded me how much I missed having family and old friends nearby. And if I left, I would miss you, most of all."

He bent to kiss her passionately, sliding his fingers into her loose golden hair, and cradling the curve of her head.

"I love you," he told her, his voice rough with need. "I want you to stay with me, Summer. Forever."

"Yes," she told him. "I want that, too. I'm so sorry about everything that happened. I never meant to mislead anyone. I just thought it was my problem, so I had to fix it on my own."

"Promise me you'll ask for help next time you need it. Promise me that from now on, we work as a team… a *real* team."

"I promise."

∞∞∞

Summer

Then Brock's mouth was on hers, and she couldn't think clearly anymore as his kiss stirred all of her senses, hard and demanding.

She wound her arms around his neck and pressed herself against his hard chest, wanting more. He answered her need by plunging his tongue into her mouth and boldly exploring every sensitive surface.

He let his mouth trail down her throat, nipping and biting the way she loved.

Summer moaned as jolts of sensation shot down like lightning to the tips of her breasts and to the already throbbing place between her legs.

Panting, she slid her fingers through his short hair, craving more of those delicious caresses that hovered on the knife's edge between pleasure and pain.

His hands dropped to her hips, and he pulled her against him. He was already hard, the length of his erection pushing boldly through his sweatpants.

She made a protesting noise when Brock finally ended his kiss and drew back. Wanting more, she tried to pull his head back down to her.

He laughed, sounding as breathless as she felt. "Is it just me, or are we both wearing too many clothes right now?"

"Definitely." She gasped as he bit the side of her neck, following the sharp caress with a lingering swipe of his tongue. Her knees went weak.

She needed him so badly that it actually hurt. These past few hours had been hell, thinking that she'd ruined everything.

But miraculously, he hadn't held anything against her. He was still hers. She was the luckiest woman on earth.

She pushed her hips against him, hoping to encourage him to take the next step.

He only chuckled, his breath tickling the side of her neck. Then he bit her shoulder and slid his hands down from her head to cup her breasts.

His thumbs slowly stroked her nipples the way she loved, sending jolts of pleasure straight down to the pit of her belly. She arched into his touch, moaning with need, feeling pleasure so intense that she thought she might actually come on the spot.

"Please," she panted. "Please, Brock. I need you!"

"Good," he said.

His teeth closed around her throat, sending hot, liquid arousal pooling in the pit of her belly. Then he grabbed her hand and pulled her down the hall into his bedroom.

They undressed each other with fumbling haste, dropping and kicking aside their garments.

When they were both naked and stretched on the bed, Brock traced a wickedly tantalizingly line from her breasts down past her belly button.

"Now, I'm going to taste you. And I want to hear you come apart while I'm licking up every drop of your sweet honey."

He moved over her and urged her knees apart, exposing her swollen, needy core to his hot gaze. "I'm going to make you scream, Summer."

She had no doubts.

He bent and kissed her belly, then blew a teasing puff of air between her thighs that made her arch and gasp. Then he kissed his way slowly up the inside of each thigh.

He took his time, making her squirm with need before he finally reached the hot, swollen place at the top of her legs.

Summer whimpered as Brock blew another teasing breath across her aching, sensitized flesh.

"You want me to lick you? Kiss you? Maybe even use my teeth?" he asked huskily.

"Yes!" Summer cried. "All of the above!"

She was so wound up that she figured that she was going to come, and come hard, as soon as he actually touched her.

She inhaled sharply as he dipped his head between her thighs. The tip of his tongue, wet and warm, circled her in a torturous tease, then slid lower.

He explored each inch of her, leisurely, sensuously, while her arousal climbed to mind-blowing levels.

She panted and shook beneath him as he continued to caress her, keeping her on the edge of climax but never letting her fall over the edge.

"Are you ready to scream for me?" Brock asked her, his breath hot against her inner thighs.

"Yes," she panted.

His tongue darted out and lightly touched a place that sent lightning racing along every nerve.

She stiffened, and a loud whimper escaped her.

Brock chuckled. "C'mon, Ms. Fancy Pants, I know you can do better than that."

He resumed his efforts, teasing her with the tip of his tongue until she was shaking and trembling. She had never needed to come so badly.

"Please," she begged him. "Please, Brock."

In reply, he gave her a long, deliberate lick. She felt the slick scrape of every bump on his tongue and thought she might die of pleasure.

"Oh, God," Summer said fervently.

Then he closed his lips around the exquisitely sensitive bud at the core of her need and drew it into his mouth with hard suction.

Summer arched off the bed and screamed as a sweet, wave of unbearable pleasure swept her over the edge of a cliff and plunged her into the maelstrom of a powerful climax.

Her breath came in sobbing gasps as intense shudders wracked her for long moments.

Brock's mouth on her gradually became lighter and lingering, and she began to float down from the storm that had nearly drowned her.

He moved up against her, his hands braced on her shoulders, and kissed her long and deeply. She returned the kiss eagerly, her body tingling with the aftermath of her climax.

She felt relaxed and suffused with a golden glow like warm sunlight.

"Ready for more?" Brock murmured, his lips brushing her neck.

"God, yes," she said, her fingers digging into his shoulders. "I can't wait."

He cradled her face between his hands, and his mouth covered hers in another of his demanding kisses. The sensation dizzied her, and the hot throb between her legs sprang back to life.

She loved everything about him—his touch, his scent, his taste. The way he looked at her... the way he held her. The way he was kissing her now, devouring her as if he were starving in the desert and she was the sweetest manna.

He bent his head, slowly, oh so slowly. His tongue darted out to circle her nipple before he drew it into his mouth.

Summer whimpered. She thought she might climax again just from the intense sensations rushing down her spine and gathering between her legs with every flick of his tongue and press of his lips.

He teased her sensitive nipples to hard, aching points, alternating his caresses between her breasts. She squirmed with intense, renewed desire and clamped her legs around his hips, rubbing herself shamelessly against him, a slow, sensual slide against his stiff shaft.

He rose to his knees and reached for a condom packet. Handing it to her, he slipped his hand beneath her legs, hooking around the backs of her knees and pulling her forward as he lifted her hips and spread her legs even wider.

He looked fierce and hungry as he lined himself up and slid into her, thick and hard, stretching and filling her with a satisfying burn.

As his hand moved to her waist, she wrapped her legs around his hips and dug her bare heels into the small of his back, taking him in all the way. It felt *glorious*.

Brock began pounding into her with the fast, merciless rhythm that she'd been craving, each stroke rubbing all the places that pleasured her.

It felt good, so good in a wicked, primal way. She clutched at his shoulders, and he buried his face in her neck, growling as he moved in and out of her with relentless strength.

Anticipation coiled tighter and tighter with every hard stroke rubbing against her, until she cried out and convulsed, her legs tightening around him as another long, intense release tore through her.

Brock grabbed her hips with bruising strength and went into her deep and hard.

He bit her shoulder as he shook and groaned over her, driving himself deeper inside her as he came.

Brock sprawled over her, panting, his skin hot against hers. He kissed her, slowly and lovingly.

"That was amazing," she told him. "And I love you so much."

Brock

Abigail phoned in the morning, while he and Summer were enjoying a late and leisurely breakfast. Since they had already closed the diner for two days, they were planning to enjoy this unexpected day off.

Brock put her on speakerphone.

"I'm sorry about what happened yesterday," Abigail began. "I let my shock and disappointment get the better of me. I thought you should know that I have complete faith in you, and that I'm impressed with everything you've done so far. I intend to honor our deal."

Summer breathed loudly in relief and sagged back against her chair. But Brock had more questions.

"And what about Summer?" he asked harshly. "What happens to *her* half of the deal?"

"Oh, you needn't worry about that," Abigail replied. "Now that we've both had a chance to calm down, I intend to have a long talk with her."

Brock looked over at Summer. It looked like she was trying to curl in on herself, to make herself smaller.

"You don't seem to understand, Abigail," he said. "Summer and I are a package deal now. If you intend to honor the deal we made, then you need to honor *all* of it. Not just the part with me."

Abigail audibly sucked in her breath. *"What* did you say?" She sounded indignant.

"Whatever you decide to do about our deal, Summer and I are going to continue working together at The Yummy Cowboy Diner. And you know what? My accounting software has this neat report that predicts future profits. Even without your deal, I'll be able to pay off everything within five years."

Abigail remained silent for an uncomfortably long time. Summer had straightened in her chair and was staring at Brock, open-mouthed. He grinned at her.

"So, you're that serious about my granddaughter?" Abigail asked finally.

"Yup. She's my partner, in *every* sense of the word."

Summer's smile took his breath away. He reached for her hand and kissed her knuckles.

"Good. I won't change the deal for either of you. And I apologize for having reacted so badly to the news." Abigail sighed into the phone. "Kenny Stinson is a bitter old troublemaker, and I should've known better than to listen to him. Please tell Summer that I owe her an apology."

"Tell her yourself. She's here with me. And you're on speakerphone."

"Hi, Grandma," Summer said, her voice shaking.

"Oh." Abigail paused for a long moment, as if thinking over what she wanted to say. "Summer, dear, will you forgive me for my harsh words yesterday? I was wrong to accuse you of lying. I have no excuse for the way I behaved, only regrets."

"Of course I forgive you," Summer said. "And I'm sorry for not telling you what was happening with SummerTime. I got caught up in trying to fix everything myself, and forgot to ask for help from the people who love me."

Abigail sighed. "I'm glad we've cleared the air. And I'd like to continue the terms of our deal, if you still want to."

"I do," said Summer. "I love you and I'll see you soon, Grandma."

"Love you, too, sweetheart."

When the call ended, Summer leaped up and flew into his lap. "I don't deserve you, Brock!"

He laughed and pulled her close to him. "So, now that everyone's kissed and made up, are you finally ready to consider expanding The Yummy Cowboy Diner into the Cooperman building?"

"Didn't we agree to wait until next summer to see if the numbers support the investment?" She laughed. "Just because I agreed to move in doesn't mean that I'm going to turn into a doormat."

He rested her hand on the sweet curve of her ass. "I don't expect you to. Besides, arguing with you keeps things interesting, Fancy Pants."

Epilogue – Summer

The Yummy Cowboy Diner
Three months later

"You guys!" Marlene burst into the kitchen, her weathered face alight with excitement. "You're not gonna believe who just walked in!"

It was another busy Friday night at the diner. Summer, Brock, and their two line cooks were working together in the kitchen. They moved like a well-oiled team, quickly pushing out orders that came in on the new computerized ticketing system.

Summer had finally won her battle to buy an integrated POS system for the diner. Once he got used to the new way of doing things, Brock grudgingly agreed that yes, it was easier to keep track of tickets, receipts, and inventory with the new system. Not to mention that it hooked into their existing bookkeeping and payroll program, eliminating the need to enter information manually. That saved hours of work.

"Someone who's got you all in a lather?" Brock asked dryly. He never stopped basting the steelhead filet in his pan with lemon-garlic sauce.

"No, silly!" Marlene responded. "Eric Charles! Here! In our diner!"

"Who the fuck is Eric Charles?" Brock asked.

Summer answered. "Isn't he the star of that cowboy soap opera? *The Merrills of Montana*?"

"Yes!" Marlene turned to her. "There's a group of people sitting with him, and they're all wearing *The Merrills of Montana* t-shirts." She was practically spinning on her toes like a ballerina. "This is really going to put Snowberry Springs on the map!"

Summer finished slicing a filet of bison, cooked rare, and topped it with a creamy peppercorn-and-Cognac sauce. "I guess I should go out and introduce myself," she said with resignation.

Brock shot her a look. "You a big fan of his? Gonna ask for his autograph?"

Summer shook her head. "No, it's customary for the executive chef to personally greet VIPs. You need to come make nice, too, Brock."

She looked down at her white chef's coat, checking for stains, then straightened her skullcap. It was embroidered with The Yummy Cowboy's logo, as was her coat. She usually made the rounds of the dining room at least twice during each dinner service to greet their guests and ensure that everyone was happy.

Brock grumbled under his breath, but said, "Fine. Let me just finish this ticket."

"His group is at tables sixteen, seventeen, and eighteen," Marlene volunteered.

Summer glanced at the ticket she was working on. "Oh, the peppercorn bison. I'll deliver his meal myself. Can you pick up the bison meatloaf and steelhead for that table?"

"Fish for table sixteen," Brock said, and slid the plate with the lemon-garlic steelhead fillet on a bed of couscous onto the pass. "Meatloaf coming right up."

She finished plating her peppercorn bison. Then she and Brock followed Marlene out into the dining room.

It had been a very busy autumn so far. Business at the diner was booming, and she and Brock were currently consulting with an architect Winnie recommended. They wanted to find the best way to expand the diner into the neighboring brick building without destroying a piece of the town's history.

The police had finally caught up with Gregory Brandywine in late August and arrested him for embezzling money from both SummerTime and his software company.

The money he'd stolen was gone, either spent or hidden away in an offshore account. And the arrest had hit the news wires, which meant that Summer's already-shaky plan to reopen SummerTime was suddenly under pressure because her creditors now knew the whole story.

Greg's arrest had been followed by more good news, though a little bittersweet. A major restaurant conglomerate owned by William Fiamme, a big-name celebrity chef from Sonoma County, contacted Summer in early September. They offered to purchase SummerTime for a healthy sum, clearing the last of Summer's debts.

Fiamme and his lawyers agreed to Summer's condition that Maggie and the rest of her staff would be rehired when Fiamme Enterprises took over the restaurant's operations.

Summer was asked to stay on as consulting executive chef at a generous salary. She would be in charge of developing new menus and dishes, as well as keeping her name associated with the business.

Her contract with Fiamme called for her to visit San Francisco frequently and meet with Maggie and the restaurant's chefs. She was also expected to make herself available for media interviews and meet-and-greets with the conglomerate's major investors.

All around, it was a very sweet deal, allowing her to live in Snowberry Springs and spend most of her days at Brock's side in The Yummy Cowboy Diner.

Summer and Brock delivered the meals to table sixteen

and introduced themselves to the tall, silver-haired, ruggedly handsome actor who played a ranch owner on the long-running Western series filmed in the area.

In turn, Eric Charles introduced them to his wife Brianna, who worked as a producer on the show, his director, and assorted production assistants and wardrobe staffers.

"Call me Eric, everyone does," he boomed when Summer addressed him as "Mr. Charles."

"Thank you so much for coming to The Yummy Cowboy Diner," Summer said, smiling. "I hope you enjoy your meal."

The actor was already chewing his first mouthful of the bison. He swallowed, looked up at her, and declared, "Damn, this is good. I think I'm gonna have to buy a house in town, just so I can eat here every day!"

"The fish is wonderful, too," said Brianna. "Though I wish you guys served wine. Or at least beer."

"Sorry about that," Brock said easily. "But we don't have our liquor license yet."

It was the white lie he and Summer had agreed upon when asked why the diner didn't serve alcohol.

"But you should definitely leave room for dessert," Summer added. "We have an absolutely *amazing* pumpkin mousse cheesecake tonight, as well as tiramisu, apple crisp, and a flourless chocolate truffle torte with huckleberry sauce."

The rest of the dinner service flew by quickly. Marlene turned up at intervals to report on their celebrity guests—they loved their meals and went into raptures over the pumpkin cheesecake.

When all the guests had departed, and the kitchen staff were gearing up for the nightly cleaning, a familiar voice called, "Knock-knock."

A moment later, Autumn entered the kitchen.

"Sis!" Summer went to hug her. "What are you doing here? Is everything okay?"

"Everything's fine," Autumn said. "I came to get the scoop on Eric Charles's visit tonight."

As Summer told the story, Marlene winked conspiratorially at Autumn, and edged past them and disappeared down the hallway leading to the back door.

Okay, Marlene must have a hot date with Chris tonight, thought Summer.

But Marlene came back inside almost immediately, followed closely by a grinning Jenna, who carried a miniature white bakery box embossed with **Jenna's Java & Bakery**.

Brock walked over to join them. Autumn whipped out her phone and began filming them.

"What are you doing?" Summer asked her sister. "At least give a chance to put on some lipstick!"

Then Brock went down on one knee in front of her.

As Summer gaped at him, Jenna handed him the bakery box. He popped open the lid, revealing a chocolate cupcake frosted with dark chocolate ganache, Summer's favorite treat from Jenna's bakery.

His Gran's antique sapphire-and-pearl engagement ring sparkled from the top of the cupcake. It was embedded in a rosette of ganache.

Belatedly, Summer realized what was happening. Autumn was grinning from ear-to-ear, and so were Marlene and the rest of the kitchen staff.

His face flushed, Brock cleared his throat. "Summer, you've turned my life upside-down in the best possible way. You gave both The Yummy Cowboy Diner and me a fresh start. I love you so much, and I want to spend the rest of my life making you happy. I want to fill our cottage with kids and good food and even better memories. Will you marry me?"

She stared down at him, speechless for a long moment. Then, in a choked voice, she said, "Yes! Yes, I'll marry you. Living and cooking with you makes me so incredibly happy, Brock, and I want to keep doing more of both."

A huge smile broke over his features. He tugged her down and seated her on his knee before leaning in to kiss her.

Everyone around them applauded. When Brock released her lips, Summer looked around the circle of friends and family, and knew that she'd come home to Snowberry Springs, and to Brock.

Thank you so much for reading this book! If you'd like to hear about future Snowberry Springs books and receive an exclusive bonus story featuring Summer and Brock's wedding, plus recipes for some of the dishes featured in this book, please sign up for my mailing list at **https://tinyurl.com/ytjxu668**

Next up is Winnie's story, *Flippin' Cowboy*.

When her two-timing fiance leaves her at the altar, home renovation expert Winnie Snowberry needs refuge.

Life sucks and her career is in flaming ruins after the network cancels her successful *Restoring Seattle* show. Now Winnie's beloved Grandma Abigail is begging her to come home to Snowberry Springs and restore the town's historic inn. And if Winnie can bring the inn back to life and revive her dying hometown, maybe she can also salvage her career?

Well, it's not like she's got anything else going on...

Except, on Day Two Winnie discovers the building's co-owner is Nick Evans, a local historical preservationist extraordinaire who happens to be all muscled cowboy, sexy grins, and arrogant digs. She can't decide whether she wants to kiss him... or kill him.

Nick hates her trademark pink toolbelt. He can't stand that he's forced to work with a "fake celebrity flipper" who probably can't tell a screwdriver from a nail gun. And above all, he hates that he's attracted to her.

Then a surprise discovery of the inn's scandalous past puts the whole project in jeopardy. Will they get the town's only hotel ready in time for visitors to the town's First Annual Railroad Festival?

And can two contentious flippers unite to become a team... of the heart?

Flippin' Cowboy is a standalone enemies-to-lovers romance with heart, humor, sizzle, and a guaranteed HEA. It's the second book in a series about a small Montana town on the brink of a great reawakening.

The End

Books by Ophelia Sexton

Snowberry Springs Ranch (Small Town Contemporary Western Romance)
- *Yummy Cowboy*
- *Flippin' Cowboy – Coming soon*
- *Protective Cowboy – Coming soon*
- *Wounded Cowboy – Coming soon*

Bearpaw Ridge Firefighters Books (Small Town Paranormal Romance)
- *Heat (Bearpaw Ridge Firefighters Book 1)*
- *Smolder (Bearpaw Ridge Firefighters Book 2)*
- *Ignite (Bearpaw Ridge Firefighters Book 3)*
- *Flame (Bearpaw Ridge Firefighters Book 4)*
- *Burn (Bearpaw Ridge Firefighters Book 5)*
- *Ash (Bearpaw Ridge Firefighters Book 6)*
- *Smoke (Bearpaw Ridge Firefighters Book 7)*
- *Blaze (Bearpaw Ridge Firefighters Book 8)*
- *Ember (Bearpaw Ridge Firefighters Book 9)*
- *Christmas in July (Bearpaw Ridge Firefighters holiday novella)*
- *Inferno (Bearpaw Ridge Firefighters Book 10)*
- *Scorch (Bearpaw Ridge Firefighters Book 11)*
- *<u>Sophie's Christmas Dad (Bearpaw Ridge Firefighters holiday novella)</u>*
- *Spark (Bearpaw Ridge Firefighters Book 12)*
- *Combust (Bearpaw Ridge Firefighters Book 13)*
- *Sear (Bearpaw Ridge Firefighters Book 14)*
- *Rob's Holiday Honey (Bearpaw Ridge Firefighters Book 15)*

Bearpaw Ridge Firefighters Book Bundles:
- *Bearpaw Ridge Firefighters Boxed Set #1* (Books 1-6)
- *Bearpaw Ridge Firefighters Boxed Set #2* (Books 7-9, plus novellas and short stories)
- *Bearpaw Ridge Firefighters Boxed Set #3* (Books 10-12, plus novellas and short stories)

Rocky Mountain Smokejumpers (Paranormal Romance)
- *Hard Landing (Rocky Mountain Smokejumpers Book 1)*
- *Jump Point (Rocky Mountain Smokejumpers Book 2)*
- *Free Fall (Rocky Mountain Smokejumpers Book 3)*

Beast Warriors (co-authored with Bliss Devlin) (Paranormal Romantic Suspense)
- *Fugitive: A Werebear + BBW Paranormal Romance (Beast Warriors Book 1)*
by Bliss Devlin and Ophelia Sexton
- *Hunter: A Werebear + BBW Paranormal Romance (Beast Warriors Book 2)*
by Bliss Devlin and Ophelia Sexton
- *Leader: A Werebear + Dragon Shifter Paranormal Romance (Beast Warriors Book 3)* – coming soon!

Made in the USA
Coppell, TX
15 December 2023